London Borough of Tower Hamlets

910000081400000

D0625701

STARBOARD

Books by Nicola Skinner

BLOOM: THE SURPRISING SEEDS OF SORREL FALLOWFIELD

STARBOARD

STORM

STARBOARD

NICOLA SKINNER

Illustrated by Flavia Sorrentino

HarperCollins *Children's Books*

First published in Great Britain by
HarperCollins *Children's Books* in 2021
Published in this paperback edition 2022
HarperCollins *Children's Books* is a division of HarperCollins*Publishers* Ltd
1 London Bridge Street
London SE1 9GF

www.harpercollins.co.uk

HarperCollins*Publishers*
1st Floor, Watermarque Building, Ringsend Road
Dublin 4, Ireland

1

Text copyright © Nicola Skinner 2021
Illustrations copyright © Flavia Sorrentino 2021
Cover illustrations copyright © Flavia Sorrentino 2021
Cover design copyright © HarperCollins*Publishers* Ltd 2021
Getty Images: Print Collector 11br, 183; **SS Great Britain Trust:** 11t, 194;
South American Pictures/Tony & Marion Morrison: 13, 361
All rights reserved

978-0-00-842244-8

Nicola Skinner and Flavia Sorrentino assert the moral right to be identified as the
author and illustrator of the work respectively.

A CIP catalogue record for this title is available from the British Library.

Typeset in Goudy Old Style 12pt
Printed and bound in the UK using 100% renewable
electricity at CPI Group (UK) Ltd

Conditions of Sale
This book is sold subject to the condition that it shall not, by way of trade or
otherwise, be lent, resold, hired out or otherwise circulated without the publisher's
prior consent in any form, binding or cover other than that in which it is published
and without a similar condition including this condition being imposed on the
subsequent purchaser.

MIX
Paper from
responsible sources
FSC™ C007454

This book is produced from independently certified FSC™ paper
to ensure responsible forest management.

For more information visit: www.harpercollins.co.uk/green

*Dedicated to the memory of
Isambard Kingdom Brunel, who dreamed up a ship, and
created beauty out of nothing, and Ewan Corlett, who saw
her beauty when she was next to nothing,
and brought her home.*

And for the people of Bristol, of course.

'What is done in love is well done'
Vincent van Gogh

PART 1

'What will become of me?'
Diary entry, Isambard Kingdom Brunel, 1824

BRISTOL EVENING POST, 19ᵀᴴ JULY 1843

THE SHIP OF DREAMS SETS SAIL!

THEY CALL HER 'THE SHIP OF DREAMS'. The men who built her call her 'the Mammoth.' Others are calling her 'the greatest experiment since the Creation'. But her name is the **Steamship *Great Britain*.** And today thousands gathered to see her maiden voyage from Bristol's harbourside.

She is the largest, fastest, lightest ship the world has ever seen, and a credit to the man behind her: **Isambard Kingdom Brunel**, the most famous British engineer of our time, as daring as the ship herself, rapidly making a name for himself, despite his shortness of stature, as a giant of the Victorian age.

Brunel said: 'I put so much care into this ship, I believe she will last for ever, and never tire, never hesitate, never break.'

THE SAILING TIMES, 19th JULY 1970

SHIP OF DREAMS RETURNS TO BRISTOL
A BROKEN WRECK

How the mighty have fallen. The once celebrated SS *Great Britain*, at one time the world's largest, most glamorous ocean liner, has returned to the docks of Bristol a shadow of her former self. Eighty years of neglect and mistreatment have left her broken, mutilated, nearly done for.

The engineer behind her, Isambard Kingdom Brunel, is long dead. She also came close to a lonely death in a watery grave out in the Falkland Islands. Only the efforts of a few saved her from certain ruin, and brought her home. But it was a sorry ship that returned back to the very city that had seen her built with such love and care.

It is hoped that she can now be repaired, and one day opened to the public as a museum ship on Bristol's harbourside, for children and adults alike to visit. But one thing is certain: after going round the world thirty-three times, her travelling days are over.

Surely.

- 1 -

PRESENT DAY, BRISTOL
TUESDAY

LIKE A LOT of people, Kirsten Bramble had no idea what was missing from her life until the moment she came face to face with it. But it wasn't her usual sort of accessory, like a delicate bracelet or a tiny backpack. It wasn't pocket-sized, for starters.

It was a ship.

A big, old, gleaming ship.

An *iron* ship.

And it tugged at Kirsten's heart like a magnet.

Normally, when Kirsten saw something beautiful that she liked, she bought it. Up until recently, that had been easy to do because she was a reality-TV star. A much-loved one, with a glittering TV career ahead of her still (despite what some people were saying) and a generous pocket-money allowance. (Perhaps not as generous as it had once been admittedly, but Kirsten had a plan to fix all that, so everything was *totally* fine.)

But this ship looked out of reach. She wasn't sure it was

even for sale. Yet her hands twitched a little with all the wanting.

The ship's name was the SS *Great Britain*. Kirsten had thought this was quite funny back at school, when Mrs Walia, her class teacher, handed out sheets explaining where they were going on their next school trip.

The SSSS Great Britain? she'd thought. *We're going to see a snake?*

But Mrs Walia had explained that it was pronounced Ess Ess *Great Britain*, and the 'S's stood for Steam Ship, and there were no snakes involved. She said the ship was full of history, and had been round the world loads, and now she was a museum ship, and they were going to explore her.

Kirsten's class boarded the school coach and an hour later they were in a car park by the harbourside. When she got out of the coach, Kirsten saw something gleaming and massive just beyond a gate and her heart beat faster, even then.

The back of the ship faced the car park and the ticket office. The only way to approach it was through the gift shop. So, when you first came face to face with the ship, it was actually face to bottom. But even that was a thing of beauty.

Why were golden unicorns stuck on to the ship's backside? Who knew? *They look wonderful*, thought Kirsten

Bramble, walking underneath them, imagining she almost saw one of them give a proud snort.

The ship rested on a thick pane of glass that looked a little like water. And it shone in the sun like a huge black swan.

Kirsten slowly walked round the left side of the ship. It radiated a mysterious power. It made her stop walking. It made her hold her breath. Her eyes couldn't properly take it in all at once. Her eyes felt utterly useless, even though she had two of them. Two weren't *nearly* enough to see this ship properly. She wanted to look at it for ever. Even at the end of that, she suspected she wouldn't be quite finished.

It was so glossy. It seemed to drink in all the light around it and radiate it back so that it was practically glowing. Her fingers twitched again. Kirsten looked around. All of her classmates had gone on ahead. None of them had waited for her. She looked back up at the ship's shiny hull and sighed.

Her thoughts were interrupted by the sound of someone coughing. 'Looks like you've got it almost as badly as me,' said a short man abruptly. 'Marvellous, isn't she?'

'*She?*' said Kirsten, spinning round to look at the man. Where had he come from? He hadn't been there a moment ago.

'Oh yes,' he said, staring at Kirsten with dark, clever eyes.

'*She*. It's the first and most important lesson of seafaring: all ships are *she*. And this one, I'm sure you'll agree, is more *she* than most. All 3,847 tons of her.'

'Right,' she stammered. 'Um, have we met before?'

The man had a face she could have sworn she'd seen somewhere. It was his eyebrows and sideburns. Not to mention his tall black hat. Very familiar. He looked significant. He glanced at her, and Kirsten had a sense of ferocious daring.

'Have we met?' he said. 'Anything is possible with the right calculations. I don't like to rule anything out.' He tucked his hands into the pockets of his waistcoat, rocked back on scuffed brown boots and looked up at the ship. 'Almost alive, isn't she?'

Kirsten said nothing, because that was *exactly* what she'd been thinking. She half expected to see the ship's sides gently moving in and out. Together, she and the funny, short little man gazed at the SS *Great Britain* in silent appreciation.

In the pages of Kirsten's history book in class, the ship had seemed – well – almost forgettable and a bit dull, if she was honest. Just a black-and-white photo from another century washed up on the page, like driftwood from the past. But now? Now that Kirsten was actually *standing by the ship itself*? It seemed almost impossible the vessel in front of her was the same one in the book.

They *were* both black and white – that was true. But *this ship* had a glossy black hull that shone like satin, and a delicate white trim that went round her middle like a ribbon. The ship in the book was easily held within the photograph. But in real life she looked like nothing could ever contain her at all.

There were six tall masts sticking out from the ship's huge deck. They had flags strung between them. As these fluttered and flapped in the breeze, it was honestly as if the ship was tossing her hair and peering around for someone to dazzle and charm.

This ship seemed to flick away the ship in the book as easily as a panther swatting away a fly, as if to say: 'Me? History? *Are you* sure?'

- 2 -
A NARROW DART

KIRSTEN LET OUT a besotted sigh. The short man – who'd gone very quiet over the last few minutes (and had been watching Kirsten almost as intently as she'd been looking at the ship) – grinned. 'Yes, I'd say you've got it very badly indeed,' he said. 'Just like me. Still smitten after all this time.'

He patted the ship with stubby, ink-stained fingers. 'I come back every year to see her, you know,' he said in a confiding way. 'By rail naturally. Check it's all still tickety-boo.'

Kirsten looked at the part of the ship the man had patted. It had grown even shinier at his touch. 'Tickety-what?' she said, turning back to him.

But there was no reply. He'd disappeared. He must have wandered off without saying goodbye. *What a funny little man*, she thought, sniffing the air, which for a moment smelled strongly of cigars.

She shook off her enchantment and circled the outside of the ship – which took *ages*, as it was so vast – until she located the rest of her class. They were gathered at the front, listening to a woman with red hair and a badge that said

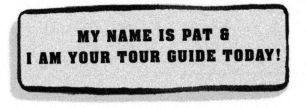

**MY NAME IS PAT &
I AM YOUR TOUR GUIDE TODAY!**

The front of the ship was as narrow as the back was wide. And it steadily got narrower and narrower, ending in a sharp point like a big needle.

'We call this the bowsprit,' said Pat, pointing at the long white needle sticking out from the ship. 'It connects the front mast to the prow, and would have kept the sails taut—'

But Kirsten Bramble, who didn't usually go around thinking about ships and their innermost feelings, found all of a sudden that she did. She sensed that the long bowsprit wasn't there to keep the sails taut at all. The bowsprit was the ship's *longing*.

It seemed so obvious suddenly. *The ship was yearning for somewhere.* This had sharpened her into the narrowest, pointiest dart, so she could get there quicker. And you didn't have to be a genius to work out where.

The ship was pointing, as clearly as she could, towards the ocean.

- 3 -
ARE YOU *THE* KIRSTEN BRAMBLE?

THE WAY TO board the ship was the same way as boarding a plane: from the top, not the bottom. Kirsten and the rest of her class explored the museum next to the ship and from there walked up five flights of stairs, which ended at a high, narrow bridge. This led to the **SS** *Great Britain*.

One at a time, the children walked over the bridge.

The biting April wind plucked at the ship's rigging.

The wires went ZING.

The metal went PING.

The rigging went DING.

Everything felt bright and loud.

Up close, the ship's extreme shippiness was almost too much.

Really, thought Kirsten suddenly, *she should come with a warning.*

Halfway across the bridge, Kirsten stopped walking completely, suddenly dizzy. She didn't have a head for heights and the bridge was very high. The pinging, zinging and dinging, not to mention the squawking of the seagulls overhead, all seemed extremely loud and extremely close. Kirsten hesitated, even thought about getting off so she could find somewhere to sit and calm down, but then Mrs Walia turned round and gave Kirsten a look that said: *Get a move on.*

So Kirsten got a move on and hurried over the bridge.

Later, much later, when she tried to pinpoint the precise moment when the day had tiptoed over the very thin line between *educational class trip* and *complete and total nightmare*, she'd trace it all back to then.

It was the hurrying that did it. Most people board a ship, but Kirsten fell on to this one. She landed on her hands and knees on the decking. Pain burst open in her hands. She sat up and turned them over. In each palm were two thin wooden splinters, sharp and unexpected.

Mrs Walia grabbed her hands and pulled Kirsten roughly to her feet.

'Ow!' said Kirsten. Both splinters had just been driven in deeper and a jolt of energy ran through her.

'You're pale,' said Mrs Walia. 'Even paler than usual. Are you all right?'

Kirsten looked at her palms again. The splinters were so deep in her skin she doubted they'd ever come out. The ship was now inside her.

'I – my hands,' she muttered, but Mrs Walia was fretting about the rest of the class, so she nudged Kirsten on, towards the middle of the deck. Kirsten stumbled after her classmates.

The rigging and the colourful flags stretched above and around her, catching her in their midst. She felt as if she'd wandered into the middle of a radiant spider's web. The sky above had turned the brightest blue she'd ever seen. Her heart felt odd.

From a big dressing-up basket on the deck, her classmates were pulling out frilly dresses, bonnets and waistcoats. They held them up to each other, laughing easily. Kirsten watched them, feeling a different kind of wanting, one she couldn't fix with a credit card.

'It's all about getting in character for the tour,' said Pat, the guide, breaking into her thoughts. 'This is a Victorian ship, so we dress up as Victorians. Now – this petticoat might be your size?'

Kirsten looked at the garment on offer and came back down to earth.

'Is that . . . *second-hand*?' she enquired, wrinkling her national treasure of a nose.

Mrs Walia cleared her throat. 'Oh, really, Kirsten. You're not a celebrity when you're at school; we've talked about this. You're a *schoolgirl* on a class trip, so how about a little cooperation?'

'Oh, I *thought* I recognised you,' said Pat, peering into her face. 'Are you *the* Kirsten Bramble? From the telly? What's the name of your reality show again? *Find My Dad a Girlfriend*?'

'That's me!' Kirsten produced her famous smile automatically. 'Except now it's just called *At Home with the Brambles*. We've sort of evolved—'

'Oh, I used to be such a big fan!' said Pat, and the wattage of Kirsten's smile flickered. Then the woman began to babble, looking embarrassed.

'I mean, er, still am, of course. Nearly applied myself when it all started, *adored* your dad, what a total character, watched it every Saturday, but then it started to feel a bit intrusive, if you don't mind me saying, felt sorry for you, if I'm honest, love, struggling to make friends in Series Three, that wasn't quite as feel-good as the first two series, plus I'm not sure about that woman, what's her name, watch out for her–'

Kirsten decided to end it there. 'Lovely to meet you!' she said quickly. 'Thank you for watching! And don't forget to tune into the Jade Cooper chat show this Friday night!'

Pat's eyes grew wide with awe, and Kirsten knew she'd impressed her.

'You're going on *The Jade Cooper Show*?' she said. 'Wow.'

'I know,' said Kirsten smugly. 'With Dad. And we'll be dropping some exclusive teasers for Series Five. Seven p.m. Friday!'

This all came out in a smooth, practised manner because she was nothing if not professional. As her management team liked to remind her: '*Every conversation is a chance to promote yourself and the Bramble brand, Kirsten.*'

Pat held up the lacy, old-fashioned skirt again. 'So . . . no petticoat?'

Kirsten shook her head.

- 4 -
A FEW YEARS AGO

FOR THE FIRST seven years of her life, there had been no such thing as the Bramble brand, and Kirsten had not been famous at all. She'd just been plain-ordinary Kirsten, who lived with her dad in Brimmerton, South Bristol.

Now Brimmerton wasn't particularly fancy. Brimmerton had one playground with a rusty swing, one Spar and one pub, the Pigeon's Mangled Foot. But, if you liked swings with conversational squeaks, eating crisps fresh from the shops, or playing computer games with your best friend, Olive, then Brimmerton was *great* for that.

The people who'd designed their block of flats weren't really good at naming things, so Kirsten and her dad lived at Number 12, Block 3. Their kitchen window was covered in cat stickers. Their front door was yellow and they had a little garden.

Kirsten's dad was a nice man with a melancholy smile who taught maths at secondary school. His name was Mick Bramble. Kirsten called him Dad. He loved salted peanuts, speaking in slightly confusing maths metaphors and Kirsten. He loved Kirsten the most. He had adopted her when she was tiny, and it had been the two of them together ever since. (Three if you counted Pricky Bill, their cat, who did as he liked and was very good at that.)

But, just after turning seven and a half, Kirsten decided that the only thing missing from their life was a girlfriend for Dad. Someone to hold his hand at the school gates while he waited for her. Whenever she went to Olive's (Number 9, Block 2) for a sleepover, Dad spent the evening alone, eating peanuts, watching telly. This, Kirsten suddenly felt, was not enough. What he needed was True Love. He needed to go on some *dates*. And that was a fact because she'd decided it was.

Luckily, she knew what to do about this situation. She'd watched enough U films to know that, if you wanted to find a girlfriend for your dad, all it took was imagination and guts. (Not *actual* guts – that would be weird.) If he wouldn't make an effort to find love, she'd find it for him instead.

'I'm honestly very happy with our life as it is, love,' he'd told her when she first suggested the idea. 'I *love* teaching maths, and Pricky Bill, and spending time with you. Trust me, this is the good life.'

Then his eyes had gone all misty, like they always did just before he talked about maths. 'You see, you and me, we're two triangles, and together we make a square. And what is a square, Kirsten, at the end of the day? It's a building block. It's *bedrock*. It's solid.'

'Right,' said Kirsten, only half listening, as she was busy watching an instructional video about uploading content.

'But, if another triangle came along, what would we be? We'd be lopsided. We'd be *a right trapezoid*. And, believe me, that's a very complicated thing to be.'

Kirsten barely glanced up from the screen. 'Yeah, but one day I'll grow up and move out, and then you'll be a sad triangle on your own, eating too many peanuts. So go and brush your hair, please, and put on that nice green shirt of yours.'

And because he doted on her – and calculated, with some professional satisfaction, *that the statistical probability of anyone actually watching the video Kirsten wanted to make and providing the projected desired outcome was significantly low* – that's exactly what Mick Bramble did.

Once they were both ready, they went into the garden. It was a Friday night, late summer. The roses were out. Life seemed soft and kind. It was the perfect setting for finding True Love.

'What should I do?' Dad asked, nervously eyeing the mobile in his daughter's hand.

'Why don't you – erm – sit at the picnic table and smile?

No, not that *mopey* one. Haven't you got another one that we can use?'

'This is just how I smile,' said Dad. 'I'm not sad – I just don't like my teeth.'

'Mmm. How about you do some gardening, then, and I'll film you, and do the talking?'

'*Great*,' said her dad, more enthusiastic. 'I can catch up with the weeding!'

Kirsten switched on her mobile, found the VIDEO settings in CAMERA, pressed the REVERSE button so the camera was on her, and pressed RECORD .

'Hi, I'm Kirsten Bramble,' she said. 'And I'm looking for True Love for my dad. Here he is.'

Then she pressed the REVERSE button so the camera was on Dad and, while she filmed him, Kirsten said that he was a nice man and could do maths, which was good if you had homework, and he was kind to animals, and people too, and usually let her choose whatever she wanted to watch on the telly, and he'd make someone a great boyfriend if those qualities were what you wanted in one. And, if they weren't, you probably needed to sit down and have a good long look at yourself.

She was quite proud of her film, which seemed really factual, concentrated on his unique selling points and had a good action shot of Pricky Bill trying to kill a leaf too.

Also, when they watched it back on Dad's mobile, Kirsten was pleased with how the light in the garden flattered his skin and didn't show how tired he looked in real life.

('*Wow*, thanks, love,' said Dad when she pointed this out.)

Then she persuaded him to upload the short, wobbly clip on to the internet.

While he'd been banging on about triangles, Kirsten had done some research on how to make a video grab people's attention. Like, *loads* of attention. Enough attention to attract True Love. It was all about hashtags. So Kirsten made up a few:

#GirlfriendForMyDad
#DateMyDad
#TrueLove #LoveNotMaths #YouCan'tKissMaths
#MustLoveCats

She was *good* at this.

Then a button had come up on the screen and it had basically said:

**UPLOAD YOUR VIDEO TO THE INTERNET?
WHERE MILLIONS OF PEOPLE CAN SEE IT?
ARE YOU SURE?**

HAVE YOU PROPERLY THOUGHT THIS THROUGH, HON?

She and Dad had looked at each other. He had gulped. Smiled his melancholy smile. Kirsten had pressed YES.

And – *well*. Neither of them had been in any way prepared for quite how famous, how fast, that video would make them.

- 5 -

THE SHOW MUST GO ON

FIRST CAME THE newspaper people. Then the television people. Next came long-term contracts and signing things. Finally, there was the award-winning ITV show. The format was simple: every week, Dad would be sent on a date with a different woman, and then Kirsten would meet her to see if she liked her.

They never had much luck finding Dad a girlfriend. His heart didn't honestly seem to be in it, but that didn't matter. Everyone loved the show, and his reluctance to go on dates just became a part of their brand and made people laugh. Even his catchphrase of 'What's this one's name, then, and what time can I go home?' was quoted in pubs and bookies and offices up and down the land.

'That Mick Bramble,' people would laugh, 'he's no Romeo, is he?'

Then came the spin-offs, the Christmas specials, the Christmas single . . .

And even after Dad *did* get matched with a girlfriend – Edwina Clippity, an unstoppable force of determination who insisted they were perfect for each other and who somehow bulldozed her way into their life – the show didn't stop. Even though they'd done what Kirsten had set out to do, the cameras just kept on rolling because they had a huge team behind them who said they were an 'established brand'. So the show became about *them*.

Sometimes Dad would act as a 'love expert' for other single men looking for love. The advice he gave was always dreadful, and the public lapped it up. They'd done a 'walking in the country' show called *Rambles with the Brambles* where they'd been chased by cows, and everyone thought this was brilliant. Occasionally, the series would just be about Kirsten, like when she struggled with school for a bit after finding fame . . .

. . . because it hadn't taken long for Kirsten to fall out with her best friend, Olive, and most of her classmates at Brimmerton Primary. (Also, she had boasted *a teeny bit much* at the beginning of all this, and been quite annoying, it had to be said.)

This was something no one had warned her about.

She'd felt so lonely at her old school that she'd tried, for a term, to attend a posh private school in Clifton. But she hadn't liked it very much there either and they'd teased her terribly. So she'd gone back to Brimmerton Primary and tried to carry on as normal, but Olive didn't seem to want to talk to her at all by then, and everyone else had moved on, and formed different gangs she couldn't find a way into. Kirsten was kept so busy filming after school that she gradually drifted apart from all the other children.

After a while, she just put up with not having many friends at school and pretended she didn't care. (Most of Series Three had been about this, which had actually been a little embarrassing, especially as the producers had called it: *Get My Daughter a Friend.* In the end, they did find her a best friend called India-Rose, who auditioned for the role, and didn't go to her school, but was very good at learning lines.)

There was, Kirsten had come to understand, literally no end in sight to their TV career at all.

They left their tiny garden flat, they shut that yellow door one last time and got into a removal van and moved into a big white house on the other side of Bristol with Edwina Clippity called

which had astronomical running costs, but which Edwina had *insisted* was the right house for them.

Edwina Clippity was tall and skinny and loved suede furniture and her new-found fame. Pricky Bill also loved her suede furniture, but he did that with his claws, giving Edwina significant looks as he did so. When Pricky Bill died of old age, Edwina said they couldn't get any more cats.

Edwina had confiscated all Dad's salted peanuts and hired a gardener and persuaded Dad to stop teaching maths as she thought he needed to be at home, with her, working on True Love. (This apparently meant watching reruns of the show and working out in their private gym. Kirsten missed her dad's squishy tummy. Cuddling him now was like trying to cuddle a bag of new potatoes.)

A few months ago, their management team had said that audience figures were dropping quite a lot. They said Dad needed to make more of an effort to show enthusiasm, that the show wasn't raising the laughs it used to. They said what Kirsten had done last summer hadn't helped and they hoped she wouldn't do that again. (Kirsten said she wouldn't.)

Then ITV announced that they wouldn't be renewing their contract for Series Five. They would always think of the Brambles as part of the ITV family, they said, but they'd taken them as far as they could career-wise.

Then their bank manager and their accountants said they were living beyond their means and if they couldn't keep up their mortgage payments they might lose the house. To cope, Edwina went on a shopping spree. Again.

All of which meant that the new series of *At Home with the Brambles* – which had been picked up by a smaller TV channel called 24-Hour Reality! – *had* to be a hit, or Series Six would be called something like *Hanging with the Hasbeens: Remember the Brambles?*

Fortunately, their latest agent, Keith O'Keefe, had secured an interview slot with Jade Cooper on her Friday night prime-time chat show.

'I pulled a lot of strings,' said Keith. 'This is your chance to show the nation what made them fall in love with you in the first place, all those years ago. I want you to go on, talk about how excited you are about this new series, make a gorgeous, heartfelt apology for what you did last summer, Kirsten – Mick, don't forget to smile properly – and the job's a good 'un.'

What Keith didn't say, but might as well have, was: '*Don't mess this up.*'

Kirsten Bramble was only eleven, but once in a while she felt much, much older.

Of course it wasn't always easy, but that was show biz. She had built this life for her, and Dad, and she felt responsible for it, and for him. She wasn't about to throw it all away because she was a true professional, and would do everything to keep the show on the road. And, no matter how tired or occasionally lonely she felt, *this* was the good life, and she would protect it.

So, when she strode out on to *The Jade Cooper Show* on Friday, she would dazzle like she'd never dazzled before, or her name wasn't—

- 6 -
BACK ON DECK

'KIRSTEN? KIRSTEN BRAMBLE? Hello?'

Pat and Mrs Walia were looking at her impatiently. Mrs Walia gestured at the basket of dressing-up clothes. 'You have to choose *something*, Kirsten,' she said. 'You know our motto at Brimmerton Primary—'

'Never use the far right toilet after Wednesday?' muttered Kirsten.

'—education is best when it's immersive,' said Mrs Walia.

'Oh,' said Kirsten. 'You meant the *official* motto.'

'Go on, love,' added the tour guide encouragingly. 'Have a browse. Don't be shy.'

Kirsten rifled through the dressing-up basket. All the best things had been taken already. Then she saw it. A tiny gleam of gold winking up at her from the very bottom of the basket. Maybe it was a vintage sequinned top – she *loved* sequins – so she reached for it eagerly . . .

. . . and pulled out a hat.

It was dirty white with a navy peak. The only vintage thing about it was the dead woodlouse that fell out.

Kirsten stared at the hat. Glued to the front was a gold anchor. On the navy peak were two garlands of golden leaves. The sun hit the gold in a certain way.

It's nice how it does that, she thought. *Mesmerising, if you like that sort of thing.*

'How lovely,' said Pat. 'You found the captain's hat! I forgot we had that! Haven't seen it in years . . . almost thought we didn't still have it at all—'

Above, the seagulls shrieked like delighted children at a party.

Kirsten wasn't usually into hats. She decided to put it back in the basket. Maybe she'd just look at it one last time though.

It glimmered in her hands like a small scrap of magic. They really did catch the sun, those gold bits on the peak. The whole thing was grubby but oddly endearing. A forgotten hat putting on a tiny valiant show, as if to say: *'Pick me!'*

She didn't toss it back in the basket. Feeling reckless,

Kirsten put it on. It was too big for her head and it smelled funny.

'Oh, what a shame,' said Pat. 'It doesn't fit you after all. Do you want to swap it for something else?'

'No,' Kirsten Bramble heard herself saying, which was weird because she sort of did.

'Right,' said the guide. 'That's you sorted then, *Captain*. On with the tour.' And she ushered the entire class towards the sticky-outy door that was in the middle of the deck. 'This is the *companionway*. Follow me.'

As Kirsten walked down the stairs into the **SS *Great Britain***, she turned over her aching palms and had a funny thought. *The ship is inside me now* – she glanced at those splinters – *and now I'm inside the ship.*

She had an eerie feeling of being swallowed up whole BY SOMETHING and never coming out the same way again.

- 7 -
THE BEEHIVE

OUTSIDE IT WAS bright and dazzling. But inside the ship was not. It was dark yet glimmered. It was empty but full. It smelled of furniture polish and secrets. And, underneath that, a dash of something else: the faded perfume of thousands and thousands of lives; passengers long gone, but whose traces seemed to still linger, stored in the ship's huge body like the most delicate cargo.

Pat began to take them through the ship one chamber, one room at a time. It was as if they were exploring a massive beehive, thought Kirsten suddenly, and you knew there was a queen somewhere, you just hadn't met her yet.

That magnetic pull she'd felt outside was stronger now.

They were ushered out of one dark corridor into a large, wood-panelled room, simply furnished with benches, its walls studded with portholes through which the bright April sunshine poured.

The children arranged themselves round the room, laughing at each other's Victorian outfits. None of her classmates were keen to stand near Kirsten Bramble and that was only partly because of the smell of her hat.

'This is the *promenade saloon*,' said Pat. 'Where the first-class passengers would read the newspaper, play cards and make polite conversation . . .'

They followed her out of the saloon and into another corridor. Was it the same corridor or a different one? Who could tell? The ship's insides had a peculiar labyrinthine quality. The usual laws of physics seemed fluid. Normal rules about what was right, where was left, and how those two things should *not fidget* or swap places didn't seem to apply here.

Someone SCREAMED.

The class squeezed round a doorway and stared at the bleeding man inside. Silently, he held out a mangled hand. Kirsten glanced at her own painful palms and gave the injured man a grimace of sympathy. Bending over this man was another man cradling the patient's hand. He gazed into their eyes. The room stank of antiseptic.

No one moved. The two men were staring at them, unblinking. Realisation rippled across the children.

Someone said: 'They're . . . fake!'

Everyone relaxed.

It was true. In the dark surgery, the mannequins *almost* looked like real people, until the children saw the tiny telltale scratch marks on their waxy-looking faces, the small but giveaway specks of glue in the depths of their extravagant sideburns.

'They *are* fake,' said Pat delightedly. 'But wonderfully convincing, as you've just discovered. And you'll find quite a few of these fibreglass mannequins – both passengers and crew – dotted round the ship, complete with replica *smells*, to help you picture what each voyage would have been like in the nineteenth century. You've just discovered the ship's surgeon.' She pointed at the man bending over. 'Isn't he a magnificent chap?'

Kirsten looked at the surgeon, and he looked back at her: glass eyes staring at her solemnly, as if trying to read her symptoms. For a moment, she sincerely believed he was going to tell her something important. Then she gave herself a shake, and walked away quickly.

Spotting the mannequins became one of the highlights of the tour. And, as the children went further and further into the ship, dressed in their crinolines and top hats, it became harder to differentiate between the mannequins and the humans, so that every time they turned a corner they'd brace themselves for a minute, not sure of what, or who, they'd find.

In the upper-class berths, where the people who had paid most for their journey had once slept and lived, were mannequin men in top hats and black suits and bonneted women with pretty ringlets and pink cheeks. The bedrooms here were small but relatively comfortable cabins, with only a few beds, curtains, a window and a door you could shut for privacy. There was even a dining saloon: a very long room on the lower deck, with linen tablecloths, marble pillars, a truly disgustingly patterned carpet, and a small group of mannequin musicians, hands poised over their violins, to entertain them.

'No expense spared for these passengers,' said Pat.

Down in the lower depths of the ship, called steerage, the rooms were more cramped, with less space and privacy. There was no dining saloon, no musicians, just two rough wooden tables pushed up against a porthole.

Here there were thirty bunk beds arranged in two lines, facing each other, down a long corridor. In some of the beds were the curled-up figures of mannequins having a pretend sleep under rough blue blankets. On the walls were keepsakes – drawings, sheets of music, old-fashioned Victorian photographs of unsmiling relatives. Hung between the cabins were makeshift curtains of plain linen to show how the steerage passengers tried to keep their privacy in such crowded quarters on long voyages.

Kirsten also spotted two mannequin women in ragged dresses pulling each other's hair, and three thin, pale children poised over a wooden train set between two bunks. Near them, a separate mannequin in a faded dress was bending over a bowl in a retching position, looking pale and sorry for herself.

'Victorians got horribly seasick,' said Pat, 'and of course it was worse in steerage. Although this one –' Pat beamed at them all – 'is actually pregnant. Lots of babies were born on the ship during her many voyages. She truly was bursting with life.'

In more ways than one, thought Kirsten, keenly aware of how each part of the ship seemed to contain its own special kind of light. Some corridors and rooms had a golden, soft light; others were dark and shadowy and bluey grey. These colours played and danced through the ship continuously, as if they were passengers too.

There was also a huge kitchen crammed with copper pans and flickering flames, and in the middle of it all was a large red-cheeked cook in a stained apron, hunched for ever over a bubbling vat.

Last, they visited the engine room – a cavernous space the height of a double-decker bus, right in the heart of the ship, around which the middle and lower deck had been built. Within it was a huge metal wheel that turned continuously.

Here that magnetic pull on Kirsten's heart became even stronger. Perhaps the ship *was* a bit magnetic; she was made of iron, wasn't she? But *Kirsten* wasn't made of metal, so why did she feel that connection between them? Her chest felt like it would burst.

'This is a perfect replica,' Pat said, interrupting her thoughts, for which Kirsten was thankful, 'A perfect replica –' she pointed to the grey wheel within the cavernous space – 'of the crankshaft engine the ship once had. It was the biggest engine in the entire world at the time, made specially for her and no other ship in the world. The measurements are unique to the SS **Great Britain**, much like our hearts are to us.'

WHOOSH,
WHOOSH,
WHOOSH

went the ship's metal heart in agreement, as it turned round and round endlessly, tirelessly.

Kirsten gulped and felt peculiar under her captain's hat.

Along with the other children, she pretended to admire the very old Victorian diving suit tucked away in the corner of the engine room, which Pat explained had been stuck in there as a prank back in the 1980s and was too heavy to move.

Then it was question time.

Kirsten's classmates asked questions mostly about the mannequins, and what the fake vomit was made of, and how did they get it to be so lifelike cos it smelled just like it. Pat asked if there were any questions that weren't about the mannequins, and everyone shuffled their feet.

Mrs Walia told them all to say thank you very much to Pat, and everyone did, and then Mrs Walia said they were running a bit late and it was lunchtime. This caused a rush for the staircase. Kirsten hesitated, unwilling to be part of the stampede. She had a finicky dislike of school crowds, partly because she sometimes got pinched in them. She found herself right at the back of the queue as everyone stomped and stamped up the stairs and out.

Then her feet stopped moving on a curious impulse.

All of a sudden, she was completely alone.

There was something surprisingly nice about having the ship to herself. She saw life, suddenly, as a large heavy chain of many links stretching backwards and forwards, with her in the middle. As if in sympathy, she heard the ship's own chains clank gently around her.

Kirsten closed her eyes. And, in that private, sneaky way

that they sometimes have, her soul secretly asked something of the ship.

And the ship, which had been watching her and fancied a spot of MISCHIEF, decided to do something even sneakier and grant it.

- 8 -
BEND A LiTTLE CLOSER

AFTER A FEW seconds of stolen peace, Kirsten opened her eyes again. She felt completely lost, with no idea how to get out. She vaguely remembered she was on the lower deck, broke into a run, stumbled, then – she was never quite sure how afterwards – fell against a door that swung open into a room.

There are two types of silences in the world.

The first is *proper silence*: the total absence of noise. Like an empty classroom during the summer holidays. The second type isn't really silence at all. It's caused by things trying to be quiet. It's a silence full of life – where things wait and watch. This room definitely contained the second type of silence and not the first. Everything in it seemed to observe her.

Kirsten thought they'd been shown all the rooms in the ship, but she'd have remembered *this*, if only for the weird green wallpaper patterned with twisting tendrils and crests picked out in fading gold leaf. Here the light was black and brown and green, flecked with gold; as dark and rich as soil.

The walls seemed alive, appeared to ebb and flow around her, as if the room wasn't certain what size, what version of itself and what dimensions to present to her. As Kirsten walked tentatively inside, it grew gigantic one second and small the next. It was all very peculiar. She'd never come across a room that undulated around her before, like a jellyfish.

All the walls came right up to her, the ceiling lowered until it was touching her head, and she found herself in a tiny box. A moment later, they all backed slowly away, and she felt, curiously, like a foot that had just been measured for a shoe.

'H-hello?'

But, as the sound of her voice was absorbed into the wallpaper, the room seemed to shake itself into a more normal size, and what had just happened seemed as if it had never happened at all.

Kirsten glanced over her shoulder and saw a golden plaque on the door:

the sign said. The words felt like a wink in the dark.

The hat on her head grew warmer and tighter. Kirsten took two further steps into the odd room.

One.

Two.

Just like that.

Now she saw three pieces of furniture. A wooden chair with a frayed leather seat. A mahogany desk. And a lamp, on the desk, with a green glass shade.

Stretching out beneath this lamp, like an elderly person soaking up sunshine from a green sun, was an old map.

Kirsten put her rucksack down on the floor, walked up to the desk, and gazed down at the faded paper.

Once, it would have shown the world. Now it showed almost nothing but its age. Only a few wavery lines here and there revealed what it had once been, and even those were as thin as a strand of hair and about as ready to snap. The only thing keeping the map tethered to the world were those brittle threads, and once they finally disappeared it would be completely blank.

'Seen better days, map?' Kirsten muttered.

And, in reply, the map rippled, as if in agreement.

Kirsten double-checked. It was *definitely* rippling. Like there was something within the map itself.

The lamps on the wall spluttered and went out. The

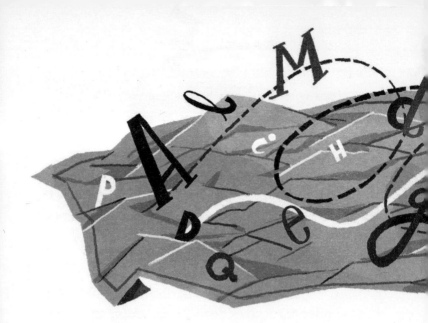

room grew darker yet the map grew brighter. Like a pancake in a frying pan, it bubbled. Indigo lines began to spread across the paper like branches, and form themselves into shapes. But they weren't islands and countries.

Kirsten gasped.

They were words.

Bend a little closer, human.

'Wh-what?' said Kirsten.

The words faded into the brittle paper as if they were being drunk back somehow, and then:

Take that look off your face. It will interrupt my reading.

'Your – your reading?'

Most people read maps, stated the map.

Kirsten nodded. 'That's true.'

I am a map that reads people.

'You're a map that reads *people?*'

Yes. I read people.

Kirsten had to stifle the urge to laugh.

You're smirking because you're frightened, said the map.

'I'm *not*,' said Kirsten stubbornly.

You're frightened and, what's more, you are lost. It's written all over you, as clear as fresh ink.

'I'm not *lost*,' scoffed Kirsten. 'I know exactly where I am—'

A true sign of being dreadfully lost, said the map, *is being overly concerned with knowing exactly where you are. Now come a little closer.*

'But – why?' said Kirsten.

Well, for the same reason, of course, that people use maps. I'm going to read you to work out a route.

'But why do you need to work out a route? You're just an old map. You're not going anywhere.'

Oh, we are.

- 9 -
THE READING

KIRSTEN LAUGHED WITH relief. She'd realised the truth. This wasn't an actual *speaking* map. This was a tourist gimmick, and all it was doing was reading from a preprogrammed script. Basically, it was as fake as the mannequins.

'Very funny,' she said. 'Ending the tour with a talking map – it's entertaining, if a bit bizarre.'

Believe me, this is totally normal. It's your way of doing things that is bizarre. Humans reading maps? How utterly outlandish. What will **you think of next?**

'Hey—' said Kirsten.

Now bend closer so I can look at you properly. This light is rather dim for human-reading and you're not a particularly clear one, either.

It was hard to resist the map's bossy tone. Kirsten bent down till her nose was just a few centimetres away from the map.

Not that close! You've gone all blurry, the map spat abruptly, spraying ink into her face. **Retreat! Retreat, for the love of god! Boundaries, girl!**

Kirsten backed away, wiping the ink off her face.

Now stand still and keep your eyes wide open.

She played along and did as instructed.

All of a sudden, she really did feel as if she was being scrutinised. There was an odd pressure on her chest, as if something had pressed against her and peered into her heart. Then, for a couple of bewildering seconds, the pressure seemed to run along a line, as if an eyeball – or something *like* an eyeball – was darting back and forth, reading her.

Then it stopped.

Her mind raced. The map had rifled through her heart, just as she'd rifled through the dressing-up clothes. What had it seen?

On the map, a blot of ink appeared in the middle of the parchment, like a creature from the deep swimming to the surface.

Ah.

There was something worrying about the way it said that.

As I suspected.

And then a baffling sequence of numbers appeared on the map:

51.44° N, -2.60° E

48° N, 13° E
45° N, 30° E

Eventually, all the letters and numbers came together and then, in a second of energy, they fused into a shape, and the shape was . . .

X

There was a polite, strained silence. Then the map wrote:

We're going the long way round.

Kirsten bit her lip. She was suddenly desperate to laugh, to expel all her nervous energy.

Take some time to absorb the full magnitude of my markings, said the map grandly.

Kirsten tried to gather herself, and said in a slightly shaky voice, 'I get it. X marks the spot. *Brilliant*. And this happens every time, right? To anyone you "read"? They all get the same result?'

I am weary of this conversation now, said the map, and it was true: the map had grown thinner and more faded in the last few minutes. **It is tiring reading ungrateful people.**

There was also something laboured about the ink it

produced for this sentence, as if the reading had cost the map a great deal of effort.

Please take a journey away from me. By which I mean go away.

'Fine by me,' said Kirsten. She peered around, wondering if there was a button for the map so she could switch it off. Her attention was caught by her reflection in an old speckled compass that hung on the wall.

She was still wearing that dirty captain's hat, she really should take it off, but everything else was still something to be proud of. There was that lovable girl from the television. There she was.

Glossy brown shiny plaits on either side of her face framing a cute, white, heart-shaped face. Not to mention the most sparkling green eyes in the business. (Even if she did have to use eyedrops now, but that was an industry secret her public didn't need to know.)

She practised her smile. Those dynamite dimples appeared right on cue. Despite the smattering of tiny stress pimples that had appeared overnight on her chin, she still looked like _the_ Kirsten Bramble: the cute girl next door who made parents look at their _own_ children and feel, just for the tiniest second, ever so slightly disappointed.

Didn't she?

Kirsten felt her heart twist with insecurity. The brown

flecks of rust on the compass glass made her look a bit worn out. She'd given four brilliant series, and three years of her *entire life*, to ITV, which was, basically, like, 45 per cent of her existence, and then she'd just been dropped like a hot potato . . .

And she knew who for.

She kept hearing one new name a lot. *Daisy.*

Daisy was seven. Kirsten didn't know where Daisy had come from exactly, but all of a sudden she appeared to be *everywhere*. Daisy lived on a sheep farm with her shepherd dad, who was considerably more handsome than *her* dad, much as it pained Kirsten to admit it, and more enthusiastic about being on the telly too.

As far as she could tell, Daisy and her dad spent most of their time rescuing tiny lambs from hills and then bottle-feeding them in the evening in front of perfect roaring fires. Daisy had just been snapped up for a nine-series prime-time show called *Daddy and Daisy – A Simple Life in the Country*. Nine series? *Nine?* Who wanted nine series about two farmers and their sheep?

Apparently, Britain did.

Every time Kirsten put the telly on, Daisy was there. Sitting on the studio sofa where *she*, Kirsten Bramble, rightfully belonged, wearing denim dungarees and going into long, incredibly boring anecdotes about *sleeping on straw under the stars* and the beauty of the outdoors and what her favourite lamb was called.

Well, two could play that game. Kirsten and Dad were going to go on the Jade Cooper chat show and tell lots of endearing stories about sleeping on proper beds and the beauty of being a *brand* and what Kirsten's favourite part of being *really successful and popular* was called—

There was a cough behind her. Kirsten whirled round, surprised, to see a stocky girl with round red cheeks and dark frizzy hair staring at her from the doorway of the Captain's Cabin. The girl was swamped by the frilly pink dress she wore. On her head was a peach-coloured bonnet tied under her chin in an unenthusiastic bow.

Oh no.

Not Olive. Anyone but *her*. Anyone but boring old *Olive Chudley* with her unsettling, serious grey eyes. Was there anything worse than being anywhere near your ex-best friend when you weren't best friends any more?

'I've come to fetch you,' said Olive Chudley. 'Everyone else is off the ship. What have you been doing? What's that on your face? *Ink?*'

Kirsten surreptitiously tried to rub it off. 'Maybe.'

'And what's *that*?' Olive pointed to the parchment behind Kirsten. 'Have you been reading something?' She tried to peer past Kirsten. 'What is it? It looks . . .'

'It's *nothing*,' said Kirsten quickly. 'Just a joke map. Pointless really.'

There was the faint sound of ink spluttering indignantly behind her, which Kirsten concealed with a loud cough.

Olive scratched her nose. '*Everyone's* waiting for you outside. Mrs Walia's not happy, and you've missed packed lunch, and so have I cos I was looking for you. The bus is waiting. Come on.'

'I was leaving anyway.' Kirsten grabbed her rucksack and walked out of the Captain's Cabin without looking back.

Behind her, the map on the table stretched and then went completely still. It felt like a nap, you see.

- 10 -
THE BEAUTIFUL TOFFEE APPLE

ON THE SHIP'S vast top deck, the world had grown very bright. After so long in the darkness, the sunshine felt almost supernatural, and made Kirsten squint. The ship seemed to quiver around her, like a racehorse ready to sprint. Everywhere felt full of movement and agitation, and for a moment Kirsten thought she could hear the WHOOSH, WHOOSH of the ship's heart, even though they'd left the engine room far behind.

Kirsten walked to the side and peered down, slightly sick with dizziness. Her class was gathered in a group on the tarmac below, back in their school uniform, looking really pleased at the prospect of Kirsten getting into trouble.

'What *have* you been doing, Kirsten?' called Mrs Walia.

'Sorry,' said Kirsten. 'I got, um, a bit lost? But I'll get off now.'

And, for two seconds, that was nearly true, and this story would have ended right here and now, after the very ordinary-looking full stop you'll find at the end of this sentence. (Don't stare at it or it'll feel embarrassed.)

But, fortunately for everyone who likes a tale with a bit of length to it, *just* as Kirsten was about to turn right, towards the front of the ship where the little bridge lay waiting to take her back to normality . . .

. . . she saw something else.

Something worth turning the other way for.

It was the steering wheel at the back of the ship.

It glowed in the sunshine like a beautiful toffee apple.

Where had that come from, and why hadn't she noticed it before? She wanted, suddenly, to be near it, and *who was she to question that?*

WHOOSH, WHOOSH,

went the ship's engine quickly.

So, instead of turning right, Kirsten turned left.

'Where are you going?' said Olive, looking confused. 'That's not the way off.'

'Hold on, Einstein,' murmured Kirsten. 'Wait.'

When she got to the steering wheel – which took a while, as it was right at the back of the ship – she stood behind it and looked ahead and was completely undone by what she saw.

The entire ship lay before her like a huge silver path.

The span of her! The outrageous, unapologetic size of her! *Here I am, this is my space and I am going to enjoy it*, she seemed to say, her deck stretched out in front of Kirsten like a promise and, with it, a dizzying array of colours and life: the wooden planks of the deck, shining in the sun, the bright flags, the immaculate black railings on either side, the large gleaming funnel in the middle of the deck, the white bowsprit that pointed out to sea like an elegant finger. And, beyond the ship, the jewelled colours of the Bristol harbourside: the slate-grey water, delicate sailing boats, pink terraced houses of Hotwells, that curiously bright and dazzling blue sky, the fluffy clouds that looked as if they'd just come out of the tumble dryer . . .

It was like standing in the middle of a kaleidoscope.

For an old black-and-white ship from the past, thought Kirsten, *she's good at making the right-now more colourful.* And that was the beginning of it all really. Her palms began to tingle and fizz. Now it was no longer enough just to be near the steering wheel.

She wanted to hold it.

So she reached out and . . .

. . . very, *very* lightly . . .

. . . put both hands on the ship's wheel and the ache instantly vanished.

As Kirsten looked at the large wheel, how shiny it was, how lovely, like the beginning of something, the brim of the captain's hat – that was funny, she'd forgotten she was wearing it – slid forward.

All she could really see now were two things.

One: her hands.

Two: the steering wheel.

There may as well have been nothing else in the entire world.

She felt a sudden desperate yearning and she wasn't sure if it was hers or someone else's. She was full of it: right up to the brim with it. Seagulls shrieked. Flags flapped. Kirsten's heart pounded. The beating of the ship's engine seemed to pick up. Even the droopy bonnet ribbon under Olive's chin perked up and fluttered.

Then everything suddenly went quiet, apart from the one word that boomed in Kirsten's head.

GO!

Her hands gripped the wheel a little tighter.

And, just like that, the ship – the dry-docked museum ship that shouldn't have been able to move at all – *lurched forward*.

- 11 -
OUT OF THE DOCK

THE SS *Great Britain* was an old ship, and a valuable one. Her iron hull had patches of rust and in some places her metal was thin and battered. To prevent this part of the ship from deteriorating any further, the bottom half of the hull was enclosed in an airtight chamber topped by thick glass.

For further protection, and to guarantee she didn't wobble from side to side, her hull was surrounded by thick reinforced steel poles. The entire ship was kept away from the water of the harbour itself by a thick concrete wall called a caisson.

You could say the ship was trapped by steel, and glass, and concrete.

But, the moment Kirsten touched the steering wheel, those reinforced poles began to buckle and break, and cracks inched their way across the glass panels.

The air filled with the sound of snapping and smashing and breaking, which would have been bad enough without all the screaming too. Kirsten was so frightened, she gripped the ship's wheel even tighter. (Which made everything worse, unfortunately.)

There was a dreadful pause as if the entire world was holding its breath. Then the poles holding the ship in place snapped. The glass around the middle of the ship broke and fell to the floor. Kirsten's stomach went *whoosh* into her mouth. Olive screamed, then turned to face Kirsten. The two ex-best friends stared at each other for four whole seconds, which was twice as much as their usual annual average.

It was chaos round the ship itself. People were running about in panic like ants round a doughnut, trying to avoid the broken metal and glass. There was a lot of arm-waggling, and not in celebration.

The ship began to move. With painful scraping sounds, she inched her way across the concrete slabs, past the broken mess of glass and poles, towards the open water of the docks, like a thirsty person crawling towards an oasis.

'What – why?' said Olive, pale and terrified, holding on to the railing for safety. Kirsten could not have put it better herself.

Only one thing now separated the ship and the water: the caisson. This was the impenetrable, indestructible, extremely thick wall that lay in front of the hull, the final barrier between the ship and the water that she had not touched for fifty years.

A man shouted: 'The caisson will hold her! The caisson will hold her!'

The caisson did not hold her.

The top of the ship's vast iron hull pushed at the caisson patiently. A silent, intense debate seemed to take place between the two. Then the indestructible wall snapped in half as easily as an ice-lolly stick and the ship broke through it and into the water.

Everybody around and aboard the ship went absolutely silent, united by one thought alone:

How is she moving?

And then water cascaded up and under the ship, easing her way out, and finally the SS *Great Britain* landed with a splash in the water of Bristol's Floating Harbour. Kirsten could almost feel the ship give a victorious wiggle with her backside, like a fish swimming away from a hook.

When Kirsten looked back towards the dock, she saw, just for a second, that funny short man with the tall black hat standing slightly apart from the crowds.

While everyone else was dashing around in a fluster, he remained quite still, smoking a cigar with an undeniable air of pride.

- 12 -
SPLISH-SPLASH

FOR AT LEAST thirty seconds after this shocking escape, the only sound was that of the small ripples gently breaking against the ship as she glided through the water.

On the other side of the river, in the weak spring sunshine, people enjoying a lunchtime drink at the Grain Barge Pub lifted their glasses and cheered. Bristolians loved the harbourside, and were fond of rejoicing in anything that happened there, even when it was clearly a mistake.

Kirsten and Olive turned to each other awkwardly.

'Do you think there's someone in the engine room making it move?' said Kirsten, after a pause.

'But h-how?' stammered Olive, her sardine-coloured eyes wide with shock under her bonnet. 'This is a museum ship, not an *operational* one. I mean, there's nothing down there apart from a replica engine, right? No coal? No fire?'

Kirsten had forgotten how clever and earnest Olive could be.

'*Too clever really, for the feel-good programme we're going to make with you,*' the telly people had said to Kirsten all those years ago. *'And it's a shame about her hair. And her ears. And her smile. And those feet. And her shoulders. And her gums. And her cuticles. And she gets quite scratchy and breathless when she's nervous – have you noticed? Apart from that, we totally love her, but sadly not quite enough for now. Have you got any other best friends we could use?'*

Kirsten's thoughts turned, panicked, to the grumpy map below deck. What if it really *was* a human-reading map, not a gimmick? Perhaps it would know why the ship was moving? And, if it did, maybe she could tell it to turn the ship round and everything could go back to normal?

'I'm – er – going to the loo,' she told Olive.

'No!' stammered Olive. 'Don't leave me all alone!' Then she went bright pink. 'I mean – it's just—'

Kirsten bit her lip, remembering something about Olive, how she sometimes felt when confronted with unexpected stressful situations. Shortness of breath, panic attacks . . . Was she having one now? If so, what should Kirsten do?

Olive closed her eyes. 'I'll be fine. Go. Just – don't take too long. I'm going to sit down and wait to be rescued.'

'Okay,' muttered Kirsten and slipped away.

Back inside the ship, she hesitated, unsure. She had no idea where the Captain's Cabin actually *was*. She'd found it by accident before. She looked one way, checked the walls – it wasn't there. She glanced the other way. It wasn't there either.

And then suddenly it was – an open door with the golden plaque saying:

It had materialised. From somewhere else.

The ship had a room on the loose? And why had it come looking for her?

It was as if the . . . Kirsten pushed the thought away, but it gently came back.

As if the room was making itself easier for her to find.

- 13 -
THE SECOND READING

IN THE DOORWAY, Kirsten took a deep breath. She was trembling all over, and her legs felt extremely unsteady. The walls rushed at her, then retreated. Once Kirsten could step into the room, she approached the parchment.

The lamps flickered. The map rippled.

YES? it wrote.

'It's me.'

I can see that. I'm old, not blind.

'Oh. Well, it's just that, um – the ship is – moving, and – you'd said something about going somewhere? But I don't want to go anywhere. I think there's been a mistake?'

Are you saying I'm not very good at reading humans? Is that what you're saying? The ink was spluttery and thick and the words came fast.

No point making an enemy of the map. 'No, I'm not saying that. But this shouldn't have happened.'

Everything is going according to plan.

'It's *so* not.'

That's your opinion.

'I know—'

But it's not fact. Human opinions are generally like barnacles on a rock – not very pretty, largely useless.

'Wait a second—'

I don't want to just sit and stare at you all day, you know. What do you want?

'I want you to read me again, find the *real* truth inside me, which is – like I said – that I don't want to go anywhere, and this is all a huge mistake. I've got big plans after school today. I'm going shopping *actually*, to find an outfit for *The Jade Cooper Show* on Friday—'

The map stared at her. Then all its four corners lifted up, in a small but definite shrug.

Kirsten went a bit pink. 'So – yeah. I think there's been an error.'

I don't normally do second readings. My energy is not what it was. But I will, just this once, because frankly I'm beginning to wonder if this is a mistake too.

'Oh,' said Kirsten, feeling slightly insulted.

Come closer. Look straight at me. Try not to think about anything . . . That was quick!

'Hey—' said Kirsten. And then that weird scanning sensation began again in her chest, as if her heart was being inspected.

The map began to glow. A flickering collection of dark blue lines arranged themselves. Disturbing words like . . .

Here be monsters

and

Sea of unimaginable depth

and

Oh no, here they come! Make way! It's the dreaded doldrums

. . . appeared briefly, then   v a n i s h e d.

Then all these things fused into a small but recognisable ship of dark blue ink. It glided across the map towards a large whirlpool. Then the tiny ship fell into the whirlpool and disappeared.

And Kirsten had no idea what any of that meant, but it didn't look good.

'Well?' she prompted.

My reading was correct. You have a journey to make. You are the chosen one. There will be hunger, possible madness, fear . . .

. . . Oh, wait! I wasn't meant to tell you any of that. Ignore that last bit. Pretend you never saw it.

'But – *where* are we going?' spluttered Kirsten. 'And – and – don't I have a say? Shouldn't I choose if I'm the chosen one?'

You want to choose?

'Yes? I mean – yes.'

Go on then.

Her mind went blank. In theory, she knew there were a lot of places out there, but it was very hard when put on the spot like this . . .

Just as I thought. You aren't ready. One day you will be but not now. Because you're so lost.

Kirsten wished the map would stop saying that. 'You've got this all wrong!'

Your heart has spoken.

'Not the last time I checked, it hasn't. Can't you listen to what I'm telling you now properly, with my mouth?'

Mouths? I hardly ever listen to mouths. How can you

expect something so tiny and cluttered to reveal anything big?

'Um – if you'd looked into my heart *properly*, all you'd have seen was that I want to go back to Bristol.'

This has nothing to do with what you want. Goodness me, you humans and your wantings. The way you feed them, like they're precious pets.

'Never mind what I want then. I – *need* to go back.'

And that's exactly where we're going, said the map.

'Back . . . to the dock?'

No. Somewhere much more important. But we are, in a manner of speaking, very much going back.

'Huh?'

There are things that must be named. There are people who must be forgiven. There are truths to be revealed. All these things must be done on this journey. Only then can it end.

'But – but – who's meant to do all of that?' said Kirsten, firmly hoping the map would say something like, **Oh, Doris down the road**.

You.

'Sorry?'

Actually, you and the ship. Your needs are eerily tangled up with each other, which is why all of this is happening. She chose you. You chose her. Embrace it.

'What?'

Do you really not understand any words at all? Have you been to the doctor about this?

'I understand *lots* of words *actually—*'

The first destination is decided. You will learn something from each destination and, when the time is right, you will choose the final destination, and that will be the most important one of all.

'*Each* destination?' Kirsten went rigid with terror. 'How many are you planning exactly? What is this, a cross-country bus route? And why can't you go into detail? What's with all the secrecy and weird riddles?'

Loose lips sink ships, my girl. You're going to have to work it all out for yourself.

'Why?'

Heavens to Betsy! scribbled the map furiously. *If I spoon-fed all the knowledge to you now, why, it wouldn't be much of a journey, would it? It'd be over before it had begun. And that would be bad, because a long, painful and baffling voyage is just what the doctor ordered.*

'It's *not*.'

It is actually. I checked with the ship's surgeon and he's in perfect agreement with me. Based on your recent appointment—

Kirsten suddenly remembered the mannequin surgeon who had stared at her for a moment or two. 'That wasn't an *appointment*,' she spluttered. 'That was *one second of accidental eye contact—*'

Yes, he's so good he often doesn't need longer than that. Anyway, he said you have a classic case of the heebie-jeebies.

'The *what?*'

Textbook apparently. So advanced that only sea air can cure it.

Kirsten had *had it*. 'You mean a *lifeless dummy* and a *talking map* are making decisions about my life? I want to make a complaint!'

On the contrary, it is I who should be complaining. It's really not good for my health to stare at a human for too long, and we must press on. Time is not on our side . . .

'Wait—'

If I read you much longer, I'm going to go human-eyed, and then I'll have parchment-ache all afternoon.

'But—'

I'm folding you up and putting you away now. Please enjoy the first stage of your journey.

Oh, and sorry for the complete lack of seatbelts, but they haven't been invented yet.

There is no dining cart today.

Toilet on middle deck is a bit blocked. Avoid if you can.

The map went blank.
And the ship
continued to move
through the water.

- 14 -
THE VOICE

A COLD, CLAMMY sweat broke out on Kirsten's back. She gripped the edges of the desk for support.

How could she make all of this just not happen? She eyed the map. If she ripped it in half, maybe its bizarre prophecies would suddenly stop, and so would the runaway ship?

She got as far as picking up one corner, but . . . found she couldn't do it. The map was so fragile. And – essentially – alive. She couldn't destroy it. But she could think very, very bad thoughts about it, at the very least.

She let it fall back on the table and squeezed her fists hard against her eyes, desperate not to cry. Then a voice spoke inside her head and it wasn't her own.

'Captain,' said the voice. 'There there, Captain.'

The voice didn't belong to anyone else she recognised either. It sounded like it belonged to someone old. *Very* old. It was basically very strange, very new and very old. It was also, curiously, quite maternal and gentle.

'Don't take on so,' the voice continued. 'I know old Flatty doesn't have the best people skills. But it knows a thing or two about a thing or two. You can't be read by a better, fairer map than Flatty.'

Kirsten stared round the dark room, her tears and her terror momentarily forgotten.

'What? Who are *you*?' she whispered.

And the voice spoke again. 'I would have thought that was obvious, darling.'

Kirsten blinked. 'Are you . . . um . . . a ghost?'

There was a strange silence, and then she heard the voice again, as clear as if someone was speaking right in her ear. 'A *ghost*? Darling, please! Guess again.'

But Kirsten didn't want to guess.

She turned on her heel and fled.

- 15 -

THE MAMMOTH SPEAKS

KIRSTEN WASN'T SURE how she managed to stagger back up the staircase. She'd gone down hoping to make the situation better. *That* hadn't gone well. And now, above deck, things were also dreadful.

Word had apparently spread throughout Bristol that the historic **SS *Great Britain***, a source of pride for the city, was somehow on the move for the first time in over fifty years. Casual onlookers had plainly decided to treat this as a cause for celebration, rather than the disaster it *actually* was.

So there was waving and cheering, tooting of car horns and clapping all along the harbour, as the runaway ship moved gracefully through the water.

'What took you so long?' said Olive, lifting a worried face to Kirsten. Her usually red cheeks were pale, and in her large taffeta dress and bonnet she looked like a crumpled china doll sitting cross-legged on the deck. She had an old, cracked mobile phone in her hand. 'I've been trying to call Mum, but can't get through.'

It took Kirsten a while to tune back into reality after the

map's disturbing talk about journeys, not to mention the strange voice in the Captain's Cabin.

Then, looking at Olive's phone, she realised with a jolt of dismay that she'd left her mobile in her bedroom that morning.

'Um . . . right,' she said falteringly.

Then all conversation dried up. A few years ago, she'd have already been halfway through telling Olive about the map and the voice.

But now she had a new best friend. She thought, fleetingly, of India-Rose, her best friend since the end of Series Three. India-Rose didn't go to her school and they didn't have much in common, but she was photogenic and the producers had been very insistent. Their episodes together usually involved them having sleepovers, or pillow fights, which were staged and choreographed. (Once, Kirsten had suggested that India-Rose have a sleepover *without* being filmed, just for fun, and India-Rose had said she was busy.)

Kirsten's stomach churned. She only just made it to the railings of the top deck in time before she brought up her breakfast.

Olive got up, took a few uncertain steps towards her and thrust something into her hand. A half-opened pack of tissues.

'Thanks,' mumbled Kirsten, wiping her mouth.

Olive gave a casual shrug. 'It's okay. I feel sick too.'

Kirsten turned from the railings and looked at her properly, close up, in the bright light of day.

There was a new scar just next to her right eyebrow. How had she got that? Cycling? Judo? Was she still into those? And since when had she had her ears pierced? Olive was completely unknown to her now. Kirsten didn't even know which secondary school she'd be going to.

'Can I please borrow that?' she asked Olive, pointing at her mobile. 'I want to try and phone Dad.'

Olive handed it over. 'There's not much battery left,' she said. 'Sorry it's a bit cracked.'

'It's fine,' muttered Kirsten. 'Thank you.' She hastily tapped Dad's number into the battered phone, but got a busy tone. She *could* try to phone Edwina or her agent, Keith O'Keefe, or even – at a push – India-Rose. But she didn't know their numbers off by heart.

'No reply?' said Olive as Kirsten handed it back, shaking her head.

'Well, look, never mind.' Olive rubbed her nose roughly and gave a shaky smile. 'They're bound to come and fetch us soon. Either that, or the ship will stop. There's no way it can keep moving. I'm sure it will just grind to a halt in a minute or two.'

She looked uncertainly round the massive deck as the ship moved slowly along the harbourside. 'Right?'

'She,' corrected Kirsten faintly.

'Huh?'

'You call ships *she*. Someone, um, told me once.'

Her mind was working overtime. Would the ship really stop, like Olive thought?

That map downstairs doesn't seem to think we'll be grinding to a halt soon.

She groaned.

Olive put her head to one side. 'You look dreadful. Why don't you go to the front? Might make your motion sickness better. I'll stick around here. I'm going to try Mum again . . .'

While Olive tapped patiently away at her phone, Kirsten turned and did as she suggested, burdened with worries. Not only was she desperate to speak to Dad, but there was that mysterious voice she'd heard in the Captain's Cabin too.

I would have thought that was obvious, darling. What *had* that voice been? Her imagination?

All of a sudden, there was a loosening inside Kirsten's head, as if her brain was making space for something.

There was a strange silence, and then she could hear the voice again as clear as if someone was right next to her. 'Oh no,' it said. 'I'm not your imagination at all. I'm *real*. I'm the Mammoth. I'm the SS *Great Britain*. I'm the *ship*.'

Kirsten gripped the rail as they left behind the floating harbour, and reached the River Avon.

PART 2

'She had set her own rules, and did not follow theirs'

Ewan Corlett, *The Iron Ship: The Story of Brunel's* **SS *Great Britain***

- 16 -
A HERO IS BORN BUT DOESN'T LiKE iT

'YOU'RE THE WHAT?' said Kirsten. 'You're the – WHAT?'

'I shall not repeat myself,' said the voice. It was a strong, deliberate voice – as if every word was a piece of metal being beaten out with a hammer. 'Any lady worth her sea salt knows that. It gives society the mistaken impression that she's not worth listening to in the first place. I say things once, twice on occasion, but never thrice.'

'But – but – why can I hear you? What's going on?'

'Because *you're* my next captain, Captain,' said the ship. 'Just like old Flatty said. Perfect candidate for the job. You're hired.'

'I'm your *what*?'

'Oh, do start taking things in properly, Captain. Give those grubby side-holes on your face a scrub and a mop, will you?'

'My *side-holes*? Do you mean my ears?'

'I suppose so. Bit pathetic, aren't they? I'm always surprised they work at all. Now listen, is anyone going to bring us some champagne? I don't normally start a journey without at least a bottle. I do *adore it*, especially when the glass goes SMASH and the crowds go YAY and the bubbles pour down me, tickle-tickle-YUM.'

Kirsten felt a bit wobbly on her legs all of a sudden. The ship continued to speak into her brain. 'See if you can find a waiter nearby, will you, and give him a nudge? Because there is a proper way to do this, you know. Champagne at the beginning, champagne in the middle and champagne at the end, yes? But nothing else – honestly. I don't like to make too much of a fuss.'

The difficult thing about talking with a ship, thought Kirsten wildly, *is that you aren't sure which bit to look at when it – she – is talking.*

'I knew this was going to happen from the moment I felt your feet on my planks, Captain. You wanted to *go*. There was something inside you that needed the best, most important ship in the world so badly. Luckily for you, I checked my diary and guess what? I'm free.' She gave a wiggle in the water.

The shiny black bolts on the railings all appeared to swivel in their bearings like eyes and regarded Kirsten.

'Well, I'm not,' said Kirsten.

'You're quite a *bit younger* than my last captain admittedly,' said the ship, ignoring this. 'And a girl, which is new. But, as Isambard himself thought, and I should know because

I was inside his brain for years and years, you have to keep trying new things, and you have to be prepared to make mistakes, in the pursuit of perfection.'

Flags fluttered merrily above Kirsten's head.

'I'm not a mistake,' she muttered.

'Jolly good. Do you know,' the ship went on happily, 'I've always *loved* this bit of a journey – when I've met my new One, and we're just setting off, and my insides are freshly packed and mopped and cleaned, and all the little people inside my belly are excited and well behaved . . . The beginnings of things are always so wonderful, aren't they? They've always been my favourite part. It's endings I try to avoid. Endings are sad and leave me empty. All my little passengers go troop, troop, troop out of me and, after carrying them, getting to know them, keeping them safe, I never see them again. Endings are bad.'

'Oh,' mumbled Kirsten, overwhelmed.

'But never mind! We move on! That's what ships do. You're a quiet one, aren't you? Struggling to express your gratitude?'

'You could say that.'

'You mustn't worry about a thing. We wouldn't be doing this if you weren't right for the job. Old Flatface and I both think—'

'Flatface? The map?'

'That's the one. Tempting to ignore, on account of it not being a ship, and being quite useless on water and what have you. But if there's one thing Flatty knows, and knows well, it's its onions. And Flatty always works out the best routes.'

Kirsten tried to swallow, but her throat felt too dry. 'How are you and, um, Flatty connected?'

'Well, it's rather difficult to explain to a human because the engineering of it all is incredibly sophisticated, and Flatty says you're not the brightest spark in the furnace—'

'Try me,' said Kirsten through gritted teeth.

'Well, in basic terms, Flatty is kind of my guardian. Flatty looks after me. You could say Flatty's my brain.'

'Ships . . . have . . . brains?'

'*Everything* has a brain if you know where to look. Apart from a few humans I've known over the years, but that's to be expected. Very poor substitutes for ships, your lot.'

'Humans are *not* substitutes for ships,' said Kirsten indignantly.

'You can say that again. Anyway, as a brain, Flatface is exceptional. Even if I haven't understood it completely in years. You see I move and Flatty does most of the strategy.'

'Pardon?' said Kirsten.

'I'm the most important and biggest ship in the world, Captain. I can't waste time on things that are small – like details. The way I see it is that I control what happens up above deck extremely masterfully, darling, but everything down there, below my planks, all those little rooms and cavities full of the past and old stories, I leave well alone as much as I can.'

Kirsten opened her mouth, then shut it.

'Old Flatty seems happy down there, stewing in thought, ruminating with ink, and once in a while it says something wise, which is nice. Flatty tells me where to go, and that's where I go. I live in the present; it's the only way to live. I don't *question things* or overthink. I leave all that to Flatty. Follow?'

'Not really.'

'Capital. Thinking too much makes one heavy. I was built to be light and fast.'

Kirsten decided to be firm with the ship. 'Listen. You've got the wrong girl. I'm *not* your captain. This is a mistake, that's all.'

There was an awkward silence. Kirsten noticed vaguely that Olive had stopped fiddling with her mobile and was slowly walking up the deck towards her, but then the ship started to speak again.

'I *was* expecting a bit more excitement from you, Captain,' was her eventual prickly response. 'Don't all children love ships and the dazzling promise of adventure on the high seas?'

Children? thought Kirsten hazily. She hadn't thought of herself as a child in years. She was an entertainer. She was a popular TV personality. But a child?

'I don't know,' she admitted. 'Not this one anyway.'

'Well, regardless, this is how it works. Captains – that's *you* now, darling – steer. *I* dazzle. I do all the moving; you hold the wheel; Flatty does the planning. It's a very effective division of labour. So why don't you take the helm and–'

'No,' said Kirsten, as loudly as she could inside her brain. 'Look, if you're thinking that I'm going to come along on some sort of magical mystery tour with you and a faded map, I'm sorry, but unless you've cleared it with my agent, that's not happening.'

The ship said nothing. From somewhere on the deck came the sound of footsteps coming closer. Kirsten stared out past the front of the ship. They had left the busy harbourside behind, and were now on the sludgy, windy River Avon, snaking out between the hills and woods of outer Bristol. They went under the high arch of the Clifton Suspension Bridge. A few people on the bridge had stopped and were peering down at them, open-mouthed.

Kirsten gave them a wave and a dazzling smile, ever the professional, then resumed the argument.

'Look, I *can't* just nip off on a spontaneous ocean crossing. I'm part of a very popular, award-winning television programme. My new series is about to air soon. We've got a big publicity drive I need to be around for . . . and also you can't just whisk someone you don't know off on a journey and not even *tell them* where they're going.' Kirsten's words began to pick up speed, like a sled going downhill.

'First of all, this isn't *Swallows and Amazons*. This isn't the 1950s when children just – went to the sea and captured smugglers and came home in time for tea. I don't have a pork pie in my pocket and a wonderful sense of fun. This is *the twenty-first century*, I'm not allowed to eat pork pies because I'm on a strict calorie-controlled diet, I have a schedule to keep and a contract to stick to and lots of publicists to keep happy. I'm *not* a captain.'

'You *are*.'

'I'm totally wrong for this job. I can barely *ride a bike*, let alone drive–'

'Steer,' muttered the ship.

'–steer a ship. See, I don't even know what it's called! I don't know what *anything* on a ship is called! I don't know what's front–'

'Bow,' said the ship.

'–and what's back–'

'Stern,' said the ship.

'–or what's left or what's right–'

'Port, starboard. Yes, you are rather rusty admittedly . . .'

'I'm hopeless with geography, I can't read winds, I barely know what the oceans are called and—'

'Are you always this obsessed with your failings, Captain? I only ask because they're extremely *dull*. Will they go on much longer?'

'I just can't, okay?' The sigh Kirsten let out was as large and ragged as a seagull's wing. 'I hope you understand.'

'I understand perfectly,' said the ship kindly. 'I understand you need this journey more than I thought. Looks like I got you out *just* in time.'

'Argh!'

screamed Kirsten as Bristol grew smaller behind her.

'So exciting!' said the SS *Great Britain*.

'What's going on?' Olive had stomped up the deck and was standing next to Kirsten, peering out from her bonnet. 'You've been standing here, muttering to yourself, doing weird gestures with your hands like you're having an argument with someone . . . And why did you just scream?'

'*Just because*,' said Kirsten, trying to sound normal,

despite every cell in her body shrieking in panic. The last person she wanted to tell was Olive Chudley.

Their mutual glaring was interrupted by the sound of someone shouting into a loudspeaker right behind them.

- 17 -
RESCUE ATTEMPT

COMING UP BEHIND the **SS *Great Britain*** was a small speedboat, with the words

BRISTOL WATER
AUTHORITY

painted on the side, waggling slightly in the eddies and swirls the ship was leaving in her wake. The little boat overtook the ship and began to cruise along her length, starboard side.

'Are you okay?' shouted a woman with a megaphone.

'No!' screamed Olive. 'We are *not* okay! Please get me off this ship!'

Kirsten flinched a little.

'How many people are onboard?' asked the woman on the rescue boat.

'Just me and her!' shouted Olive, glancing at Kirsten.

'Got any idea what's making the ship move?'

'None!' said Olive, looking terrified. 'You mean you don't know?'

'Not a clue,' said the woman. 'All we know, and honestly it's a good place to start from, is that it's not us, and it's not anyone back at the dock either.'

'Then who is it?' screamed Olive, while Kirsten tried to look innocent.

'Very good question. Let's try to rescue you girls, all right? We're going to throw up this rope ladder,' shouted the woman, 'and what we need you to do, right, is tie it to a railing, okay?'

There followed several attempts to make the rope ladder go over the railing. Each time the people on the speedboat threw the ladder, the ship seemed to rock a little, or go a little faster, or swerve to the side.

Kirsten thought she could hear an odd hiccuping sound from within the ship's belly. Was she . . . *laughing*?

After twenty minutes of throwing the ladder and watching it land in the water each time, the crew below looked perplexed and defeated.

'Can't you keep trying?' Kirsten begged.

The speedboat rocked unsteadily in the water below them.

'Unfortunately, rescuing you is much harder than it looks,' admitted the woman.

'Well, if anyone's doing any rescuing, it's me,' muttered the **SS *Great Britain***. 'Tell her.'

'If we stay here, we'll capsize,' said the woman. 'Very strange. Must be some new currents we weren't aware of. Not to panic. I expect the big cheeses will get involved – look out for them when you get to the Bristol Channel. You can't miss 'em. Cheerio for now!'

Olive saw the little boat fall back and gave a tiny sob. Then she frantically began to rip at her dress and bonnet. 'I can't – breathe—' she gasped.

Kirsten eyed her nervously. Olive's skin had taken on a clammy sheen. She began to make desperate fluttering gestures with her hands. Kirsten ran to her and began to unzip the Victorian dress with shaking fingers.

Olive hurriedly pulled it over her head, gasping for breath. Now she looked like the schoolgirl she was, in her grey trousers, white shirt and grey Brimmerton Primary cardigan.

'Thanks,' she panted, ripping off her bonnet and throwing it on top of the discarded dress. Then she sat down on the deck and stared out at the River Avon with a wide-eyed look of disbelief.

'Still get them then?' said Kirsten quietly. 'Panic attacks?'

'Yep.'

'Sorry,' said Kirsten.

Olive shrugged. 'It is what it is. Sometimes I count – that helps.'

Silence fell over the deck. Once Olive's colour returned,

Kirsten took a few steps away. The ship continued to chug further up the river.

Her geography wasn't the *greatest*, but even she knew that, if you followed them for long enough, all rivers led to the sea.

This was worrying. Were they really destined to reach the ocean? By themselves? On a rusty old ship that hadn't sailed for . . .

'Over one hundred and thirty-five years, Captain. My last journey was in 1886.'

You're reading my mind now? thought Kirsten, not wanting to alarm Olive further. *I didn't give you permission to do that!*

'I'd like not to, but you are thinking *rather loudly*. I hope you're not going to be doing this all the way to New York.'

'*New York?*' gasped Kirsten out loud, before she could help herself.

'What?' said Olive, looking up.

'Um, nothing,' said Kirsten, moving even further away from her ex-friend and towards the front of the ship.

'What do you mean *New York?*' she hissed once out of earshot.

'Didn't Flatty tell you?' said the ship.

'No, Flatty most certainly did not,' said Kirsten through gritted teeth. This must be the *first destination* the map had threatened her with.

'Oh yes. I used to go there *all the time* in the first flush of youth. In fact, getting to New York is *why* I was built. I was transatlantic, darling. Great times. Back and forth across the Atlantic Ocean, everyone excited, banquets every night, quadrilles and port and the finest silver . . .'

'Really,' said Kirsten.

'I expect the New Yorkers miss me dreadfully. Whenever I sailed into their harbour, they'd line the dock to see me, bring their little kiddywinks out, and all their photo-makers would go *flash POP pop* and bring out the most beautiful sheen on my hull. Prepare yourself for adulation: it can be quite exhausting if you're not used to it . . .'

'Right,' said Kirsten, glancing up at the fluttering flags around her.

'Old Flatty wants me to embark on a victory parade, I think,' said the ship contemplatively. 'A chance to revisit old haunts. One last journey, for old times' sake, give my public a spot of razzle-dazzle. Once you have it, you never lose it, darling—'

'Razzle what?' said Kirsten.

'And, by the way, less of this *old and rusty*, please. I *may* have been born in 1839, but there's no need for that sort of language. I mean, look at New York. That city's been calling itself New since 1664. So, if New York is still New, then so am I.'

Even through her shock, Kirsten couldn't help noticing what an interesting voice the ship had. Prim and cool like a cucumber sandwich, yet as playful and rough as a teething puppy. Despite being a vessel made of iron, she sounded very human at times, but her accent slipped about all over the place. Sometimes she sounded like the merry men in the Pigeon's Mangled Foot's beer garden, and then in the next second her metallic voice would make a whirring sound, as if it was shifting cogs, and turn into something more precise and clipped.

Kirsten thought of all the different people who would have had a hand in making her – the labourers, the welders, those who forged her and built her, the shipbuilders and Isambard Brunel himself . . . Had all their accents and sayings somehow seeped into her planks and metal plates, and shaped her voice just as they'd shaped her form?

And underneath all of that lurked something else too, something that peeped through the other elements like a playful child playing hide-and-seek, and that was different altogether – not human at all but darker and brighter and harder and more liquid, and Kirsten had the oddest sensation that *that* voice was the truest of all, but the hardest to reach. It was like trying to glimpse a secret underwater.

Despite herself, Kirsten found it intriguing. It was a voice of mystery, packed with nearly two centuries' worth of experience. The ship might have an ego to match her size, but at least she wasn't boring. It was hard to know what she'd do or say next, and that was what made her so exciting.

- 18 -

THE HERO IS STILL SOMEWHAT RELUCTANT

ON THE NARROW strip of muddy river water that twisted out of Bristol, the ship continued to talk at Kirsten. Her favourite topic of conversation soon became dazzlingly clear.

'Friendship, relationship, comradeship, leadership . . .' the ship went on smugly. 'Notice a pattern?'

'That's—' Kirsten floundered for words.

'Worship, fellowship, partnership—'

'Oh, stop saying words with ship at the end! It doesn't mean anything. That's not how things *work*—'

'It's exactly how they work, darling. Humans always come adrift when they don't have enough *ships* mixed in with their most important things. You need me more than you could ever know.'

As the ship moved down the River Avon, their surroundings began to change. The pretty cottages and back gardens gave way to factories, cranes and grey flyovers.

This was Avonmouth, the edge of Bristol, where the city met the ocean, the last bit of urban sprawl before they reached the Bristol Channel, and it seemed as if everyone there had crammed themselves up against their office windows or scrambled to the roof of the nearest multistorey car park to see the SS *Great Britain* on the move again.

Olive had recovered enough to pick up her mobile and had joined Kirsten at the prow, trying to phone her mum again. 'I just can't get through!' she said. Then she dialled 999 and shouted into the receiver that she was on a historic ship and it was heading for the ocean.

'They just hung up on me,' she said, stunned. 'Said I was wasting police time. Me? I'm a Girl Guide.'

She walked unsteadily away from Kirsten, as if she needed a moment to collect herself.

Kirsten had a sudden idea and began to speak to the ship under her breath. 'Look, why don't we just stay here for an hour or so, you can, um, give them a spot of the old razzle-dazzle, and then we can go back?'

'Return? We've barely started. I do question your approach to life. A captain who doesn't want to be a captain? I've never come across such a lot of old flotsam in my life. You *look* like a captain.'

'How?' Kirsten quickly checked herself over, but saw only her school uniform: a smart grey skirt and cardigan, pristine white shirt and knee-length socks and glossy black leather school shoes. 'I'm eleven! I look *nothing* like a captain!'

'You've got a captain's hat—'

Kirsten's hands flew up to her head. *That stupid hat!* 'It's from the dressing-up box – it's just a *prop*.'

Kirsten could have sworn that the sides of the ship actually *lifted* in a shrug.

'Looks like a hat,' said the **SS *Great Britain***. 'And you've a bit of me inside your hands. We're bonded. We're meant to be. We are to experience the joy of GOING. It's called the wander-thirst, and there's no point fighting it. Fighting your wander-thirst is such a colossal waste of time, darling.'

Kirsten stared at her palms. She hadn't *asked* for those wooden splinters. She'd *tripped*! She'd had vertigo! She wasn't good with *heights*. This wasn't destiny – this was just being uncoordinated at an unfortunate time!

'Look, don't take this the wrong way, ship, but you're not seaworthy. I saw the rusty patches around your hull, and they're *huge*.'

'I'm not *what?*' said the ship sternly, with all the might of her iron voice.

'Seaworthy,' repeated Kirsten quietly.

'Say that again,' said the ship, sounding dangerous. The water around them began to get choppy as the **SS *Great Britain*** zigzagged wildly in the water.

Kirsten was a quick learner. 'No. A lady never repeats

herself. Anyway, it's true. You're a *tourist attraction*. You're not, like, meant to actually *sail on the sea any more*. You don't even have any coal . . . Speaking of which, I can't understand how you're moving at all. Do *you* know?'

Olive had turned round and was looking at Kirsten curiously, but Kirsten was too caught up in this row to notice.

'You wanted to go. I wanted to go. Together, we went,' said the ship firmly. 'Sometimes, that's the only fuel you need. Listen, darling, I've got a million nautical miles under my belt, and you don't get *that* without learning a few tricks of the trade along the way . . .'

'That doesn't make any sense!'

'Oh, you don't think a magnificent vessel designed by the *greatest engineer of the Victorian era* makes *sense*?'

The ship was clearly rattled, and the argument seemed to have the effect of making her pitch and roll in the water. After one violent movement sent Kirsten and Olive tumbling, Kirsten hurried over to the steering wheel.

Then she took a deep breath

and turned it slightly,
to straighten the ship. It
wasn't as easy as she thought.
The wheel was stiff and
awkward, and didn't move at all
beautifully, despite its appearance –
but it did rotate just enough for Kirsten
to straighten the ship, stop the wild jerking
movement, and manoeuvre them out into the grey
wide water of the Bristol Channel.

The land fell away, the river turned into the sea,
Bristol dwindled into just an opening behind them,
and suddenly the world had skipped into the complete
unknown and dragged Kirsten along with it.

- 19 -
'I'M STEERING IT WITH MY MIND'

A SECOND LATER, Olive peered under the brim of the grubby old captain's hat and into Kirsten's eyes with unnerving directness. 'Okay, this has gone on long enough. What's going on?'

Kirsten played for time. 'Going on?' She gestured at the ocean and the ship. 'Apart from the obvious?'

Olive's eyes narrowed. 'Going on with *you*. Your lips have been moving, as if you're talking to yourself. Plus –' Olive's voice had the tone of someone wrapping up an argument – 'you just *steered the ship*.' Her eyes filled with suspicion. 'This isn't an episode of your show, is it? I haven't just been . . . I dunno – pranked?'

She looked around nervously for cameras, visibly cringing. Olive *hated* them, hated posing, hated being the centre of any kind of attention. It had been one of the reasons her audition for Kirsten's show had gone so badly; that and the fact she hadn't made the tiniest effort.

'No!' said Kirsten. 'Honest!'

This did not seem to reassure Olive – if anything, it

made her more worried. 'Then what is happening? It's not *fair* if you know something and you're not telling me . . .'

Olive's breathing was beginning to change. Hurriedly, Kirsten said, 'Okay, I'll tell you. The truth is, I've accidentally activated the ship by mistake.'

Olive rolled her eyes and looked frustrated. 'This is not the time for stupid *jokes*, Kirsten. We're actually heading towards the open sea, and I don't know if you noticed but there are no adults or lifeboats around—'

'It's not a joke! I swear! I know it sounds crazy but . . . the ship is moving because of me. Because I'm onboard. I'm steering it with my mind, or she's steering me – or something.'

Olive began to walk away, shaking her head. Kirsten followed her. She was beginning to regret embarking on this confession, but one thing she'd learned from nearly four years of shooting an *extremely popular, award-winning* reality-TV show was that you couldn't just abandon a scene once you'd started it: you had to *see where it went*. That was what their director always said.

'Olive. Listen to me. *Please*. I'm not lying. We – that is, me and the, um, ah—'

'Ship?' said Olive witheringly.

'*Yes*. Honestly. We can talk to each other. I can hear her voice; she can hear mine. We're on a *mission* apparently.

Oh, and there's a rude map downstairs that reads people, and spits ink in your face if you get too close, so avoid that if you can—'

Olive scrunched her entire face up in a way that was almost impressive. 'Uh-huh.'

'Anyway. The map thinks we, that is, me and the ship, ha ha ha ha, have to, um, *do* something together. Something about finding lost things? It said loads of stuff, to be honest. It was a bit overwhelming. And we're going to New York first, because everyone there wants to see the ship again, and I picked the wrong hat out of the dressing-up box and Mrs Walia drove two splinters into my hands and the ship thinks I'm the captain.'

Kirsten moved a hand wearily across her forehead with a professional dramatic flourish. 'Basically.'

Olive gave Kirsten a sudden smile, which looked dangerously like pity. 'Oh, now I understand. I know it's been sort of weird for you, this last year, what with the show struggling a bit, and ratings plummeting, I've heard. It can't have been easy . . .'

'This has nothing to do with that,' said Kirsten indignantly. 'I'm not losing my marbles! I *am* communicating with the ship telepathically! We've been kidnapped and we're going to New York! And then other places! I think!'

Olive muttered something like: 'I *knew* things were bad.'

Then gave Kirsten another entire smile, which made two in three years. 'You need a lie-down.'

'I actually don't.'

But Olive had walked ahead to the companionway and was holding the door open for her. 'Let's get you out of the sun and somewhere quiet. Then I'll try the police again.'

It was hard to argue with Olive when she was in that sort of mood.

Inside the ship, Olive turned smartly on her heels and headed right. And then she stopped so abruptly that Kirsten walked into the back of her.

'This door – this room—' stammered Olive. 'They've moved around.'

'Yup,' sighed Kirsten. '*She* does that.'

Both girls looked up at the door they were now facing. It had a sign on it that said:

But, as they watched, the sign shimmered and flexed and the words rearranged themselves. Now the sign said:

'I *told* you!' said Kirsten, triumphant. 'I wasn't lying!

This ship is . . . alive!'

The effect on Olive was electric. Colour returned to her cheeks and her eyes grew a little brighter. 'Did it – did *she* say anything about this door?'

Kirsten tried to remember the baffling set of instructions the map had revealed earlier. 'It wasn't the ship, it was the map. It said I have to find things? And name things? And that truths must be revealed? And . . . oh, so much more. Apparently, I have the heebie-jeebies.'

'What are they?'

'Something bad.'

To Kirsten's surprise, Olive smiled. 'You know what this is, right?' she said, jerking her head at the door.

'A nightmare?'

'No. It's a quest.'

'Huh?'

'A *quest*. Come on, Kirsten, you used to be good at this sort of stuff. It's just like *The Hidden Realms of Zeleth*. You know, on level three, when we had to unlock the secret door that led us to the Tribe of Helpful Toads? That took us eight weeks to work out!'

Kirsten stared at her. '*The Hidden Realms of Zeleth*? That stupid game we played on your dad's console?'

Kirsten didn't know why she called it stupid. She'd actually loved *Zeleth*, the endless afternoons in Olive's lounge playing it together. They'd really got into it. KIRSTEN THE INVINCIBLE and MIGHTY OLIVE had been their wizard names. And they'd roamed strange lands, trading things with villagers and monsters to help them on their way. The worlds in *Zeleth* may have changed from level to level – sometimes they were mazes, sometimes abandoned castles – but the essential rules of the quests never did.

'Stupid or not,' said Olive firmly, 'I know one when I see one, and this –' she looked at Kirsten's hat and then at the door – 'is a quest.'

Kirsten shook her head. 'This isn't a quest, it's a misunderstanding.'

But, even as she protested, she wasn't so sure. The air around them felt very crackly. Maybe this whole thing was just a tiny bit questy.

'I'm right,' said Olive simply. 'I'm getting definite *open this* vibes from that door. I bet there's something important on the other side. It might be a talisman or a special potion . . . Something to help you get home. That was what the, um, talking map said you had to find, right?'

Kirsten tried to turn the door handle. 'It's locked.'

'Course it's locked!' Olive widened her eyes. 'How many open doors have you ever seen on a quest? Come on, Kirsten – this is basic-level stuff.'

It was a fair point. Kirsten knocked on the door with her knuckles. Nothing happened. But all her senses, quivering and taut, detected the tiniest movement from the other side – like the secret inside had blinked. What would she have done when playing *Zeleth*?

I shall use my Overwhelming Powers of Persuasion.

'Can you – um – please open the door?'

SHHHHTTTTP

There was a soft sliding noise, then two very faint thumps, as if the secret had fallen to the floor. Olive gasped. Kirsten thought about being sick again.

The handle moved slowly down and then flew up.

The door swung open . . .

- 20 -
PERMISSION GRANTED

. . . INTO A TINY, dark storage room. It was empty.

Kirsten felt intensely relieved. Olive had sounded so convincing, she'd almost got caught up in the whole thing . . .

Until her eyes adjusted. Standing in front of them was a short, undernourished, barefoot boy dressed in rags, regarding them warily.

The barefoot boy suddenly blinked, and Kirsten and Olive both gasped and took a step back. Then he slipped out of the shadows and stepped tentatively towards them. Shorter than Kirsten, he came up to about her shoulders.

'Are you - lost? Were you on a school trip too?' she asked, although he didn't look like he'd been on one, she thought privately. Not with those dirty, ragged trousers, bare feet and a cream shirt with streaks of mildew in its folds.

'School?' said the boy. '*School?* I'm not at school. I'm a *boy*, Captain. A boy, for the ship.'

'I'm not a captain,' said Kirsten wearily.

'You got a captain's hat on.' He sounded wistful, and a little bit envious.

'It's a long story,' said Kirsten, trying to sound conversational, all the while shocked at how dirty and unkempt the boy looked. Who could have let him get into such a state? And what was a *boy for the ship* anyway? She glanced at Olive, who seemed to be thinking the same thing.

The boy gave them a hesitant smile, and the effect on his face was curious. It was as if something thick was moving across his face, like yoghurt.

Olive spoke gently. 'How did you get stuck in there then?

'Some people locked me in here. A long time ago.'

He shifted slightly and light from a porthole fell on his face. Now they could see what was different about him, why his skin rippled so oddly when he moved his mouth and opened his curiously glassy eyes.

He wasn't a real boy, he was a mannequin.

And he'd been locked in a broom cupboard. That was why they hadn't seen him during their tour.

For a moment, the three children stared at one another, and they were all so still and so silent that, if you'd been looking at them, you wouldn't have been able to tell, immediately, who was fake and who was flesh.

He glanced back at the dusty cupboard he'd been in and shuddered with relief.

'Were you in there long?' asked Kirsten, suddenly feeling sorry for him.

He shrugged, and the movement seemed to take a huge effort, as if his body had been still for a long time.

'I couldn't tell you exactly,' he said after a while. His voice was low and quiet, but, even in the few seconds since he'd come out of the room, seemed to flicker with eagerness. 'All I know is I was on my usual watch, and then one of the grown-ups picked me up and said something about how no one wanted "this exhibit" any more.'

'So they got rid of you because—' Olive prompted.

'"Cabin boys aren't very exciting. He's not got much of a story, has he? He's not a hero, just a dogsbody. Let's put him away for a bit." That's what they said anyway. It was years ago! I didn't know I was meant to be exciting, Captain! I thought I was there to keep the ship clean. Except they never gave me any fresh water to do it, just that mop –' he gestured behind him – 'which they threw in after me.'

The more the boy talked, the more liquid and lifelike his face became, as if it had been stiff from lack of use before. He gave the mop a look of regret, then tugged at his synthetic hair, which dislodged a spider. All three of them watched as the spider slowly floated down to the floor, and scuttled away across the patterned carpet.

'You must have been in there a while,' said Kirsten, dazed.

'They really tickle too,' stated the boy. 'Are we on the move? I felt the ship quickening.'

'Yeah, we are,' said Olive.

'Unfortunately,' added Kirsten, surreptitiously kicking the ship.

'This is *so questy*,' said Olive, beaming as she looked round the ship in a new way. 'You were telling the truth then.'

'Yep,' said Kirsten flatly.

Olive hesitated, then went a bit pink. 'I thought you were talking rubbish earlier. Sorry. It's just you've seemed so preoccupied at school recently, and always seem so tired – Mum said the stress of being a show-biz telly star has got to you?'

'Well, now you know. And she's wrong by the way. I'm *fine*.' With some effort, Kirsten produced one of her famous dazzling smiles. 'Don't worry about *me*. I'm better than ever. I've got a new agent, a new contract, we've just wrapped Season Five *and* I'm going on *The Jade Cooper Show* this Friday—'

'*Great*,' said Olive.

'It is *actually*,' said Kirsten. 'A great promotional opportunity.'

'Sounds *really* fun.'

'Have you got better plans for Friday night? Or are you going to be hunched in front of a computer game in your lounge as usual?'

Olive gasped. The air almost caught and crackled between them.

The mannequin boy watched them both curiously. 'Permission to go above, please, Captain?' he said.

'Above?' said Kirsten, flustered and cross.

He glanced at the rough boards above them with eyes that shone. 'Up there,' he said. 'I haven't been for years.'

'What? Oh. Yeah. I guess.'

The boy looked at her and seemed to hesitate. 'Sorry, Captain, but technically you're meant to say: permission granted.'

Now this Kirsten could do. Give her a line to say and she'd say it. 'Oh, right. Permission *granted*.'

As she followed him and Olive out on to the deck, Kirsten reflected uneasily on the situation. For almost four years, she and Olive had both done everything they could to make sure they were never left alone with each other.

But now each other was all they had.

Well, technically, they also had a mannequin. But still, you get the point.

- 21 -
TIME FOR SOME FACTS

IN THE BRIGHT April sun, out on the deck, there was no mistaking the boy for a human. He was clearly a grimy fibreglass mannequin, made in a factory. But the joy on his face as he felt the first caress of sunlight was anything but manufactured.

He tilted his head back till his eyelids clunked shut over his glass eyes, then stood completely still. With his arms outstretched, palms facing the sky, he was like a faded flower trying to drink in all the light all at once. Then he began to explore the deck, stopping every now and again to grin and close his eyes again.

Olive tore her gaze away from the mannequin. Then she looked at Kirsten with a no-nonsense, Girl Guide air. 'Let's deal with the facts. Facts are always reassuring if you number them, so that's what I'm going to do right now.' She lifted a trembling hand and raised a shaking finger for each point.

'One: the ship is magical. Two: we're on a quest.'

'We're *not*,' said Kirsten. 'Strike that from the list.'

'Three: there's some disagreement about quest status, but

request to strike denied. Four: you and the ship are actually talking to each other. Wait—' Olive cocked her head. 'Is she trying to talk to me?'

'You'd *know* if she was. She's not quiet.'

Olive looked a tiny bit envious. 'Five: there's also a live mannequin. Six: somewhere around here there's a map that reads your soul. Seven: it wants you to find stuff before you can go home. And eight: we're being kidnapped all the way to America.'

It was like Olive had taken a heavy bag from Kirsten and was sharing the load. Kirsten gave her a brief look of gratitude. 'That's about it, yes.'

'Okay,' said Olive. 'So now what?'

Kirsten didn't have an answer for that. She was absolutely unprepared for this. For the last four years of her life, in any type of drama, she'd been given a script and a run-through. Her life had become so managed and staged and timetabled.

She couldn't have a haircut without permission from her management, couldn't sit down for a cup of tea and a biscuit with Dad without Edwina moaning about his calorie intake. There were adults and cameras and make-up brushes *everywhere*, keeping her camera-ready and perfect and very much in the right spot, at the right time, for when filming began, and no matter what happened things were always wrapped up within a half-hour segment and everything always ended with an emotionally uplifting pop song.

All of which meant that nothing had prepared her for *this actual unscripted episode of life*, and Kirsten couldn't think of a single reassuring thing to say or do. Ironically, being in the spotlight had actually made her much shyer and more tongue-tied in real life, and that seven-year-old she'd been once seemed to have been buried under layers of something else. She really *hadn't* been making it up when she told the ship she wasn't captain material. She was *not* a natural-born leader. If someone told her what to do, she'd do it, but captain a *ship*?

She glanced down at the splinters in her hands and blinked rapidly.

'I'll try Mum again,' said Olive. 'She'll know what to do.'

A few seconds later, she handed her mobile to Kirsten with a sigh. 'Can't get through. Your turn.'

Kirsten tried Dad again, but only got his voicemail. She left a message, then handed the phone back to Olive.

'You look like you want to cry,' said Olive casually.

'I was just thinking the same thing about you,' said Kirsten. 'But *I* don't.'

'Me neither. No point crying at the beginning of a quest. You'd lose focus. And points.'

Olive lifted a defiant chin at Kirsten, who raised her eyebrows back. In this stubborn manner, both girls gave each other a tiny bit of much-needed courage.

Suddenly the ship gave a delighted laugh. 'Good afternoon to you too,' she said in a manner that suggested she was speaking to someone else.

'What?' said Kirsten.

'Oh, passable, passable, can't complain. I'm more of a stationary ship these days, but the public can't keep away. Yes, bound for America again, my old stamping ground—'

'Who are you talking to?' said Kirsten curiously.

'The Atlantic, darling. The ocean I was *made* for. And we go *way* back.' The ship giggled, as if the waves beneath her were tickling her underside.

'I know these waves like the inside of my engine. Why, that's very kind of you to say so! You don't look too bad yourself – I love what you've done to your ruffles, and hello, hello, little ones, hello, currents, hello, fish, hello, cold dark patches, hello—'

The mannequin boy came running over lightly but firmly on his dirty bare feet.

'Captain,' he said urgently to Kirsten.

'I'm *not*—'

'Come and see this.'

Kirsten followed him. There was an enormous warship blocking their way.

- INTERLUDE -

APPROXIMATELY THIRTY-ONE minutes later, Kirsten's father checked his phone and found a voicemail from his daughter.

Pressing **PLAY**, he heard this message:

'Dad, it's me. I'm on a runaway ship somewhere in the Bristol Channel between Wales and Somerset. I'm using Olive's phone. Please send help! Please!'

And then there were a few strangled hiccups, which made him want to wrap her in the tightest hug. But, when he tried to ring back, he couldn't get through.

Mick Bramble phoned the police immediately, was told they'd already been informed by the dock authorities, ran out of the house and headed straight for the harbourside.

- 22 -
QUITE AN INTIMIDATING RESCUE ATTEMPT

WHILE THE **SS *Great Britain*** was curved and shiny, everything about the warship waiting a few waves ahead was razor-sharp. Maybe it had gleamed once, thought Kirsten, but all its shine had fled in fear a long time ago now.

And who could blame it?

The SS *Great Britain* was made by hand and it showed. Even though Kirsten wasn't enjoying their little trip, there was no denying the ship's beauty, so clearly forged from the best of human imagination and effort.

But the ship waiting for them up ahead looked like it had simply clunked itself into being in a massive factory. It didn't look handmade at all. It had no soul. It didn't rest on the ocean so much as flex its muscles like an immovable bodybuilder.

And it totally dwarfed the SS *Great Britain*: twice her height, three times her width. It had a hard, pointy turret in the middle of the deck, and other odd metal constructions dotted here and there too, which might as well have just said: '*BEEP-BOOP, TAKE ME TO YOUR LEADER, PUNY*

FLESH WEAKLINGS!' It certainly had no jaunty air, glossy hull or golden unicorns sticking out of its bottom. It had all the width and looks of an industrial estate.

Kirsten gulped.

The ship was basically frowning at her. It was, essentially, just one huge, grown-up, scary-looking frown on water. And it was coming to get her.

With guns. Very large guns sticking in an unfriendly way out of grey mounds.

The black lettering on the side said

which obviously made Kirsten feel all warm and fuzzy inside.

'Blimey,' said Olive. 'That must be the big cheeses the woman from Bristol Water Authority was shouting about. The Royal *Navy*. Looks like we're about to get rescued. This quest is over.' She sounded a bit deflated.

But Kirsten, despite the guns and the frowning, felt nothing but relief. The scariest hour of her life was over and she could return home to Dad, and *The Jade Cooper Show*, and all that was important and worth protecting.

'What . . . what is that, Captain?' said the **SS *Great Britain***.

'It's a warship,' replied Kirsten. 'It belongs to the navy. Massive, isn't it?'

'But . . .' The ship's voice seemed to waver. 'It cannot be? I am the biggest ship in the world. How has that happened?'

'When was the last time you were at sea? Over fifty years ago? Most ships are about this size now. Some cargo ships I've seen from the beach are as big as small islands.'

The ship groaned. 'That . . . that doesn't even look like a ship, Captain, and it makes me feel small. I don't like feeling small. So instead I shall simply refuse to accept its existence.'

'Not sure you can really do that.'

'Oh, it's very easy. I do it all the time. If something's unpleasant, I pretend it's not happening. I take anything I don't like and I store it in one of my rooms and I never think about it again. I did it for ages out in the . . . when I was . . .'

The ship paused, then concluded: 'I'm good at hiding things I don't want to face. I shall do the same with this.'

Kirsten felt a pinprick stab of sympathy. She could even empathise a little. The **SS *Great Britain*** had been the biggest ship in the world once, all the way back in the nineteenth century. But you couldn't stop progress. The world kept turning.

One day you're a sensation, ship, and then someone cuter and newer comes along and usurps you. But there's no point being bitter. All you can do is keep being you, stay positive, believe in yourself and hope that Daisy accidentally falls into a combine harvester, and I say that with nothing but love and the utmost professional respect.

The ship stopped moving completely, but the warship, undeterred, edged closer. When they were parallel to it, they became aware of the two stern-looking officers standing on its deck, staring down at them.

Kirsten felt like a small ant, about to be squashed.

One of the officers held up a megaphone to his face. It crackled with static and then spat out words.

'Looks like this is becoming a bit of a habit of yours, Kirsten Bramble.'

And Kirsten blushed because she had a feeling she knew what they were talking about.

- 23 -
A MINOR MISDEMEANOUR

THE PREVIOUS SUMMER, Kirsten had accidentally taken a sports car for a little spin. It hadn't been for long, and she hadn't taken it far, but it had *sort of* cost her the ITV contract, and she could see how, in the light of that, it might look a bit dodgy to be standing on the deck of a museum ship with a guilty look on her face.

So what happened had been this.

She'd been on a photoshoot for a fancy clothing label. She was the face of their new summer range. The photoshoot was in a huge private garden, down in Dorset, overlooking a sand beach. It was a five-hour shoot, lots of costume changes, lots of pretend ice cream to pretend to lick.

It had sounded fun but it wasn't, not after the first hour. It had been one of the hottest days of the year. All the clothes Kirsten had to wear on the shoot were definitely not made of 100 per cent breathable cotton.

'I was so *hot*—' she said quietly.

Olive gave her an awkward glance. Olive knew. *Of course*

she did. It had been all over the news.

So she'd been really hot, right? After hours of changing and turning this way and that way, and all the make-up dripping into her face, Kirsten had been asked to sit in the back of a sports car that had been hired especially for the shoot.

It had been brought out by a man wearing white gloves, and parked with care on the lawn. It was one of those roofless sports cars: red, shiny, Italian.

'So this is going to be the billboard shot,' said the shoot director. 'We'd like you to sit in the car – Kirsten at the back, and Dad and Dad's girlfriend—'

'Edwina Clippity,' said Edwina Clippity eagerly from the make-up chair, clearly enjoying herself the most out of the three of them. Edwina Clippity was really taking to fame.

'—at the front. So you'll all look like you're driving your daughter somewhere lovely on a summer's day, in your fabulous summer clothes, even though you're technically going nowhere, ha ha.'

Kirsten and Dad were ready first. While they waited for Edwina to decide on her favourite false eyelashes, they baked in the hot car, making silly faces at each other to pass the time.

'You enjoying this, Kay?' he'd said suddenly, so quietly

she wasn't sure she'd heard him at first.

For a brief moment, their eyes met in the rear-view mirror. Dad looked quite clammy. He'd waved his hand around. 'You know. Are you enjoying . . . this?'

'Yeah,' said Kirsten. 'Of course.' She dabbed at the sweat on her forehead. 'I mean – it's good, right? A dream come true? You don't have to teach maths any more, and we live in a big house, and you've found True Love. And money. Don't forget the money.'

'I didn't worry about money before,' Dad said quietly. 'And you certainly didn't. My salary was enough to get by. If anything, we worry about it more now that we have it – especially the rate at which Edwina spends it. Which is –' he grew animated – 'a perfect example of positive correlation between two variables. I used to teach a whole term on it. Great days. But as long as you're happy—' He'd given her a look then, which she couldn't figure out.

They'd both descended into silence. A few metres away, there were the happy shrieks of people running into the waves and splashing each other.

The heat was oppressive. It slowed down speech, messed up thoughts. Sweat trickled out of Kirsten's high, gelled-back ponytail and into her eyes. She looked at the sea. She looked at Dad.

And then, quite abruptly, and in what their lawyer would

later call 'a moment of madness caused by sunstroke', popular child star Kirsten Bramble clambered into the front seat, pressed the button for the ignition, felt the powerful roar of the sports car as it clicked into life and – drove.

And Dad did absolutely nothing to stop her.

Kirsten didn't know how to change gear, but she didn't need to. They went right through a hedge, then *another* hedge, then an expensive-looking fence, and then . . . on to the beach. Kirsten thought she could hear her father laughing.

She drove that sports car right up to the water's edge and then some.

When the water lapped in through the doors, she and her dad had held hands tightly and jumped into the blissfully cooling water. When they surfaced, they'd looked at each other with glee and Kirsten hadn't heard anything but the sound of them giggling at each other.

For at least sixty seconds.

Before all the telling-off had begun.

And someone leaked the story to the press.

Even though Dad kept insisting that he'd turned on the engine, and started it all, Edwina said she'd seen the whole thing, and it was all Kirsten's fault, and made sure that Kirsten was properly told off.

'You don't want your daughter to let fame go to her head,'

Edwina told Dad again and again. 'She *needs* disciplining, my angel. She's been needing it for at least five years if you ask me. You've been too soft for too long, Mick, and I say that because I love you both very, very much.'

Kirsten got off with a warning from the police in the end, but there had been some embarrassing headlines in the newspapers that had initially loved her so much.

THE DAILY NEWS

NAUGHTY CHILD STAR KIRSTEN BRAMBLE STEALS BEAUTIFUL SPORTS CAR IN PATHETIC PLEA FOR ATTENTION

THE DAILY NEWS

WE ASK THE PUBLIC: HAS THE BRAMBLE BRAND BECOME TOO THORNY? IS IT TIME TO GIVE IT THE CHOP?

Edwina, who somewhere along the line of becoming her dad's girlfriend seemed to also turn into their unofficial manager, made sure that all the rules about Kirsten's free time were tightened.

She had a chaperone on photoshoots now. *No vehicles of any kind to be allowed anywhere near Kirsten during any kind of filming or photography* was written into her contract.

And now here she was, and it had happened again. And even though this time she hadn't even *wanted* to drive the ship towards the sea – she had more than learned her lesson and, besides, she had genuinely *just been hot that one time, can't anyone even try to understand that?* – Kirsten could see how it might look to someone – someone *judgey* – on the outside.

Someone like the officers standing on top of HMS *Destroyer*.

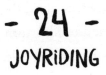

'KIRSTEN BRAMBLE,' THE Royal Navy officer with the megaphone said, 'the taking of a ship without the permission of the owner is PIRACY.'

'I'm NOT a PIRATE, and I have NOT stolen this ship!'

shouted Kirsten, as loud as she could.

She was shouting so they could hear her, but she was aware this might make her look like a hardened criminal too.

'Interesting,' said the officer. 'You say you haven't stolen her. Prove it then. Have you got an ENG1 certificate?'

'A what?' yelled Kirsten.

'*Any* certificates of seafaring competency? Have you got anything signed off by a doctor and approved by the Maritime and Coastguard Agency? Have you got your British seaman's card, which permits all British seafarers to land at foreign ports?'

'Honestly? No!' Kirsten screamed, as politely as possible.

'So where's your paperwork,' asked the officer solemnly, 'proving you have the right to sail this ship?'

'*Paperwork*,' sniffed the ship inside Kirsten's head. 'Humans and their fetish for chewed-up trees—'

Kirsten took a deep breath. 'Look, I didn't mean for any of this to happen!' she shouted. 'It's the *ship* doing it to *me*!'

The second officer on the warship took off his sunglasses and stared straight into her eyes, then lifted the megaphone to his mouth again. 'So you're saying this was completely unplanned? A crime committed spontaneously?'

Kirsten started enthusiastically nodding at the beginning of this sentence, but had stopped by the end when she realised what the officer was hinting at.

'Hmmm.' The two officers slightly inclined their closely shaven heads towards each other. 'Well, if you had no intention of permanently depriving the ship's owner of the ship, then this isn't technically theft—'

'I TOLD YOU!'

shouted Kirsten, relieved.

'You're a joyrider instead.'

Kirsten gritted her teeth. '*I'm* not joyriding the ship! She's joyriding *me*! She's . . . she's . . . she's *kidnapped* me! And there's nothing I can do to stop her!'

'That's enough of that nonsense. Now look, sweetheart,' said an officer firmly. 'Whatever's actually going on, it's stopping right now. We're going to send a few officers onboard the SS *Great Britain* and they'll escort you and your classmate off the ship and on to this one.'

Kirsten could have sworn she saw the *Destroyer* smirk.

'And then we're going to tug the SS *Great Britain* back to safety and we'll try to find out exactly how she moved all the way up the Bristol Channel to the Atlantic without any fuel and a replica engine. But one thing's for sure: her little daytrip is over. She's not seaworthy, not any more.'

The ship, Kirsten realised, had been as good as her word and fallen completely silent, which was understandable. It was even possible to feel a pang of sympathy for her broken dreams of travel and adoration, far-fetched as they were. But this was for the best. Really, when you boiled it right down, she was just an old lady yearning to be young again, unwilling to accept her age, and she'd roped an innocent eleven-year-old into her crazy schemes, and the sooner she realised—

And then there was a curious smell from behind them, of wigs and musty dressing-up clothes. Kirsten was filled with a terrible sense of foreboding.

'Oh my actual God?' gasped Olive.

The mannequins were *all* coming alive.

Kirsten counted at least four walking up the deck slowly, stiffly, as if they'd been roused from a long sleep, with even more emerging from the companionway. She started to slap herself. 'Wake *up*, wake *up*.'

A tall mannequin soldier in an old-fashioned naval coat and trousers, and sporting the largest sideburns Kirsten had ever seen, pushed past her and walked over to the railings of the SS *Great Britain*. Then he lifted a heavy silver pistol and pointed it up at the *proper* officers on the *Destroyer*.

'Don't even think about taking our ship,' he growled in a scratchy voice.

'Or we'll scratch your bleedin' eyes out,' said someone

just behind Kirsten. She whirled round to see the two mannequin fighting women from steerage swaying erratically on the deck in grubby, ripped dresses.

'Yes, I'll give you what for,' uttered a top-hatted gentleman Kirsten vaguely recognised from the upper-class quarters, brandishing a cane and looking forbidding. 'You dastardly mongrels. I've paid for my passage to the Americas, and my passage I shall have.'

Behind them stood the small barefoot cabin boy, looking thoroughly pleased with the way things were going. 'Thought we needed reinforcements, Captain,' he said, smiling proudly. 'To protect the ship.'

'*Wow*,' said Olive. 'You're, like, *totally acting independently, all by yourself.*' She turned to Kirsten with a look of utter wonder in her eyes.

'Brilliant,' said Kirsten. 'Well, this all seems like a wonderful development.'

'Thank you, Captain,' said the SS *Great Britain* modestly. 'One does one's best.'

- 25 -
'WE WANT TO BE RESCUED'

BEFORE KIRSTEN COULD say, 'Honestly, officers, none of this is my fault,' the mannequin soldier lifted his pistol in the air and stared meaningfully down the barrel at the human naval officers.

The fighting women began to shout colourful Victorian curses and shook their fists, looking like they were having a thoroughly lovely time.

The mannequins seemed ready to go to war.

Olive and Kirsten exchanged an uneasy glance. 'How many of them do you think are down there?' asked Olive.

Kirsten was about to reply when the portly mannequin cook they'd last seen in the kitchen, in a stained apron nearly bursting at the seams, ran straight between them on short little legs, huffing and panting and waggling a large chef's knife in front of him as if he was ready to slice anything out of his way. He was closely followed by the ship's surgeon, the man with the bleeding hand, a few children and one or two young ringleted ladies from the first-class accommodation.

'Wow,' said Olive. 'They're – they're – they're – they're – they're—'

'They are,' said Kirsten. 'Yes.'

An officer onboard the *Destroyer* looked confused. 'We didn't – we weren't told there were additional passengers onboard,' he said into the megaphone. 'Our report said it was just two young girls we had to retrieve—'

'It's . . . hard to explain!' Kirsten shouted into the wind. 'But can you just *hurry up* and rescue us?'

'You *are* being rescued!' shouted the mannequin soldier next to her, who took a moment from brandishing his pistol to give her a look of disappointment. 'We're rescuing you from these absolute pirates here. Is that not clear?'

'Pirates?' spluttered the megaphone on the *Destroyer*. 'We're in the Royal Navy! How dare you? This is *treason—*'

'Forsooth and gadzooks!' shouted the soldier. 'I'll have you know I'm an officer of the Royal Marine. And I am sworn to protect this ship and all who sail on her.'

'*They're all thinking for themselves,*' muttered Olive. 'This quest is on a whole other level!'

'We're not in the navy, but we *are* a force!' shouted one of the fighting women, holding up a mucky fist. 'And we *love* a bit of fisticuffs. Come any closer and we'll show you how much.'

'Yeah,' jeered the other woman. 'Just you wait till you

see my ear-ripping move—'

'Ooh,' winced her companion. 'You don't want to be on the receiving end of *that*, laddie, I can tell you—'

'So give us freedom out into the Atlantic or there shall be a price to pay,' said the mannequin soldier, and he waved his pistol with a theatrical flourish.

The officers onboard the *Destroyer* looked at each other in alarm, and then glanced behind to shout a command at someone else. Kirsten didn't hear all of what was said, but she caught a few words: *reinforcements* and *criminal elements*.

'No, please, don't listen to them,' stammered Kirsten. 'We *want* to be rescued. Olive? Olive, tell them.'

But Olive, who had spent quite a lot of the last hour trying to phone her mum or looking stressed, was now, frustratingly, staring at the mannequins with a definite look of love in her eyes that Kirsten recognised from all those afternoons playing *Zeleth*.

'Er, yeah,' she murmured now, staring at the fighting women. 'Rescued. Great. What she said. That.'

'Say it like you mean it,' muttered Kirsten crossly.

An extremely loud whirring noise filled the sky.

'What – what is that?' gasped one of the top-hatted mannequins from the first-class quarters. 'It's – it's a mechanical – it's a flying . . . metallic – bird?'

'It's a *helicopter*,' gasped Kirsten, relieved.

The men on the *Destroyer* gave the mannequin soldier a triumphant look, one that distinctly said: *You've lost.*

The green helicopter came nearer. It had

emblazoned on the side.

Kirsten began to wave eagerly from the deck.

'YOOOO-HOO! OVER HERE!'

It was all over. And not a moment too soon.

The helicopter's propellers made the ocean churn around them, and salt spray splashed over the deck and whipped their school uniform around. Kirsten felt the captain's hat get whisked off her head.

Good riddance, she thought.

The helicopter was now immediately above the **SS Great Britain**.

A soldier in camo was leaning out of the open door, holding an armful of thick rope, and Kirsten realised what would happen. The soldiers were going to drop the ropes on to the ship and then climb down, and then there'd be grown-ups on the ship, and she could have a little cry, and then everything would go back to normal, and the mannequins could stop being alive, and she could go home to Bristol and get an extremely early night.

She crossed all her fingers for luck.

The rope fell on to the deck with a thud. The first soldier began to descend the rope ladder.

His black boot was just centimetres away from the top of the ship's middle mast when something very peculiar began to happen.

- 26 -
A WHOLE OTHER GEAR

THE **SS *Great Britain's*** mast started to *move*. Slowly at first, then picking up speed. The five other masts began to spin too. They whirred round like an electric whisk. Kirsten's heart fell. The soldier hesitated before climbing a little way back up the rope.

'If he puts one foot on that mast, it'll get ripped off,' muttered Olive.

As the masts began to get faster and faster, in a mocking imitation of the whirring propellers of the helicopter, everyone onboard the **SS *Great Britain*** threw themselves face down on the deck.

Through the flying mess of masts, wires and her own despair, Kirsten risked a glance up towards the helicopter, and thought she caught a glimpse of defeated faces. There was no way anyone could land on the deck without being turned into cake mix by the masts.

For a desperate moment, the helicopter hovered, as if wondering what to do.

'Well, this has been fun, and I do appreciate the social

call, but we have places to go so we'll be off now,' said the SS *Great Britain* with exquisite politeness and, underneath her feet, Kirsten felt the ship begin to thrum all over.

'Wh-what are you doing, ship?' she gasped.

'It's been a while since I did this, Captain, but I've still got it. Hold on tight – it can be rather fast. Tell the others to lie down and hold on.'

Kirsten's survival instinct kicked in. She could feel the entire ship gearing up for something and she sensed it would be gigantic. She glanced around.

'Olive! Everyone! Listen to me! Grab something! Anything!' Kirsten shouted, as the ship slowly lifted her nose, and Kirsten began to slide down the deck. At the last minute, she was able to wrap her arms round the base of a mast and saw, with relief, that the others had done the same. The captain's hat went flying past her, and she prayed, fervently, that it would end up at the bottom of the sea.

And suddenly the ship was flying away from the *Destroyer* at breakneck speed. She was faster than *anything* Kirsten had ever been on before.

And then speech and thought were almost impossible for the ship began to move at a speed that *no one* had ever travelled at before.

And as they flew across the ocean, at a bone-shaking, cheek-rippling, eye-watering velocity, the ship explained why.

- 27 -
EXPLOSION

'A COUPLE OF billion years ago,' the SS *Great Britain* said, although she wasn't so much talking, Kirsten realised with a sort of dazed confusion, as somehow *trickling* the knowledge into her brain in a funny, bright way, as if history could be passed between them like a precious parcel, 'I was a star. Up in space.'

The ship's voice seemed to break open then. That other quality within it, the one that was more liquid and yet also harder and otherworldly, grew stronger in Kirsten's mind, and she had, for a stunning and also frightening moment, the sense that she was communicating with something beyond real human understanding.

'You were a ship . . . in space? You sailed through the galaxy?'

'No. I wasn't a ship, not then,' said the SS *Great Britain*. 'I was still in my first form. I was an *actual* star.'

'Wh-wh—?'

'I know,' said the ship. 'Just listen. You don't have to

think. That will come later. I was a supernova, you see, until I exploded—'

'Oh no—'

'No, I was happy to do it; it was my time. Anyway, within that explosion, a lot of chemical processes happened, and I was turned into iron – fused, you see. Dying stars are quite productive in that way; their explosions are wonderfully inventive. Life, death, stars, ships, darkness, brightness – they're all so much closer to each other than we realise really, darling—'

The deck and the ocean around her were just a murky streak. All Kirsten could do was close her eyes, hold on tight and listen.

'Anyway, after the explosion, which was all rather exciting, *bang-bang-bang-bang* and what have you, I fell because I'd just become iron, which is too heavy for space. I landed on the nearest planet, which happened to be this one. And I stayed, undisturbed, in a bog somewhere, for a bit – four or five billion years roughly.'

'Were you lonely?'

'Oh no. I had *lots* of ferns to keep me company. Wonderful companions, ferns. Very droll. Then there were all the dinosaurs, of course. *They* were interesting . . .'

Kirsten gulped.
The world flew past her.
She was literally
clinging on for life.
Her skin would be
flayed off her face
by the wind
if they went
any faster.

The ship, however, was talking as lightly as if they were out for a casual Sunday stroll, twirling their parasols. '*Anyway*, after several aeons passed, I was dug up by some industrious Victorians who were exceedingly fond of metal, and my new life began when I was turned into—'

'—the ship,' said Kirsten, finally understanding.

'Yes.'

The ship's flickery, almost supernatural voice was fading a little here, and now she sounded more Victorian again, which was just as well because hearing her supernova voice was like standing a bit too close to a fire.

'So you see, Captain, we're the same, me and you.'

Kirsten nearly laughed but didn't, because they were going so fast she had no idea where her mouth was any more. 'How's that then?'

'We're both fallen stars.'

Kirsten flinched.

'I'm – I'm not *fallen*. I'm—'

'Ooof, that's enough. I haven't moved like that since I fell from space, so I'm a bit out of practice. You could say I'm a tad . . . rusty . . .' And, as she laughed at her own bad joke, the ship finally slowed down.

Kirsten glanced over her shoulder to the back of the ship. They were surrounded by the grey waters of the Atlantic, and the *Destroyer* was nowhere to be seen. She didn't know exactly where they were, but at a guess she'd say a couple of hundred miles away from Bristol now the ship had sped across the ocean like a comet.

'They were going to *rescue me*,' she said sadly.

'Darling, you have got to get your eyes tested,' sniffed the ship primly. 'That wasn't a rescue. That was just an ending.

And endings, as we all know, are bad, and must be delayed as much as possible. So come on now, shoulders back, lift up your booms, straighten your gaff and eyes front, Captain. Oh, and did you manage to find any champagne?'

'I conceal things from myself'
Private diary entry, Isambard Kingdom Brunel, 1824

- 28 -
INTERNATIONAL WATERS

OLIVE AND THE mannequins slowly unpeeled themselves from the ship. The air filled with the sound of the mannequins slowly getting to their feet, their limbs squeaking slightly from the novelty of it.

Kirsten, however, remained exactly where she was – slumped in a heap, face down on the deck. Everything was awful.

She'd been on the brink of going back home. The ship kept calling her Captain, but she didn't seem to be in charge at all. Olive was in the middle of some sort of quest *obsession* and didn't appear to care about reality any more. Every time they were on the brink of being rescued, the ship managed to outsmart everyone: warships, helicopters . . .

And those splinters in her hands really hurt.

As the treacherous ship chugged along the grey Atlantic Ocean, Kirsten contemplated what might be happening back on land. The level of serious phone calls that might be flying between her management team and the school.

'*She's on a ship?* Without a chaperone? Joyriding again?

This goes against everything in her contract! Jade Cooper cannot know, or they'll cancel her appearance this Friday! Keep it from the press! Who can we sue? Fetch her back at once!'

And Dad would be so worried. Had he got her message?

'Have you any idea how much trouble you just got me into?' she said roughly to the ship, wiping her tears away. 'Didn't you hear what those men said? I don't have any of the right paperwork to steer you. Even you calling me Captain is against the law. We're breaking practically every single nautical law there is.'

'Not any more we're not. They can't touch any of us, not now,' said the ship calmly. 'We've just passed into international waters.'

'What does that mean?'

'We're in a part of the sea where no one can tell you off. This ocean doesn't belong to Great Britain, you see, so they can't come and arrest you. That's the beauty of marine law. You're free to move as you wish.'

'Oh,' said Kirsten. 'I didn't know that.'

'Yes, all you have to do is sail international waters for ever. If you land in a port, of course, you can be arrested. Best way to avoid that is to commit to a life of endless adventure and endless beginnings. Something to think about?'

'No,' snapped Kirsten. 'I'm going to think about how I can end this voyage, and get back to Bristol, and prepare for my interview, and forget any of this ever happened, if you don't mind.'

'Ah, youth,' said the ship sadly. 'Truly wasted on the young.'

Below them both, the grey international waters continued to flow past, and the flags fluttered faster than ever. And, even though the ship was driving her bonkers, Kirsten realised with a terrible feeling of doom that she needed the SS *Great Britain* if she wanted to survive.

- 29 -
SHOW-BIZ STUFF

Kirsten looked up from her sulking. While she'd been talking to the ship, the mannequins had been taking in the fresh air. And it seemed to be doing wonders because they were now moving almost naturally, had congregated in small groups and were chatting to each other.

She couldn't see all the way down to the prow, but it definitely looked as if their numbers had swelled. Time to face facts: all the mannequins inside the ship had come alive. So she had *that* to deal with too.

'Captain?' said the cook. 'What time shall I prepare dinner for tonight, please?'

'Can you tell us where we're going, Captain?' lisped a little boy in large knickerbockers.

'May I take your temperature, Captain?' enquired the ship's surgeon.

'This is all a huge mistake,' said Kirsten through gritted teeth. 'Please stop talking to me. I'm *not the captain.*'

'I'll say,' said a top-hatted mannequin. 'It goes against the natural order of things. You'll be asking for votes next.'

'Can I borrow your phone?' Kirsten said abruptly to Olive. 'I'd like to try Dad again.'

But Olive shook her head. 'There's absolutely no reception here,' she said, holding out her mobile and pointing at the blank screen. 'We *are* in the middle of the ocean, and my network's *rubbish* at the best of times, and there's no Wi-Fi.'

Kirsten felt like crying.

'Look,' murmured Olive hastily, 'I know this is a difficult, um, time, but look at those people.' She pointed to some of the children and passengers from steerage.

Olive's eyes were brighter than usual and there was a pink tinge to her cheeks.

Kirsten regarded her wearily. 'They're not people. But what's your point?'

'Well, I think they might be a bit frightened. And I reckon if you were to just say – well – a few encouraging words, as their captain, it would comfort them.'

Kirsten jutted her jaw out. 'But I'm not their captain! How many times do I have to say it?'

'Can't you pretend? Do some of your show-biz stuff? Look at them. They need a pep talk. This is definitely *your* role, right? It feels like the right thing to do.'

Kirsten had to admit that Olive had a point. The mannequins looked overwhelmed. Even the soldier's bluster had left him. He could be heard confessing to the fighting women that he wasn't sure how to shoot a gun anyway. Three of the mannequins were holding on tightly to the nearest masts as if terrified of sliding off the ship if they let go. One or two monocled passengers looked as if they wanted to cry.

'Come on, you're always saying emotional stuff on your TV show, aren't you?'

'*Am I?*' said Kirsten meaningfully. 'How would you know?'

'We have it on sometimes,' said Olive, squirming. 'Remember the heart-to-heart you had with your dad halfway through Series Two, when he told you he was tired of dating and wanted the series to end?'

'*Yeeeeeah,*' said Kirsten slowly.

'But you begged him to carry on? And you said – what did you say? Something like: *didn't he think you deserved a mummy, just like all the other little girls at school?*'

Kirsten felt a stab of remorse at the memory.

She'd never particularly wanted a mummy; Dad was enough parent for her. But the producers had asked her to say the line anyway.

'*It'll be telly gold,*' they'd told her. '*We have to keep him dating, it's the whole point of the show, and you want the show to continue, don't you, Kirsten?*' They'd looked at her with their greedy eyes and Kirsten hadn't known how to say no.

So she'd said it and Dad had cried.

'*Who am I to deny you the chance to be part of a proper family, love?*' he'd said. '*I've been so selfish. Forgive me.*'

The show had ended with them both hugging while a sad song played in the background, and viewing figures had been the highest ever.

'Well, my mum said it was the most moving thing she'd ever seen,' said Olive. 'You're *good* at this sort of stuff. Speaking aloud, putting on a show, getting people emotional . . .'

'I . . . I don't always come up with what I say on the show, you know. I'm given a script, and I have a director—' Kirsten felt a flicker of irritation at how little Olive knew about making reality TV. 'A lot of it is scripted.'

Olive widened her eyes. 'Oh, I didn't know. Well, anyway, why don't you just say something encouraging and nice? I don't think it needs to be complicated. *This is your captain speaking. Don't worry about anything*—'

And, for a second or two, Kirsten did try. But the words weren't there. A whoosh of something dry and gritty blew into her heart, and she gave up.

'I'm *not* their captain, and I'm not in the mood. *You* say something inspirational if you're so bothered about it. *I'm* going downstairs.'

And she turned away abruptly without looking back.

- 30 -
'WHAT CAN I GET FOR YOU?'

BELOW DECK, KIRSTEN had a vague ambition to lie down in a furious heap somewhere. It was as good a plan as any other. She stomped up and down the ship, looking for the Captain's Cabin to crawl into and sulk.

To her surprise, it was trickier to locate than usual. When she eventually tracked it down, hiding away between the kitchen and the larder down in steerage, the room didn't feel quite as welcoming as it had before. In fact, it seemed distinctly hostile.

For starters, it wasn't letting her in.

The door was stuffed with a tightly wound plug of green-and-gold wallpaper. It was as if the entire room had scrunched itself up and then wedged itself in the doorway, as tight as a fist. When Kirsten touched the squeezed-up room gingerly, it folded in on itself even tighter, like a Venus flytrap, *scrunch, scrunch, scrunch*. The message was clear. No entry.

'Fine!' she shouted to the balled-up room. 'I didn't want to come in anyway!'

She drifted into the ship's galley instead. It was massive and, despite having no windows, full of a gentle glow that came from the many copper pans strung on the walls. So different, she thought suddenly, to the cold white kitchen back at

True Love Heights

'Hungry?' said someone behind her.

Kirsten jumped.

'Now what can I get for you?' said Cook.

'Really?' Having brought up her breakfast and not eaten her lunch, Kirsten was ravenous.

'Oh yes,' said Cook. 'I'd be delighted to serve you anything, Captain. It would be my honour.' He waved an expansive arm around.

'Well, I'd love something organic and low fat, ideally protein-based, and steamed, not fried.'

'Righto,' said Cook. 'How about a lovely bit of glazed tripe?' And he proudly put a plate of something grey in front of her. A fork was placed in her hand.

'Go on. Eat up. Before it gets cold.'

Kirsten prodded at the tripe reluctantly under his eager eye. It was as hard as glass. Realisation flooded her. It was fake. All the food in the kitchen was fake. Of course it was. She was on a museum ship. *Everything* was a prop.

Her bones froze with fear. This was actually happening. They were in the middle of the Atlantic Ocean with no grown-ups, no mobiles, no food and no way of shouting for help. She gave a big despairing sigh and gazed up into the mannequin's eyes.

He immediately looked concerned. 'Something wrong with the tripe, Captain?'

'It's not—' The vulnerability in Cook's face made Kirsten bite back the next word. 'It's not that it doesn't look delicious—'

'She's just realised that she's got some important seafaring discussions to have with me, Cook,' said Olive suddenly, appearing at Kirsten's elbow out of the gloomy shadows.

'Well, when you come back from your seafaring discussion,' said Cook expansively, as cheerful as a sunbeam, 'this will all be waiting for you. I got tinned tripe, tinned pig cheeks, tinned jelly, tinned pilchards, tinned quince, tinned—'

'Thank you so much,' said Olive, and she gently pulled Kirsten away, leaving Cook to his enthusiastic recital.

- 31 -
SHIP'S RATIONS

THE GIRLS MOVED through the middle deck, navigating their way round some of the mannequins who had drifted back below deck. Olive, Kirsten noticed, was good with them, and gave each one a smile, nod or kind word as they passed. Kirsten felt a little awkward by comparison.

After finding their way down a particularly crowded corridor - one of the mannequin children had scattered a bag of marbles - Olive led them below deck to the long, elegant dining saloon. Ten wooden tables filled the space, laid with pristine white tablecloths and silver platters of fake food.

At the sight of them, the violin players immediately burst into a concerto.

'Why are we here?' said Kirsten over the violins.

Olive lifted up both their rucksacks. 'Food,' she said solemnly. 'We never did eat that packed lunch, did we?'

Kirsten was surprised her bag didn't break, she opened the zip so quickly, silently thanking Mrs Walia for insisting all Year Sixes were responsible for carrying their own packed lunches on school trips. She was about to tear into her sandwich when, despite every nerve in her body quivering from hunger, she put it back on the linen tablecloth.

'Stop,' she managed to say through a mouthful of yearning.

'Stop what?' mumbled Olive, her mouth crammed with white bread and thin slices of ham.

'We have to –' Kirsten searched for the unfamiliar word – '*ration*.'

Olive's eyes went wide with astonishment. Kirsten understood – she was a bit surprised by herself too.

'Look: the ship has already shown us how slippery she is. She's evaded capture twice already today. We might not get rescued tonight. Which means we have to make our food last.'

With extreme reluctance, and after swallowing what was in her mouth, Olive slowly put her sandwich down. 'You're right.'

Kirsten licked her lips. 'Let's see what we've got.'

They spread their packed lunches out on the table. Kirsten's mouth watered as she spoke. 'We have one ham sandwich, almost uneaten, one hummus and rocket sourdough sandwich – shut up, it's actually very nice – totally uneaten. One packet of ready salted crisps, two chocolate bars, some fizzy strawberry laces, one pot of organic strawberry yoghurt, two bananas, one flapjack and one bag of almonds. Plus a spinach smoothie.'

'You can have the smoothie all to yourself,' said Olive solemnly. 'Honestly.'

Kirsten ignored this jibe as she continued to unpack her bag. 'We've also got . . . one small bottle of multivitamins and some vitamin E supplements. They make your skin glow. Great for telly.'

'Wow,' said Olive.

'And two bottles of water,' said Kirsten. 'And one carton of Ribena.'

'And two whole packets of strawberry Fruittellas,' said Olive after a while, emptying her pockets and gazing at the sweets fondly.

They looked at each other.

'We're going to get scurvy, aren't we?' said Olive matter-of-factly.

For a moment, the girls fell quiet as they contemplated their provisions, and the stark reality of being all alone on a huge ship in the middle of the Atlantic without any grown-ups. But each was determined not to cry in front of the other.

Blinking several times until her eyes went back to normal, Kirsten tried to think. Without knowing how long the journey would go on for, calculating exactly how to divide the food was difficult. This was what Dad would call an *unknown factor.*

She tore her thoughts away from him. 'Let's assume we're going to be rescued tomorrow and not today,' she said. 'Worst-case scenario, but it's good to be prepared. This has to stretch out across –' she ticked off her fingers – 'today, and then breakfast, lunch and dinner tomorrow. That's eight meals, *at least*, out of two.'

'Let's share my ham sandwich now, because I've started it,' said Olive, nodding, 'and the yoghurt too, because that will go off anyway.'

'And one banana each,' said Kirsten. 'For energy.'

They looked at their meagre provisions.

'Actually, let's share *one* banana,' added Kirsten. 'Just in case.'

They were just polishing it off a few minutes later, and taking cautious sips of their water, when the broom-cupboard boy came running into the dining room. 'Wonderful news! You're going to be so thrilled!'

'The navy has found us again?' gasped Kirsten.

'No!' He held a white-and-gold hat up proudly. 'I found your hat on the deck! It blew into a sand bucket! Bet you've been looking all over for it!'

He looked so delighted to have done something useful that Kirsten swallowed her bitter disappointment, forced a smile of gratitude and held out her hands.

She noticed, as she took the hat from his hand, that his grip was tight, and it took quite a few seconds before he gave it up completely. Then, his task completed, he seemed to linger, as fascinated by their faces as they were by his.

'Why don't you sit with us?' said Olive.

'Are you sure?' said the boy, looking at Kirsten, as if her word was gospel.

She thought of how long he'd been stuck, alone, in the broom cupboard. 'Yes.'

'Thank you!' he said, sitting next to Olive.

'Would you like any food?' asked Olive.

'No thank you, First Mate,' he said, patting his torso, which made a hollow noise. 'I haven't got the stomach for it. But I do appreciate you offering all the same. Much obliged.'

'Oh, please, um, don't mention it, not at all, upon my word,' said Olive, grinning a little. 'Gadzooks, this Victorian thing is *catching*.'

- 32 -
A NAMING

Kirsten looked at the cabin boy, feeling restless. 'What did you say your name was?'

He frowned. 'I'm not sure. I've just always been Cabin Boy. I don't even think I had a name when I was made, back in the factory.'

Kirsten sprang to her feet with delight. What had that mystifying map said?

THERE ARE THINGS THAT MUST BE NAMED . . .
ONLY THEN CAN IT END.

Perhaps naming this . . . dummy . . . was the key to ending her suffering! If he had a name, she could end the journey, right?

'You need a name,' she said. 'Choose something.'

He gave her an awkward smile. 'I – I can't think of—'

'Anything! Anything! Go on!' Kirsten felt frustrated. How hard could it be? 'Anything! Billy? Bobby? Babby? Bibby?'

The sound of the violins grew strange, frenetic, like wasps and flies dancing in the air. 'Just choose something! We haven't got all day!'

'Easy, easy,' murmured Olive. 'You're scaring him. And me.'

He'd stopped looking at them, was picking at a hole in his mildewed shirt.

'Sorry,' said Kirsten gruffly. 'Got a bit carried away. Do you want me to choose a name for you? May I, I mean?' she asked more gently.

He lifted his glass eyes and met her gaze. 'Please, Captain.'

But the only boys' names Kirsten could think of were the ones in her class, and she didn't think he suited most of them. With a flash of inspiration, she looked down at her socks. 'How about Marks – I mean, *Mark* – Spencer?'

'*Mark Spencer*,' murmured the boy. His smudged face filled with a happiness that looked almost human. 'I like it. Thank you so much. I shall do right by it and, if I don't, you must take it back.'

'It doesn't work like that,' said Kirsten. 'It doesn't matter what you do. Your name is yours for ever, Mark.'

Mark Spencer pressed his lips together very tightly. Then he dabbed at his dusty brown eyes and looked up at Kirsten with hero worship.

'Well?' she said to the ship. 'Have I done it? Named what needed naming? Can we go home now?'

The ship groaned. 'I don't deal with details, Captain. I told you that. *I* do the moving. Flatty does the strategy. Flatty loves a bit of a chat about the wheres and the whens. Not to mention the whats. Talk to Flatty if you want to discuss practicalities. I'm navigating waves right now.'

Kirsten turned to Olive impatiently.

'Come on,' she urged. 'We've got to talk to Fla— the map.'

Olive stood up quickly. 'The map that reads souls? Yes! Take me to it immediately.'

India-Rose wouldn't have been so keen to visit a talking map.

After a moment's thought, Kirsten turned to Mark. 'You should come too,' she said.

The musicians continued to play as the two ex-best friends and their beaming companion walked out of the dining saloon.

- 33 -
STORYTIME

THIS TIME, THE Captain's Cabin was a little easier to find: it had plopped itself conveniently opposite the dining room, and its door was wide open. The previously scrunched-up green-and-gold wallpaper was back on its walls, and it was as easy as anything for the three children to walk in. It had clearly forgiven Kirsten for her earlier moodiness on deck, but why? Because she'd had the idea for rationing food? Or named Mark? Perhaps the room sought her out when she did something captainly, but turned away when she didn't?

The lights gave a little flicker of welcome once the three children were inside.

'Wow,' said Olive reverentially, looking around with wide eyes. 'A magical Captain's Cabin.' She shot a meaningful look at Kirsten. 'Quest o'clock. How do you get the map to talk to you then? Do you have to bow down? Slot a key into a lock? *Utter a spell?*'

'Not really,' said Kirsten. 'What usually happens is I stand in front of it, and it insults me.'

They all looked at the map, stretched out like an old

skin on the mahogany desk.

'Well, go on then!' Olive was practically hopping from foot to foot.

Kirsten approached the map. Under the green light, it bubbled and rippled and wrote:

You've got company, I see.

Olive squealed and clapped her hands.

'Um – yes. We're here because I have a question. For you,' said Kirsten, feeling a bit self-conscious under Olive's gaze.

Oh?

'I named something. Like you said? I named the mannequin.' She pointed at Mark Spencer, who straightened his back proudly. 'So . . . can we go home? We're running out of food, it's getting dark–'

You've barely begun your journey, Captain. There's much left to do.

'Is there?' gasped Olive. 'What?'

There are other things that must be named.

'Look, I'm not a flipping vicar! I'm not here to just wander around christening mannequins–'

'Shh,' said Olive urgently. '*Look.*'

There are people that must be forgiven. Some things must be lost. Some things must be found. There are treasures to be treasured, and parts that are missing

must be restored. All these things must be done on this journey, and only when things are shipshape can the journey end.

'Treasures to be treasured,' repeated Olive. 'Wow, that's *good*.'

'What does it mean though?' said Kirsten.

'I have *no* idea,' she beamed. 'That's what makes it so good.' She reached for her rucksack and pulled out a black biro and a notebook.

'What are you doing?' said Mark curiously.

'Taking notes. This could be useful. Ooh! It's saying something else now.'

What time is it, children?

Olive glanced at her watch quickly, delighted to help. 'It's eight o'clock in the evening.'

As I suspected. It's storytime.

Kirsten snorted. 'Come on,' she said scathingly. 'We came in here to have a *serious* conversation.'

There is nothing more serious than storytime.

'We're eleven,' said Kirsten. 'We're too old for storytime.'

No one is too old for storytime – have a seat.

Captain, take the Captain's Chair. The other two can sit on the arms.

The three children did as the map suggested. Once they were seated – if not exactly comfortably – on the round-backed wooden chair, which seemed to give a little squeak of happiness at having company, Flatty seemed to stretch, as if limbering up before a great effort.

Here, children, it said, **is the story of the ship**.

- 34 -
MUCH GASPING

You see, before you can even think about ending this voyage, you must understand the beginning.

The very beginning. The once upon a time.

It all started with one man.

From somewhere in the distance came an unmistakable sound. The ship's huge metal heart was pounding and whooshing extra fast, extra loud.

THIS IS HIM.

And out of the parchment swam a massive pool of black ink, which slowly arranged itself into a perfect photograph of a solemn-looking man with dark, clever eyes and . . . a cigar in his mouth.

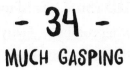

His name was Isambard Kingdom Brunel, said the map.

You see that hat? He kept an extra brain in there just for ideas. There's no other way to explain him.

'That's . . . that's the man I met—' stammered Kirsten. 'By the ship. This morning. He said . . . he'd come by train—'

Ah, yes, that sounds like Brunel. He loves to travel.

'Wait,' said Kirsten. 'I met a *ghost* by the side of the ship?'

Does that seem harder to believe than anything else? said the map.

'Fair enough,' said Kirsten.

This man, said the map, **dreamed of a ship. Now, up until this point, every ship ever built had always been made of wood.**

But he was not interested in how things had always been done.

His greatest skill was dreaming up things that didn't already exist. As an engineer, he built things from metal; he understood its secret lives. And, rather like the engines he designed, his brain never stopped whirring.

He might have been a touch on the short side, but there was nothing small at all about his ideas.

They were huge. They were dazzling. Some of them failed, as some ideas must, but others were glorious.

They changed the world.

The children in the Captain's Cabin were rapt, absorbed completely in the faded parchment map and the story within it.

The ink on the map rearranged itself into a small wooden ship, and the following words appeared.

Wooden ships could rot, warp, leak and—

The wooden ship on the map suddenly exploded in a puff of smoke.

—burst into flames.

Frankly, it was a miracle wooden ships ever got anywhere without everyone onboard dying along the way.

Brunel decided to build a ship out of something else. Something he knew best: metal.

He would create an iron ship. This would make her the lightest, fastest ship in the world. She would be a complete original: just like him.

The ink changed into a picture of a man hunched over a large desk, drawing lines. As the man's hands moved slowly across paper, the map seemed to glow with the wonder of creation, of the moment something was brought out of a heart and shaped into being. The whole room seemed to crackle with magic and love.

In September 1838, Isambard Brunel began to sketch

out his designs for the ship of iron.

Even then, she had an energy all of her own. Every time Brunel returned to her design—

Suddenly the parchment filled with numbers, and elegant curved lines, and sums, which went flying across its surface with a vital energy.

—she got bigger. It was as if just thinking about her made her grow.

She would not be rushed. Her construction took four years. She was built in the docks on Bristol's harbourside.

The picture of Brunel's study rippled, and the numbers and lines and calculations changed into a dockside scene; men and sparks flickered and rippled on the parchment, and Kirsten could almost *smell* hot metal, oil, smoke, the industry, power and the determination of the people building the ship.

Wooden ships were nailed into place, said the map, *but this ship was forged. Sparks flew. Flames burned.*

There was another puff of smoke, and a corner of the map burst into flames. Hurriedly, Kirsten blew it out, but a small scorch mark remained on Flatty, which ignored it and went on:

Down at the dockyard, metal and muscle strained together to create something entirely new.

The words then rearranged themselves and suddenly the

map was completely filled, corner to corner, with a large ink drawing of the iron ship standing proudly in the dock as confidently as if she'd been there since the beginning of time and would last until the end of it, if she had anything to do with it.

She was fitted with the most powerful engine in the world. And she was fuelled by the elements: sun, fire and the ocean itself.

The ship changed into a huge burning furnace. Kirsten kept a wary eye out for more accidental fires.

The cokers onboard the ship – the men who shovelled coal into her furnace all day long – kept her running. The fire was the magic ingredient. Fire turned the seawater into steam, you see. And the steam made her pistons pump constantly and her propeller move round.

Brunel had conquered the ocean. No longer would a ship have to rely on the wind to fill her sails. Now, with an engine, a ship could move whenever she wanted.

The men who built her called her 'the Mammoth'. Isambard called her 'his darling'. And she drew gasps of admiration wherever she went.

Now—

I beg your pardon?

The map went blank. Then:

See here, who's in charge of this story?

Kirsten and Olive looked at each other. The map seemed to be talking to someone else.

Oh, all right, fine.

Children, I've just been told I've got that wrong. Let me make a correction.

The map began to write again.

Apparently, I should not have used the past tense there, wrote the map tersely.

She very much continues to draw gasps of admiration. Everyone who sees her gasps a lot. There is much gasping. Non-stop gasping. It is literally a surprise there's any oxygen left in the world, what with all the gasping she inspires.

Olive stifled a giggle. 'Are the map and the ship having an argument over how best to tell her story?'

'I think so,' whispered Kirsten.

They turned shining eyes to each other. This was the best type of storytelling: with arguments, and flames, and ink that shapeshifted . . .

May I continue? Yes? Thank you. So kind.

Now, when the SS Great Britain *was complete, she was the biggest ship that had ever been built. She was twice as large as the next largest ship in the world at the time.*

No, I won't mention her name. I agree it's not relevant.

Yes, I will get on to the next bit now. Please can you stop interrupting? This is my turn – I'm the storyteller – I've been looking forward to this, and it's . . . Yes, I'm trying to—

Kirsten had never seen ink that sulked before.

She was launched by Prince Albert in 1843, with the roar of an entire country urging her on.

National newspapers all over the world dedicated their front pages to her. From New York to Australia, whenever she sailed regally into a dock, everyone dropped what they were doing to clap her in. Because to look at her, they knew, was to see the f . . .

. . . Future, said the map finally, with an air of determination.

What was wrong with it? It seemed to be tiring.

Kings and queens visited her and pronounced her wonderful. And everything about her – from her screw propeller to the delicate china in her first-class saloon to the furniture in her captain's cabin – was the best.

The chair holding the children gave a proud little wiggle.

She was the ship to imitate. All ships that came after her – even the ones you see today – are modelled, in some way, on her.

The ink turned into a large globe, the entire earth.

She didn't just show people the world. She made them

feel that it was theirs. Ordinary people, for the first time in their life, could get away, could start a new life, and all for the price of a one-way ticket.

And she never sank, not once, not on any of her journeys. When babies were born inside her, she rocked them to sleep. She heard people's dreams, she carried them safely and, on dark and stormy nights, she held people tightly in her iron arms until the dawn came.

She was strong and she was steadfast and she never let people down. If only the same could have been done for her.

'People . . . let her down?' said Olive.

Oh yes, said the map in shaky text. More than once.

The room suddenly grew very cold. The chair they were sitting on began to tremble.

The map stretched again, slowly this time.

Kirsten held her breath.

CELEBRATED STEAM SHIP
REAT BRITAIN
...atest, Largest and Finest Steamer Afloat will sail from
STAR LINE, PIER 23, SOUTHHAMPTON
R MELBOURNE
Taking passengers also from
EY, BRISBANE AND NEW ZELAND
Thursday, 5th June, 1874
AT 2PM
FARES TO MELBOURNE
M SOUTHHAMPTON, £8 7s 0d
DON, LIVERPOOL
DEPOSITS

- 35 -
A FLOATING SUITCASE

THE SHIP'S FORTUNES begin to change.

She was almost too wonderful, too advanced, for the times. Keeping the biggest ship in the world in tip-top condition required huge amounts of care and money—

'Sounds like Edwina,' muttered Kirsten.

—And no one had it. Repeated long journeys took their . . .

Their . . .

Toll on her, and her owners kept selling her on, unable to look after . . .

After her properly.

While she was once celebrated for her beauty, she became known for her shabbiness, and she didn't like that at all, but what could she do? No one cared. No one listened.

She had been all used up, and had given everything she could to people, and . . .

And . . .

In return . . .

Pale inkblots began to splatter on the map . . . as if it was crying.

'Are you okay?' whispered Olive.

After forty years of service to the British public, said the map hurriedly, **the ship was damaged in a storm in 1886. She was dragged to the nearest port in the Falkland Islands, where she thought she'd be repaired.**

She was not.

The port was called Port . . .

Port . . .

I must say it, even though it will hurt us both to hear the name. But the children must be told.

Port Stanley.

Those two words had an astonishing effect on the room. The wallpaper seemed to cringe. The lights flickered. The chair quaked and shuddered. The ship groaned and seemed to turn inward on herself. Even Kirsten's temples pounded. Whatever had happened at Port Stanley, the ship had not been able to forget, no matter how much she protested about only living in the present.

'What happened there?' murmured Olive, mesmerised by the history the map was revealing.

Well, she wasn't fixed. She wasn't cared for. She wasn't given the care and respect she deserved, I can tell you that.

She was stripped. As if that wasn't bad enough, she was . . . **She was** . . .

She was altered.

People cut into her. They sawed two rough doors right into her beautiful plating, starboard side. Which, I need hardly point out, was not part of Brunel's design in any way.

It completely severed the top flange of the hull girder. Absolutely shocking behaviour, as I'm sure you'll agree. One must never sever the top flange of the hull girder. You might as well slash at a Van Gogh painting with a knife.

'Why – why did they do that to her?' whispered Mark Spencer.

Because they wanted to change her. They wanted to change her very nature. They didn't think she deserved to be a ship any more. They wanted to make her a . . .

A . . .

I can't say it. I can't.

'It's okay,' said Olive soothingly. 'Take your time.'

They turned her into a storage vessel.

'A what?'

They turned the most important ship of all time into a floating suitcase. And they stuffed her full of wool.

'Wool?' gasped Kirsten.

Wool. It was really important to the Falklanders, and . . . They needed a warehouse. Someone decided a

beautiful ship designed by Brunel himself was the perfect candidate.

So they butchered her and stuffed her.

And then they robbed her.

Robbed? thought Kirsten, feeling her heart give a painful lurch. She wanted, all of a sudden, to get up and walk out, but with Olive and Mark Spencer on either side of her she felt literally wedged in: a captive audience in every sense.

Yes, robbed. People removed her sails, her rigging, her fittings, keen to make a quick profit. She needed help. She got thieves.

They took everything but her strength.

And the ship that loved to sail made no more journeys. For fifty years, she remained just like that: stuffed but full of nothing.

The ink turned into a picture of the ship as a wreck.

The entire room filled with sadness. The ship herself seemed to shudder.

Unsurprisingly, with no one looking after her, she began to leak, and rust, and decay.

In 1933, even her role as a wool suitcase was over.

She was dragged to a small abandoned cove, some three miles from Port Stanley, called Sp—

Sp—

Sparrow Cove.

They scuttled her there. They drove holes into her with a crowbar.

The three children gasped.

It was hoped she would disappear eventually, and settle in the sand.

Kirsten looked round at the cabin, and the ship. 'But she didn't, right?' she asked eagerly.

I thought you were too old for storytime? said the map.

'You win,' said Kirsten. 'I'm not.'

'Nor me,' said Mark.

'Nor me,' said Olive. 'Not this kind of story anyway.'

Very well, said the map. *I am tired . . . But we will get to the end.*

- 36 -
'WHEN THE SHIP SLUMBERS . . .'

The ship, as you rightly say, did not disappear into the sand. She was too well built, too cleverly constructed, for that.

Her ruin was a slow one. Her wooden deck rotted. Her iron hull cracked. Still she clung on, with only the crabs on her hull for company.

Thirty years passed. Thirty lonely years. She remembered, every day, what had happened to her: the cutting and the stripping and the scuttling and the crowbars.

It was not a nice memory and it shaped her in some way.

Olive gave a very, very tiny sniff.

Wait. This is a nice bit. I believe you say, in human parlance, that it will cheer you right up.

'Thank goodness for that,' said Kirsten shakily.

Just when hope was nearly over, someone . . .

My mistake . . .

. . . A wonderful human wrote a letter to The Times

newspaper, saying it was a disgrace the ship should be abandoned like that, so far from the country that made her.

Now this letter made lots of important people nod their heads over their kippers and wonder if they couldn't try to help rescue the ship after all.

She was saved. She was brought back to her city. What had been broken was built again.

And she was nearly as good as – oh, very well. As you wish. I'll say that again:

She was even more beautiful than the day she . . .

The map went silent. For a second, the three children stared at it, wondering if this was part of the story.

'Maybe it's taking a tiny break,' said Olive, and she began to scribble in her notebook, muttering to herself what she wanted to remember.

A few more seconds ticked by. Still no more words appeared.

'Olive?'

'Mmmmm?' Olive looked up, and saw Kirsten staring at her pen. 'What?'

'Can I have that?'

Olive frowned a little, then stared at the blank map. 'Oh. All right. I think I have a spare one.' She handed it over.

Kirsten unscrewed the top and stared at it. Then she put the pen down on the floor and, after a second's hesitation, stamped down on it as hard as she could. A blot of ink appeared on the wooden planks. 'Sorry,' she muttered.

Then she held the smashed remains of the pen over the map and shook it a little.

Blobs of black ink dripped on to the surface and were then sucked in.

Much obliged. As I was saying, she was even more beautiful than the day she was made.

And now the story is done. Now you know her beginning. And her near-ending. And how she began again.

The three children burst into spontaneous applause, but the map was not finished.

Now listen, Captain. Remember this: the ship's body was restored, but not all of her soul. If you want to end this journey, you must do one thing above all else. You must find the truth that she does not want to give up.

'What do you mean?'

The map was silent and still.

'Flatty?' said Kirsten. 'I mean, map?'

Sorry, said the map. *I had to check she wasn't listening. She's concentrating on some tricky waves, but there is smooth water beyond so I'll have to be quick. Peer past the dreams and you will find the truth.*

'Ask Flatty how to do that,' said Olive, eyes as bright as two diamonds.

'Where will I find the truth?'

It's terribly easy. Almost embarassingly so.

'Oh?' said Kirsten, taken aback. 'How?'

When the ship slumbers, you must explore her memories, yet make no noise and leave no footsteps. If she senses you trespassing, you might get injured.

And always, always make sure you are back in your bed before the ship awakes or you'll lose your mind.

There was a dramatic pause. The map wiped itself clean, and then, in its neatest, boldest writing yet, wrote: **AND THEN YOU WILL FIND THE TRUTH TO HELP YOU GET HOME.**

Olive, who had fished out another pen from her rucksack, was scribbling away. 'Lose your mind. Stay quiet. Terrible consequences,' she gasped. 'This just keeps getting better and better.'

Kirsten struggled to keep her voice calm. 'I thought you said this was *easy*? What does the truth even look like? How will I know when I find it?'

You will know when you know.

'But—'

One more thing, Captain. When our time is nearly up,

that is when I will need you. When you can finally prove your worth, Captain. For that will be when you have reached the peak of rare human understanding. It's hard to get to, but the views are spectacular.

A *pause.*

Oh, she's back.

No, no, you didn't miss anything. I was just talking about how wonderful you are.

And then the words were drunk back into the parchment, and the map, finally, went blank.

- 37 -
THE QUEST THICKENS

'Wow,' said Olive. 'That. Was. Amazing.' She glanced at Kirsten. 'And the quest has definitely thickened. Finding the truth? Peering past dreams?'

'You are truly fortunate, Captain,' added Mark shyly. 'I'd give anything to have such a relationship with the ship's map.'

Kirsten nodded, her mind swimming. The stories they had heard were unspeakably sad. But it was all in the past now, wasn't it? So what did they have to do with her? And how were you meant to find the truth within a sleeping ship?

Night had fallen. The ship was full of it, and her interior glow had been reduced to the few meagre beams from the wall lights that flickered here and there. Kirsten fought back a yawn. Mark Spencer took one look at the girls, swaying slightly from tiredness, and nodded to himself.

'I'll find you a berth to sleep in,' he said. He hesitated. 'Would you like me to find you separate berths or one together?'

When she'd woken up that morning, the last thing Kirsten would have anticipated was ending the day with a sleepover with Olive. A quick glance at Olive revealed she was thinking the same.

On the other hand: the ship was getting colder by the second, there were *no* adults with them, it was pitch-black outside, they were in the middle of the Atlantic Ocean, the ship was moving all by herself and they were surrounded by hopefully harmless but nevertheless slightly sinister mannequins, some of whom had weapons and who squeaked when they walked.

'Together,' they said, not looking at each other.

'Makes sense,' said Olive.

'I have just the place,' said Mark, standing up. 'Stay here while I prepare it for you both.' And he slipped away.

Five minutes later, their small barefoot companion showed them to a tiny cabin just off the first-class saloon on the middle deck. Inside it was a narrow wooden bunk bed. The mattresses were thin, but on top of each a dark blue woollen blanket had been pulled tight. On each bed was one lumpy pinstripe pillow, with no pillowcase. The room was lit by a small lantern that rested on an old trunk.

'The finest berth in the ship,' said Mark. 'I remembered

it from when I used to be an active exhibit. I hope it's sufficient?'

'Thank you so much,' said Olive quickly. She nudged Kirsten, who was thinking longingly of her large bed at home, which had silk sheets and cuddly toys all lined up in a row like an adoring audience.

'Um, thank you, it's very nice,' she muttered. Mark's pale face lit up with pride.

'May I advise the other passengers to also turn in, Captain?'

'The others? Oh – you mean the mannequins. Yes, I guess.'

Mark looked delighted to have so much responsibility. 'Goodnight, Captain. Goodnight, First Mate.'

He shut the door as respectfully and proudly as if he was the manager of the Ritz Hotel.

The girls faced each other awkwardly. The room was cramped, and they were uncomfortably close to each other.

'He's sweet,' said Olive uncertainly. 'Helpful too.'

'Very.'

'I'm hungry,' said Olive.

Kirsten's stomach muttered in agreement. They brought out the provisions from their rucksacks.

'How about we share the hummus sandwich?' Kirsten suggested. 'And let's have some of the spinach smoothie too, for – um – strength.'

They tore the sandwich in half, but Kirsten found it hard to convince Olive to share the spinach smoothie. 'I'd rather have my Ribena,' she said flatly.

'Do you want a multivitamin?' Kirsten offered suddenly. 'For –' she checked the label – 'all-round health and vitality?'

Olive shrugged. Her earlier enthusiasm had disappeared and now she seemed sad and scared. 'Suppose I'd better,' she said, and washed it down with a gulp of Ribena.

Kirsten couldn't help but feel responsible. After all, *she'd* set this entire journey off, not Olive. Olive was only there because Mrs Walia had sent her back on the ship. If she hadn't, Olive would be tucked up safe and sound in bed . . .

She felt so guilty she suggested they have a quarter of a chocolate bar each. This perked up Olive much more than the vitamins.

Kirsten couldn't help noticing that, even though they'd tried to be as careful as possible, there wasn't much food left for tomorrow. The sandwiches – the most filling thing they'd had – were both finished. Soon they'd finish the rest of their provisions.

And then what would they do?

'The ship will provide,' said the SS **Great Britain** grandly.

'Oh yes? Provide what exactly? More fake tripe?' snapped Kirsten, before feeling guilty again.

Exhausted, she sank on to the bottom bunk. She plucked hesitantly at her school uniform. She'd worn it *all day*. Then she ran her tongue across her teeth and winced. They'd brought *nothing*: no pyjamas, no clean clothes, no toiletries . . .

Kirsten let her school uniform, captain's hat and shoes land where they fell. Then she got under the blanket in her vest and pants, wrapping herself up as tightly as she could.

'Aren't you going to put your clothes away more tidily than that?' Olive muttered, folding her own away and laying them carefully on the trunk.

'I'll deal with it tomorrow,' said Kirsten through a yawn.

For a few seconds, neither said anything.

In the cold cabin, their predicament felt scary and huge. What if the ship stopped moving? What if it sank? Would anyone know? The ship had no lifeboats, no flares, no way of calling for help. A cold, hard lump of homesickness lodged itself in Kirsten's tummy. She eyed Olive, and realised she'd be feeling the same.

'Olive,' said Kirsten, 'we're going to be all right, okay? I promise.'

'How do you know though?' said Olive, through trembling lips.

'Remember what the map told us? This ship never sank. Not once. Not on any of her journeys. And she won't do it now. I just have a feeling. She might be old, and full of holes, but – I dunno. She just seems invincible somehow. Trust me.'

A small grin of gratitude flashed across Olive's face and she gave a juddering sigh. 'Okay,' she said simply. 'Thanks.'

They looked at each other, then turned away awkwardly. 'Well – night,' said Olive after a moment, climbing into the top bunk.

'Night.'

They lay there, in the darkness, for a while. Kirsten thought she heard a tiny whimper, just once, but then Olive's breathing grew more rhythmic, and Kirsten guessed she had fallen asleep.

Kirsten herself took longer. The bed was the most uncomfortable thing she'd ever slept in – hard, lumpy and only slightly wider than her. She felt the ship pitch and roll, could almost count every wave beneath her. She missed Dad. It took a while, but eventually she finally fell into an exhausted asleep too, as the ship carried them firmly over the cold, dark waters.

PART 4

'What a life! The life of a dreamer'
Private diary entry, Isambard Kingdom Brunel, 1824

- 38 -
DREAM TIME

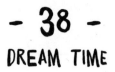

LOUD SNORING WOKE her up a while later. Kirsten peeled one bleary eye open and gazed round the silver cabin, bathed in the moonlight that streamed in through a small porthole.

The entire room seemed to shake with noise. Olive sounded like a walrus. Kirsten was surprised their bunk hadn't broken. She groaned and rolled over. She needed a wee. She struggled to a sitting position and hit her head on the bunk.

She wished she'd gone before bed. She didn't want to leave the cabin. The quietness and darkness pressed in on her, and something seemed ever so slightly off. She put one foot on the floor, and recoiled in fright.

The floor of the cabin was soft and almost spongy. Like it was alive.

She put an experimental foot on the floor again. She *hadn't* imagined it. She moved her foot around. It wasn't just one tiny spot that was soft: it was all of it.

She reassessed the sound of snoring in the room. Olive had many, *many* faults, but she had *never* snored that loudly.

If that noise wasn't coming from Olive, then who was it coming from?

Kirsten was desperate for the loo now. Reluctantly, she placed both feet on the floor, shivering at its unsettling bendiness, then tiptoed into the corridor, quietly shutting the door behind her.

The snoring was just as loud, even though she was further away from Olive.

Now she knew. It wasn't *Olive* that had woken her up. Those exhalations belonged to the ship.

She was asleep. Kirsten would not have believed it herself had she not stood on the soft, pliant floor and felt the entire vessel thrum with a deep, rhythmical breathing. In sleep, her iron body clearly softened, just like people's did.

Kirsten remembered what the map had told them. **Peer past the dreams and you will find the truth** . . . **And then you will find the truth to help you get home.**

Kirsten stood in the darkness, eyes wide as she tried to think.

For a beat, she simply remained there, marvelling at the floor that rose and fell gently under her feet. Olive was right: this was a quest. Kirsten had to find something if she wanted to get home.

Okay. She lifted her chin, as if to show the quest she was not afraid. Challenge *accepted*. Her thoughts raced. How did you go about looking for the truth within a sleeping ship?

The corridor in front of her temporarily switched direction, then switched back again. Kirsten held her breath, hoped it would stay in one place long enough for her to get to the end, then began to tiptoe into the depths of the sleeping ship, moving as tenderly as a thief in the shadows.

- 39 -
BEST OF TIMES, WORST OF TIMES

THE SHIP'S LIFE, Kirsten realised with a pang of recognition, held even more drama than her own TV show. The SS **Great Britain** had seen the best – and the worst – of people. She'd been celebrated by humanity and then wrecked by it. People had created her, worshipped her, used her then nearly destroyed her . . . and, as if all that wasn't enough, they'd restored her and then celebrated her once more.

Talk about a rollercoaster of a life. If you'd had an existence like that, then what *would* be your ultimate truth? Would you be bitter or wise, forgiving or vengeful? And where would you keep it?

All of a sudden, Kirsten felt really naughty, as if she was looking for hidden Christmas presents before Christmas, which she had actually done once.

The ship produced a loud snore, and then her insides began to shimmer. Her walls became translucent. Kirsten could see almost everything going on in her dreams all at once.

As she tiptoed down corridors and peered through walls, it became clear that when the ship dreamed, she dreamed of the past. This was a ship, Kirsten realised, of memory; a ship who'd outlived the people she'd carried, yet who still held on to some last trace of them somehow, and kept them alive that way.

In one berth, the fittings were bright, the linen was new, and there was a glamorous woman brushing out her curls . . . and then, in the next cabin, there were the ghosts of wounded soldiers staring into space with an air of shock. There were babies crying, children laughing, sweethearts muttering in corners, passengers writing at desks . . .

Occasionally, a huge wave would roll down a corridor and Kirsten would gasp and try to duck out of its way. It was only when one went crashing over her, and she emerged from it totally dry, that she realised it was a dream wave. (Because, of course, the ship didn't just dream of people – she also dreamed of the ocean; hadn't Kirsten somehow known this, ever since she'd seen her purposeful bowsprit?)

On the middle deck, the promenade saloon filled with the sounds of people dancing, but when Kirsten looked into the party she saw Victorian passengers waltzing across rotten floorboards, apparently not noticing the water pouring in through the now wrecked panels of the ship. The dreams here were mixed up; the best and the worst of the ship's past lives all in one: her worst days at Sparrow Cove, her best days as a luxury liner.

Kirsten held her breath, transfixed by the sight of beauty and decay dancing round each other, by the people laughing and the dresses flying over the crumbling floor.

Guided by nothing but the map's warning that she mustn't linger too long, Kirsten moved on. Occasionally, the ship snored so loudly that all the corridors would ripple and Kirsten would have to use every ounce of concentration to surf the floor rather than collapse on it.

For a particularly beautiful moment of time, the entire inside of the ship turned into a galaxy, and shimmered with stars and space. Kirsten looked down and saw the carpet had been replaced by the Milky Way, and she was floating on it. These were the ship's childhood dreams, she guessed – back when she was just a supernova floating in space.

In one bathroom, Kirsten saw a miniature harbour inside the washbasin, where a tiny ship pulled in to be greeted with applause that turned into fireworks that went whizzing round the bathroom. She closed the door quickly before they went flying into her face. Perhaps, she wondered, *that* was the ship's truth, the one Flatty wanted her to spot? That she longed to travel into ports once more, and be greeted with adoration? (Kirsten could kind of understand that.)

Or was there something else, something more private, that she was meant to discover?

Her wanderings took her near the engine room. Here the ship felt entirely different. It was like walking into an underground cave, where gravity and pressure and metal and earth all surged round her, creating currents her body responded to without her even realising. The air pulsed with secrets. Every single hair on Kirsten's arms stood up.

The sound of the dancing in the saloon and the fireworks banging in the basin elsewhere in the ship stopped. Nothing else existed. Kirsten could *feel* the truth nearby. Unlike the memories contained in the ship's rooms, it wasn't visible, but she could feel it. It was intense. It had a strange, pulsating warmth and sadness all at once. She recognised it; she could almost even feel it herself.

But it wasn't human. It belonged to the ship. Kirsten knew this instinctively, in a fierce, sure way. This was a truth that belonged to the ship, and it was buried very, very deeply, in a place she clearly wasn't ever meant to discover.

She turned her head. The wall next to her shimmered, and she peered through it into the heart of something large. And, for a second, she thought she saw something.

A human hand curled up on a blanket.

The wall glistened, as if the ship was crying. And then

the sound of a party started up again, and with that the roar of several feet stamping up and down a ballroom, and the truth Kirsten had stumbled across disappeared, and whatever story she'd nearly uncovered was hidden away from her again.

She spun round.

The part of the ship she had drifted into was full of shadows. What floor was she on? The corridor switched. The dreaming ship was full of trickery.

It took her a long time and several false attempts – she kept tripping over dream passengers floating through the corridors, which was extremely disconcerting, and walking into rooms she thought were cabins but weren't – before she finally wound her way back to the cabin she shared with Olive in the early hours of the morning, more by luck than anything else.

She peeled back the sheets and laid her head on the bare pillow, exhausted, frustrated with herself. Whatever that final thing *was* she'd nearly found, it was essential to her getting back home, she was sure of it. It felt like the truth – like something the ship was guarding closely.

And it had slipped away almost as soon as she found it.

- 40 -
SHIP MAGIC
WEDNESDAY

KIRSTEN WOKE BLEARILY to the sound of the ship in her head.

'I don't feel well,' said the ship.

There was something about her voice that seemed odd – slower somehow.

'I feel all stirred up and unusual. You haven't been – poking about where you shouldn't, have you? Nosing around in things that are gone? It's never a good idea. Quickest way to feel your age, you know, stirring up the past.'

Kirsten noticed Olive's head hanging upside down.

'We're still here then,' Olive's chin said wryly, peering down from the top bunk. 'It wasn't all a dream.'

Kirsten began to speak, then hesitated. Her broken night's sleep and what she'd seen in the dreaming ship had left her tired and confused.

Olive seemed to understand. She held up a finger. 'Wait.' She pushed her blanket back and landed on the floor softly. 'Breakfast first.'

They sat on the floor and brought their rucksacks out.

'Half a banana and half a flapjack each?' suggested Kirsten after a while.

'Then chocolate,' said Olive. 'And almonds.'

Once they'd shared their food, Kirsten cast a worried eye over what was left. All they had now was one chocolate bar, a packet of crisps, the almonds and the sweets. (And the vitamins, of course, but would that fill them up? Unlikely.) They were also running low on water, although they could keep their bottles topped up with the tap water in the loo. Was that drinking water though? Probably not.

Flames of anxiety burned inside her. They *had* to get home, not only to avoid starving to death, or contracting something deadly from the drinking water, but also – she did a mental countdown – because she had just over forty-eight hours before her Jade Cooper interview: the interview that would win back her public, placate the bank manager and keep a roof over their heads.

There was no time to waste. She rubbed at her eyes and spoke hastily. 'I went in the ship's dreams last night.'

'Whoa – just like the map said! That's awesome!' Olive shot her an envious look. 'Did you find . . .' She picked up her notebook from the trunk and turned its pages. 'Did you *peer past the dreams and find the truth*?'

'I found – or nearly found – *a clue*. It felt like the ship was longing for something. At times, I thought it was New

York, but then I saw something else . . . but it didn't make a lot of sense and it vanished.'

They were interrupted by a knock on the door.

'Hello, Captain,' Mark Spencer said, then nodded at Olive. 'First Mate. Having a lie-in, I see.'

Kirsten checked her watch. It was 6.45 in the morning. Mark peered uncertainly at their messy cabin. 'Have you been burgled in the night?'

Olive gave a short laugh of surprise.

'I wonder if you might be able to come out and assist me with the passengers,' said Mark Spencer. 'The fighting women need breaking up. The first-class passengers want constant attention. And the surgeon wants to know how your heebie-jeebies –' he left a delicate pause here – 'are faring.'

He disappeared. The girls hastily got ready, in very different ways. Olive easily slipped into the school uniform she'd folded tidily the night before. Kirsten picked up her crumpled clothes, then spent a few seconds looking round the room pathetically. Her school shirt was inside out from when she'd thrown it on the floor last night. Was she meant to turn it the right way round *herself*? Back at home, they had a housekeeper who did that sort of stuff. And she always wore clean uniform, fresh from the laundry, every school day – she was a showbiz star, after all. Putting on a grimy shirt was yet another challenge she was faced with, and she didn't particularly like it.

Olive opened the door and gestured to the corridor beyond. 'You first. You're the captain.'

The rest of the morning passed in mannequin management, much to Kirsten's dismay; she craved time to herself so she could work out what she'd seen last night, and how to get home. Every time she had a chance, she'd run to the deck to scan the sky and sea for signs of help, but there were none. Maybe she should just set fire to something to send off smoke signals? Where would the ship keep matches?

The mannequins, however, made concentration impossible. They clamoured for her attention like puppies.

The gentlemen from the upper-class cabins kept stopping her to ask how their passage was going, and could she tell them when they'd get to New York.

The three little children with the toy train set from steerage liked to stand and stare at her shyly whenever she passed.

The fighting women were either constantly injuring themselves or asking for gin.

Cook kept begging the two girls to approve his latest menu, and even the violinists pestered Kirsten as to what her favourite concerto was, and what she'd like to hear at dinner.

She managed to shake them off enough to share a hurried lunch with Olive: they finished off their almonds and the last remaining chocolate bar in the dining saloon. They tried to fill up with water and one more multivitamin, but it wasn't enough. Reluctantly, Kirsten agreed to open their only packet of crisps, even though that left them with just sweets for the rest of the day.

Olive clutched her stomach and groaned in pain as she shovelled crisps into her mouth. 'I'm so hungry,' she said.

'You're *hungry*?' said Mark, who was happiest when busy, and was passing through the saloon with an old hoover he'd retrieved from the cleaning cupboard. 'Why didn't you say so?'

Kirsten frowned. 'What do you mean?'

He surprised them both by going a bit pink. 'Let's just say some of the passengers here are a little – light-fingered. They've been storing food. Real food. I'm sure you can have it.'

'What?' said Olive in amazement.

Mark looked frightened. 'Oh – I shouldn't have told you, should I?'

'No, you most definitely should,' said Kirsten. 'Tell us *exactly* what you mean.'

Mark looked absolutely tiny in the vast marble-pillared room. 'Well.' He straightened his shoulders and met their eyes. 'Humans are careless sometimes, aren't they? I've noticed they're always dropping things here and there, from their pockets.'

'*They?* Do you mean the visitors? Like us? The people who visited the ship back in the dock at Bristol?'

Mark nodded. 'Yes – those human tourists. You wouldn't believe what falls out of their handbags and pockets, on a regular basis. And we all felt – all at the same time, without speaking to each other about it – that it made sense to pick up and hold on to these forgotten treasures. At first, we did it to keep the ship spick and span, you see. But then I began to wonder if there wasn't something else going on. We can't eat human food. But we *always picked up whatever they discarded*. I think—'

Here Mark's voice dropped to a reverential whisper.

'—I think the ship made us do it, with her *ship magic*. Because she was waiting for this to happen all along. She knew she'd have another captain one day, and she wanted that captain to be able to eat.'

Kirsten remembered what the **SS Great Britain** had told her the night before. '*The ship will provide.*'

Her mouth watered. 'Can you ask everyone to bring their food to the dining saloon?'

'They won't get into trouble, will they, Captain? For ... for holding on to food that wasn't theirs?'

'No,' said Kirsten. 'Definitely not.'

She coughed a little. 'Mark Spencer,' she said firmly, 'you will do me a huge honour if you ask all of the manneq– all of the *passengers* to bring their food to me immediately.'

Mark looked delighted, and ran out of the nearest exit at once.

- 41 -
SHIP'S PROVISIONS

'BLIMEY,' SAID KIRSTEN a while later. She was impressed. 'You *have* been busy.'

After Mark had assembled the mannequins in the saloon, and they'd all been persuaded they weren't in trouble, Kirsten and Olive had been proudly shown an entire treasure trove of old food and snacks, some of which dated back a decade or more. Each mannequin came forward and shyly produced their treasures, safely stored in hats, knickerbockers, pockets, the undersides of shoes for years . . .

There were unopened packets of biscuits, ancient apples, mini cheddars, rice cakes, crumbling oatcakes, malt loaves, chocolate bars, cereal bars, boxes of raisins, dried apricots – hundreds of snacks dropped by tourists and subsequently squirrelled away by a crew of mannequins obeying the inner command of the ship, who liked to save for a rainy day, and wanted no future captain of hers to starve.

As each mannequin handed over their food, one

by one – explaining where it had been stored, who had dropped it and how old it was, in the most bizarre version of show-and-tell Kirsten had ever seen – she had a sudden feeling of déjà vu.

This was exactly what she and Olive had done when playing *Zeleth*. They'd traded with the villagers. The mannequins were giving her goods, which meant they'd need something in return. But what could she give? She had nothing.

Even after eating their way through an entire banquet of wizened snacks, there was at least a whole week's worth of snacks left for the two girls to live on. It wasn't hot, it wasn't healthy, and in some cases tasted unrecognisable to what it had once been, but it would stop them from starving, and that was something.

Once Cook had commandeered organisation of the goods and taken them off into the pantry, delighted to have something to do all by himself, and Kirsten and Olive had lavished the mannequins with praise and thanks, their fibreglass companions drifted off, looking gratified.

Now the girls no longer had to worry about food, Kirsten could concentrate on the quest: finding the truth.

Kirsten and Olive had gone into the Captain's Cabin after lunch, but the map had merely opened one tiny ink eye, looked at them tiredly, and begged to be left alone after the epic storytelling session of the night before. Olive had then been pulled away by the mannequin children, who wanted to play, so Kirsten spent the afternoon wandering through the ship, looking for clues, wondering what that *hand* had meant. But there were no dreams to be seen during the day and, what's more, the ship would not consciously give away any of her secrets.

'I told you, Captain – the past is past. Also, don't keep interrupting me, please. I'm sailing to New York and I *must* concentrate. I'll tell you when to steer. In the meantime, I beg you, let me be.'

Kirsten was so wrung out and exhausted she went to bed as early as she could, hoping to get a good night's sleep, while Olive stayed up with some of the mannequins in steerage, playing card games and making her way through a packet of crisps with a best-before date of 2008.

An old stab of jealousy pulsed through Kirsten and she picked fretfully at a loose thread on her blanket. In the cold, quiet cabin, unwelcome memories began to stir.

Memories of how, in the early days of Kirsten's TV career, the producers had asked if Olive wanted to be part of the show too.

They'd both gone to the studio in London for a test shoot. 'We just want to check your chemistry as friends works as well on-screen as it does in real life,' Kirsten's then agent had said. 'Should be a total breeze, right?'

And it would have been if Olive had made the slightest effort. But she hadn't.

Kirsten stared up at the top of the bunk, squirming with resentment and embarrassment. She looked round the cabin. She played with her split ends. She polished her leather shoes with the end of her blanket. She counted the spots on her chin aloud, in Spanish. Anything, *anything*, to keep the past buried.

But it kept coming back.

Under the hot, bright lights of the studio, as the cameras began to roll, Olive had gone weird and quiet. A sheen of nervous perspiration had covered her face. She'd looked miserable – as if she'd rather be anywhere else.

'Just be natural,' said the director. 'Relax into it. Pretend we're not here, angel face.'

After ninety minutes of really awkward filming, the ITV people had taken Kirsten aside. 'She's not a natural in the spotlight, not like you, is she? Not sure she's gonna work out. Shall we start auditioning some other little girls?'

And that was enough, thought Kirsten angrily, of *that*.

She remembered something the map had said. **We are, in a manner of speaking, very much going back.**

Well, she'd gone there. And it was awful. Maybe the

ship had a point. Living in the present was the only way to live – the past was not worth visiting.

She left the cabin and stomped down the corridor to the cramped ladies' toilet where she haphazardly tried to give herself a wash with nothing but the corner of her vest. Then she rubbed her fingers over her teeth for sixty seconds. Then she went back to her bunk, lay down and contemplated crying.

I will not cry, she thought. *Crying makes you ugly.*

When Kirsten's eyes finally closed, she hoped fervently that she'd uncover the truth that night within the ship. Time was running out.

But she was so tired she slept through the entire night without waking once.

- 42 -
BURNT SUGAR
THURSDAY

THEY WERE WOKEN the next morning by a polite knocking, and Mark Spencer eagerly putting his head round the door.

'The air smells different outside,' he announced. 'I think . . . we might be approaching our first destination.'

'Already?' gasped Olive. 'Wow!'

But all Kirsten could think, as she got out of bed, was that she had accidentally slept through the entire night, and was no closer to ending the journey. Which meant – she calculated, with a lurch of her stomach – she had just one more day to get back to Bristol. The Jade Cooper interview was being filmed at 5 p.m. on Friday, which was *tomorrow*.

She had just over thirty hours to turn the ship round, persuade her to sail back the way she'd come, then disembark, rush to the shops to buy her outfit, do something about her hair, get down to London and put in a career-best performance as the nation's sweetheart.

The odds were not good.

Unless . . . She had a sudden idea. She kept it very small and quiet inside her head so the ship wouldn't hear it. Not that there was much danger of that. The SS *Great Britain* seemed so excited at the prospect of being greeted by New York again, it was unlikely she could hear anything but her own joy.

All the fixtures in the cabin rattled, and the pillows plumped themselves up quickly, as if the ship was giving herself a bit of a spruce-up.

'Oh, America, America, star-spangled thingy, land of the free! I can't wait to see what sort of welcome they're laying on for us. It was all brass bands and Sunday best last time I swung into New York Harbour. Goodness only knows what there'll be now.'

'I'll tell the passengers,' said Mark excitedly. 'See you on deck, Captain. First Mate.'

After hastily rubbing their teeth with their fingers, the girls left the cabin and headed for the top deck.

Mark Spencer was right, thought Kirsten, sniffing the cold, damp air around them, shivering in the grey mist that rose from the Atlantic. The air smelled slightly sweet and dangerous around the edges, like burnt sugar.

'Ah, yes,' said the ship suddenly. 'That's land for you. You always smell it before you see it. Every country has its own distinct aroma.'

'Does it?' said Kirsten, intrigued despite herself. 'What does Britain smell like?'

'Mustard and madness. Mostly. Hadn't you better get dressed?'

Kirsten glanced down at herself, cheeks reddening a bit at the state of her clothes. 'I *am dressed*,' she huffed. 'I can't help not having a spare—'

'You're not dressed at all if you don't have your captain's hat. And we can't *possibly* pull into a harbour without one on your head. You're not going in there dressed like that.'

'I don't want to put it on,' said Kirsten. 'It's grubby. It's got me into lots of trouble already. And I'm not the captain.'

A dismissive puff of steam came from the ship's middle funnel. 'Put it on immediately. A ship without a captain is an embarrassment, and can lead to even more trouble. Trust me.'

Kirsten didn't have the strength to argue. Also, the ship was quite scary when she was cross and made her brain ring more than usual.

'*Fine.*'

It didn't interfere with her secret plan anyway.

When she went back above deck, the buildings and smog and busyness of New York Harbour were just visible. Despite everything, Kirsten felt a corresponding thrum in her chest. There *was* something exciting about looking at land from the deck, seeing a new place get bigger, and wondering who and what was inside it. She understood, all of a sudden, why the ship loved beginnings so much, and why she'd broken through her restraints to find a few more. If you'd spent your entire life travelling the world, it must be very difficult to know when to stop.

'Are you going to stand there all day, Captain, or have you got any plans at all to grab the wheel?' said the SS *Great Britain* calmly.

Kirsten walked to the ship's stern and put her hands on the wheel. The entire deck in front of her rippled with delight. Kirsten wished the ship's enthusiasm reached as far as the steering wheel, which, if anything, was even harder to steer than usual. What had *that* slept in – glue? She'd been on bumper cars more responsive.

All the same, it was thrilling to be somewhere at last. Kirsten felt a skip in her heart when they sailed past the Statue of Liberty, and saw the skyscrapers of New York beyond.

'Ah,' said the ship. 'My public awaits.'

- 43 -
NEW YORK

BUT IT DIDN'T.

Kirsten had been led to believe that New York would be giddy with joy to see the SS *Great Britain* again. She almost expected a red carpet rolled out on the water.

But there was none of that. The people in charge of the red carpet must have been running late. If there was a crowd nearby, desperate for a glimpse of the ship's razzle-dazzle, they were being very quiet. And there was no brass band at all.

'Um – ship?' said Kirsten quietly, as the skyline drew nearer. 'Did the New Yorkers definitely know we were arriving today?'

'Oh, Captain, I can't possibly be expected to manage my schedule and my fans. I told you, old Flatty is in charge, and of course it would have told them . . .'

'But – how?'

'Telegrams, darling. The waves carry them. They do go a bit soggy, but they get there in the end.'

'*Who* gets the telegrams?'

'Oh, someone always does. Haven't you ever stood at the water's edge and got a telegram?'

'I don't know. What do they look like?'

'They don't look like anything, of course. They're *thought* telegrams. They hop right into your brain and tell you the news. That's why people look so thoughtful when they're next to the waves, darling: they're listening to telegrams.'

'Right.'

'Fishermen get them all day long. That's why some of them don't talk much: they're too busy listening to the thought telegrams. Very *nosy*, fishermen. And,' the **SS *Great Britain*** said patiently, 'of course they've been expecting us. I imagine they're just busy putting the final touches to the welcome procession.'

The skyscrapers that studded the land on either side of them stared at them with blank, shiny windows, giving nothing away. Olive and Mark Spencer stood next to Kirsten, and together they scanned the busy waterway.

They were surrounded by a crowd of sorts, but it wasn't clapping, and it didn't look delighted. It looked decidedly grumpy.

BEEP-BEEP hooted one impatient cargo ship, as they nearly collided.

HONK-HONK went a speedboat.

'GET OUT OF MY WAY!' shouted a man on a ferry.

'Um, ship?' said Kirsten after a moment. 'I'm not sure they got the . . . thought telegram. I don't think we should be here. I think Flatty got it wrong.' Feeling self-conscious and a bit stupid, she removed her hat.

The mannequins looked at each other and then, one after the other, seemed to freeze, forming a tableau of lifeless waxworks again. It was very disquieting watching the life seep out of them – nearly as weird as it had been to watch them come alive.

The ship seemed to almost droop and the wooden deck grew darker. And suddenly, right in the middle of the busy harbour thoroughfare, the SS *Great Britain* went completely still.

'W-wait a minute,' said Kirsten. 'You can't just *stop moving*. It's dangerous here.'

As if to prove her point, a crowded ferry filled with people swerved right past them, narrowly avoiding a collision, and went off angrily, making several indignant beeping noises.

Kirsten took a deep breath. She knew what she had to do. She walked back towards the ship's wheel and attempted to turn it. It was even harder to move than before. It made her veins pop and her forehead bulge. Panting, she managed to yank the ship to the side of the busy waterway. Her white school shirt was dripping in sweat by the end, making a grimy school uniform even grimier, but at least they were out of harm's way.

Exhausted, she ran to the side of the ship.

They'd pulled up just outside a busy dockside restaurant. After a few moments, the diners inside began to stare at them through the window. They looked delighted at the sight of them.

'Ah,' said the SS *Great Britain* suddenly, shaking off her despondency. 'Here we go. Better late than never. I expect the telegram was just held up in a queue or something.'

The diners were pushing and shoving each other out of the way to get out of the restaurant first.

'Just like old times,' sighed the SS *Great Britain* happily. 'They can barely restrain themselves.'

'Yes,' said Kirsten, deepening her dimples. 'They are rather excited.'

For the first time since meeting, both the ship and the girl completely agreed with each other about one thing. Together, they waited to be adored.

Once that happened, Kirsten decided, she would carry out her secret plan. But walking away from applause was impossible, so she might as well enjoy it first.

- 44 -

THE HERO REFUSES THE QUEST

BUT, AS THE little group of diners gathered outside, they began to shout up at Kirsten and the ship.

'You're in the way! Move!'

Kirsten spun round and realised there was something *behind* the SS **Great Britain**.

It was a huge white supercruiser. It was three times as long as the SS **Great Britain** and three times as wide. On the side was the name:

And she gleamed in the light like an icicle.

A languorous Italian accent began to speak in Kirsten's head.

'You heard what they said, *cara*. Now move out of the way so I can give 'em what they want.' The voice was as silky as a cat stretching in the sunshine.

Apparently, it was now Kirsten's fate to hear the voices of any passing boat or ship.

'I am goddess of the sea. And you and your old boat are obstructing my public's view, *bambolina*.'

'*Boat?*' said the SS **Great Britain** quietly, and she said the word as if was dirty. 'I'm not a *boat! I'm the most important ship in the history of shipbuilding, and you'd do well to remember that.*'

'Are you okay?' Olive was standing right next to Kirsten. 'What's going on? You look tense.'

'L-lots of voices in my head right now that aren't mine,' Kirsten stammered. 'Quite a bit to listen to.'

'Well, you may be a ship, *carina*, but you look like you from the past, and I ain't never heard of you,' said the yacht.

The ship gasped.

'But what I do know is that this is my patch, and you're taking up space with that big ol' backside of yours.'

'How *dare* you talk about my tonnage,' spat the ship. 'This is an outrage. Where is the editor of the *Evening Post*? In 1845, they dedicated their entire issue to my arrival—'

The yacht sniggered, and Kirsten suddenly felt all the fight drain out of the SS **Great Britain**. She felt uncomfortable and humiliated too. She knew what it was like to find yourself side by side with a competitor, and watch the public switch allegiance.

Kirsten had suddenly had enough. It was time to put

her secret plan into action. She was going to abandon ship.

She could navigate the crowded waterway if she had to, her front crawl wasn't bad, and then, once she was out of the water, she'd sweet-talk her way to the nearest airport and catch the next plane to England. She could be back in Bristol by evening. Which gave her just enough time to rescue the Bramble brand tomorrow. Sure, the map wanted her to find the secret at the heart of the ship or whatever, but what about what *she*, Kirsten Bramble, wanted? Had anyone thought about *that*?

She had no doubt at all this was the right thing to do. She was a hopeless captain and she was fed up of all the dreams and riddles. Protecting her livelihood, and Dad's, was more important. Also, it wasn't as if the ship was getting anything like the welcome she'd been expecting. Which just went to prove that this entire trip was a mistake. And now it was over.

Kirsten went over to the railing and glanced down at the choppy water, took a deep breath, and put her right foot on the first rung, ready to climb over . . .

'What are you *doing*?' said Olive.

'Isn't it obvious?' Kirsten said quietly.

'You're going to abandon the ship? And the mannequins?' Olive's eyes were wide with shock and betrayal. 'And leave your quest unfinished?'

Kirsten gave a tiny nod. 'Yes. Coming?'

Olive folded her arms. 'Absolutely not. *I* never walk away from a quest. What about this truth you're meant to find? What about the ship? What about the *map*? What about Mark Spencer? What's he going to do without us? But sure, you go right ahead: walk away even when people need you.'

Kirsten *thought* she heard Olive mutter: 'You've always been good at that,' but it was hard to tell over the tooting and beeping and shouting.

'Are you sure you don't want to come?' Kirsten offered one more time. But Olive just shook her head, her jaw tight. Kirsten hesitated. Then thought of everything at stake. If Olive was so keen to stay, she could stay. She had food. A bed. An entire quest to take over. She knew the ropes, and the map and Mark Spencer would surely help her out.

But Kirsten *had* to go. If she didn't make it back for the Jade Cooper interview, they'd lose everything eventually – the contract, the house . . . She quickly unbuttoned her blazer and took off her shoes.

'Captain?' said the ship quietly, and there was a break in her voice.

'I'm sorry,' muttered Kirsten gruffly, and then as

quickly as she could, before anyone else could make her feel bad, she took a deep breath, and

jumped off
the ship into
the cold
dark WATER beneath.

- 45 -
A DECISION

IT WAS ABSOLUTELY freezing. She began to swim, as quickly as she could, just to stay warm. But, once she'd gone a few metres, she made the mistake of looking back.

Olive had gone grey. She was thumping her chest. As Olive collapsed in a crumpled heap, Kirsten began to tread water, hoping that one of the mannequins would run to help her. But they all remained frozen – because Kirsten had abandoned them.

Olive had no one to help her.

Was Kirsten going to leave her now? Swim away and let Olive struggle for breath in a strange place?

I've done it once already, haven't I? Four years ago, to be precise. During that terrible audition.

A dreadful memory Kirsten usually kept deep within herself floated to the surface.

Just after Olive's reluctant audition in the television studio, Kirsten had implored Olive to try a little harder, but Olive had squirmed uncomfortably and said she hated being in the studio, and didn't like the attention, or the lights, or the people staring at her, and she didn't feel well, and she wanted to go home . . . Kirsten had begged her to make more of an effort, but Olive had said that if Kirsten wanted to make the show with another best friend then she should just go ahead and do it, she didn't care, and she was going home . . . and then she'd started to pant and clutch at her chest.

And Kirsten – who had felt so furious with Olive for embarrassing her, and not caring enough about her programme – had walked away. She hadn't even turned round. Not even when the gasps were really ragged, and she could hear Olive wheezing her name.

Someone had eventually rushed to Olive's aid, but by then their friendship was as good as dead. They didn't talk to each other at all in the car on the way back to Bristol, and at school the next day neither would look the other in the eye. Kirsten had convinced herself it was because Olive was jealous of her.

But really both of them had known the truth. Kirsten had felt let down, and so had let Olive down badly.

Kirsten let the cold dark water swirl round her. If she swam away from Olive now, she'd be betraying her all over again. If she gave up her plans, swam back to the ship now and tried to help Olive, she could make amends for an old but painful mistake. But, if she did that, she'd never make it to Bristol in time.

Kirsten looked across at the harbour, gave one last longing glance at her only chance of escape, and smacked her palm against the water in frustration at the things she was about to lose.

Then she paddled back to the **SS *Great Britain*** and, as she got closer, screamed up at the mannequins to drop down some rope. To her relief, they came alive again at her return, and began to move.

- 46 -
THE QUEST IS RESUMED

GETTING BACK ON to the SS *Great Britain* was much, much harder than either falling on or jumping off. Kirsten had to tread water for ages while Mark and the other mannequins tied ropes together long enough to drop over the railings. Then she held on to one end as tightly as she could while they pulled her back up, inch by painful inch, shivering as she was hauled up like a crab.

She landed back on the deck cold, wet, barefoot and slightly uncomfortable at arriving in such an undignified way. Once she'd got her breath back, she looked over at Olive, who was still sitting, panting, on the deck. She did look reassured at Kirsten's presence, which made Kirsten feel better about the decision she'd made.

Olive raised one eyebrow. 'What made you come back?'

'Oh, you know,' said Kirsten lightly, embarrassed.

'No.' Olive cocked her head to one side and stared at her.

'I, um, wanted to finish the quest,' said Kirsten and, even though this was only half the truth, it seemed to satisfy Olive, who lapsed into silence and broke eye contact.

Kirsten struggled to a sitting position and tried to wring some water out of her hair.

'Back again?' said the SS *Great Britain*. 'Quite right too. I expect you suddenly realised how much you needed me.'

'Yeah,' said Kirsten, reaching for her cardigan for warmth. 'Let's say that.'

'Olive?' she said. 'Have you got Wi-Fi, or any kind of connection, here?'

But, just as Olive pulled her mobile out of her rucksack, the screen went blank. They both looked at it in dismay.

'No battery,' said Olive. 'Sorry.'

And there were no plugs on the ship and no charger.

'Steer me out, please, Captain,' said the ship grandly. 'I have tired of New York, I find. They seem to have dropped their standards and are letting any two-bit strumpet in.'

They slowly moved away from the city, back into the Atlantic. Once they were safely away from the harbour that hadn't wanted them, Kirsten hurried to the Captain's Cabin.

The walls of the room, evidently unimpressed with her little escape attempt, took a while to let her in. Eventually, impatient, she fought her way to the desk with the aid of her elbows.

'I *trusted* you!' she said to the map. 'I thought you *knew what you were doing!* You said as much . . . but we weren't meant to be in New York at all. You chose the wrong destination. It was awful! No one wanted us – I mean, *her.*'

It was not a pleasant experience, I agree, said the map. **But it wasn't a mistake.**

'Why not?' Kirsten's throat was uncomfortably tight. 'All that ship wants to do is sail round the world being admired endlessly, and ignoring everything she doesn't like. It's exhausting! I can't be doing with that! I've got places to go! Urgently!'

You're right. You both have another destiny.

Kirsten clenched her fists. 'Show me. Give me a clue!'

Your journey can't be plotted on a normal map, Captain, said the map. **But I can tell you that you have rounded the gulf of understanding, you navigated the peninsula of the fickle waters of fame, and now you're sailing in the Mists of Yearning—**

Kirsten had heard enough. 'You act as if you're this wise, clever thing, but you're not, are you? You're just a stupid piece of old paper who likes to talk rubbish and tell long, pointless stories. And this isn't a JOURNEY – it's just a JOKE.'

She stomped out of the room without even bothering to read the map's reply. The walls all stared at each other after she'd left, and the gold crests on their paper began to curl and turn brown.

- 47 -
A VICTORIAN MOOD

FOR THE REST of the afternoon, Kirsten and the ship sank into a mood that could only be described as extremely Victorian. Victorians could get very sad indeed, for lots of different reasons – they all felt things quite deeply, and it was a complicated time to be alive. Their era was one of invention, ambition and progress, yet suffering too.

Not to mention all the corsets they couldn't breathe in, heavy moustaches that were quite a burden to carry about on one's face and dying in factories too young. And the smog.

They had a lot to be moody about, to be fair.

And, having been designed, built and travelled in by Victorians, the **SS Great Britain** had a similarly sensitive personality. If anything caused a loss of faith, she could slide into the bleakest of moods like any self-respecting Victorian pessimist.

'Once, my beauty dominated the ocean,' she sighed, as Kirsten went to her cabin to peel off her wet clothes, 'like the scent of roses fills a room. I *thought* that was why Flatty wanted us to go to New York, I thought that was the whole purpose of our journey, but the city wasn't interested at all. It was dreadful, dreadful, dreadful.'

'That it was.'

Kirsten herself wasn't Victorian by design, *but* felt that wallowing in despair was a reasonable response to the events of the morning. In this respect, she and the ship found themselves in agreement once more. The ship became cold and dark and motionless and silent.

Out of nowhere, a soft grey mist began to descend, like a fog, and within a few minutes it had not just surrounded the entire ship, but also snaked within it, a cloud of whispering tendrils. The interior grew vague and purposeless. In the cabin, Kirsten could barely see her own hands in front of her face. Finally, she sank on to her bed and pulled the blanket up over her head while the mist filled the room, and she thought, longingly, of her father and what might happen now.

They'd lose their contract. They'd lose their house. Was he packing his bags even now? Would he ever forgive her?

At some point, somebody sat on the bed.

'Time to talk,' said Olive.

'Don't want to.'

'Don't care. The ship isn't moving, there's this weird mist and I miss my mum. You're in charge of the ship. You need to take control and complete the quest so we can get home. We're all relying on you.'

Kirsten kept the blanket over her head. 'I'm *not* in charge. The map is. Go and talk to it if you like. I don't want to go anywhere else or speak to anything ever again. I'm just going to lie here till I die. Throw my body to the fishes – I don't care.'

'Don't be ridiculous. You *are* in charge. You have a map that talks to you. The ship moves when you steer her.'

'That steering wheel is a total nightmare and I am not going to touch it again.'

'Yes, you are.'

Something was placed on her lap. Kirsten looked down and groaned. The captain's hat. She kept trying to get rid of it, and people kept bringing it back.

'Put it on,' said Olive.

'No.'

'Put it *on*. And sit up. It's very weird having an argument with a blanket.'

Kirsten yanked the blanket off her head, sat up and put the captain's hat back on.

'There,' said Olive. 'That wasn't so hard, was it? Well done.'

Kirsten was rewarded with the smallest of grins and one Fruittella.

'I brought you some dry clothes from the dressing-up basket,' added Olive. She put a dark blue pair of trousers on the bed, a white shirt and a navy jacket with a red trim.

Kirsten looked at Olive suspiciously.

'They're the only things in your size,' said Olive sweetly.

Once Kirsten was dressed in the dry captain's dress-up clothes and had done her best to tie her wet hair back, Olive drew her knees up on the bunk and made herself comfortable.

'You never managed to finish telling me what you saw in the ship's dreams,' she said. 'Not after Mark came in yesterday morning. Can you tell me now? It's the key, isn't it? To getting home. Finding the truth inside the ship?'

Honestly, Olive really is like a dog with a bone, Kirsten thought wearily.

As they ate their sweets, Kirsten told Olive what she remembered: how soft the ship's floors were, how each room contained a memory-dream, sometimes several at once. That final feeling, right in the middle of the ship, that she'd stumbled upon, all bundled up and secretive. How it was hard to name, but felt *important*.

Olive raised an eyebrow. 'You *felt* something, but you didn't see anything? No clue?'

'Well, I did see one thing. A hand. Lying on a blanket.'

'A hand? By itself? Or was it attached to an arm?'

'I know it sounds weird. I can't remember.'

Olive's eyes grew wide. 'Oh my days,' she said. 'Have you tried asking the ship what you saw? Maybe she knows?'

'There's no point. She doesn't like me "poking around in the past". Says it drags her down. Makes her feel old, or heavy or something. She's so cagey.'

But Olive wasn't to be put off. 'Never mind. No quests are straightforward. You're going to have to go back inside her dreams and find out for yourself.' Her gaze was firm. 'And this time I'm coming with you, okay? Like—' Olive stopped herself, but Kirsten knew what she'd been about to say.

Like old times.

'If you want to,' said Kirsten, as lightly as she could. 'But I have to warn you: the ship's dream time is a bit geographically confusing.'

'What do you mean?'

'All the corridors kept switching places. It took me ages to find my way back here. It was kind of scary.'

'Right,' said Olive. 'First of all, that sounds *absolutely amazing*. Second of all—' She stared round the cabin, lost in thought, then glanced at Kirsten with an air of expertise. Solving quest problems was Olive's strength.

'Ropes,' she said firmly. 'They're going to come in handy again.'

- 48 -
DON'T WANDER TOO LONG

OLIVE'S IDEA WAS that they'd tie one end of the rope round their middle, and the other end to the door handle of the cabin. The two girls went up to the top deck to find the discarded ropes that had hauled Kirsten out of the water, and began to uncoil them to see how long they were.

'We need them to be as long as possible without being too heavy to carry, so we can wander around the dreams as much as we like, but always find our way back,' Olive explained, bent over the cords with intent. 'Like Hansel and Gretel, except with ropes instead of breadcrumbs. They'll keep us tethered to the cabin and we'll never get lost. Quick, unwind this and see how long it is.'

It was almost fun, Kirsten thought, mucking around with Olive, talking about ropes and quests. It made her think about how close they'd been . . .

The Mists of Yearning around the ship grew thicker. Lugging the ropes back to their room was heavy work so once that was done, they went to the dining saloon and settled down to an early meal, served on the ship's finest silver by Cook, of some old mini round cheeses, two packets of raisins from 2002 and ten breadsticks each, vintage unknown.

After the unusual buffet, Olive got to her feet. 'I promised the steerage passengers I'd go and learn cribbage tonight before bed. Fancy a game?'

'*No*,' said Kirsten. She couldn't understand how Olive could feel so comfortable among them, how she always had a kind word and a smile to dole out, just like the sweets. 'They're a bit creepy. Those fighting women scare me.'

'They're really not creepy, not once you get to know them. And the little ones *love* being tucked in. Why don't you do it?'

Kirsten glanced down at the floor. 'Nah.'

'Suit yourself. I'll see you at bedtime.'

Once Olive had gone, Kirsten went up to their cabin and threw herself on her bunk, unsettled and uneasy. Navigating their partnership left her exhausted. On the one hand, they relied on each other more than ever on the ship. On the other, it wasn't really a proper closeness, not like it had been. This was more about survival than friendship. But it was difficult to be confronted with what she'd lost, all the same.

She drifted into a light doze. When she next opened

her eyes the cabin was dark, and the ship was snoring once again.

Moonlight splashed on to the coiled ropes by the bed, reminding her what she had to do and how.

She lay there for a second, reluctant to begin. Her eyelids felt as heavy as rocks. She was desperate to sleep till morning.

But Olive was right. If she didn't find that truth, they might never get home. She might never see Dad again.

She glanced up, saw the Olive-shaped dent in the mattress above her. It looked like Olive had got back from her *socialising*.

Groggily, Kirsten pushed herself slowly out of her bunk. She looked over at Olive, lying on her back in her vest, black frizzy hair framing her face, frowning in thought even in sleep. Kirsten hesitated. She *had* offered to come tonight, and the rope idea had been a good one.

On the other hand – what was the point in waking her up? Olive would rather spend time with mannequins than her. And, *if* they ever got back home, it wasn't like they'd be proper friends again. It was all too confusing. Kirsten would rather do it alone.

She picked up the rope as quietly as she could, and tied one end round the door handle as tightly as possible. She unrolled the rest of it and tied the other end round her stomach. Then she set off down the corridor, tethered to the cabin behind her. The remaining rope she dropped, so it dragged and slithered behind her.

After thirty minutes of quietly exploring the ship, Kirsten felt frustrated and tired. The rope tied round her stomach chafed. The weight of it behind her slowed her down. She couldn't find whatever it was she was looking for. The ship was freezing cold. That feeling from the night before, the shimmering, powerful emotion that had seemed so significant, was nowhere to be found. Dreams were all around her, but the truth could not be seen. The ship might *seem* soft and pliant in her sleep, but she wasn't giving up what really mattered. Even level ten in *Zeleth*, with the Maze of Many-limbed Trolls, hadn't been this tricky to navigate.

Kirsten was about to give up and wind her way back to bed when she found herself, oddly, in front of the Captain's Cabin. Had it sought her out? The wooden door was shut and shimmered with beautiful, dreamy fractals of roots and golden drops of liquid sunshine, as if the door itself was dreaming of when it had been a tree.

There are dreams within these dreams, thought Kirsten.

The door began to glow. The invitation could not have been clearer. Kirsten pushed it open as gently as she could.

There was a dark-haired man inside, in a navy blue coat and trousers, staring at a globe. The room smelled of limes and a deep, rich whisky. She sniffed in appreciation and the sound startled the man in blue, who widened his eyes in astonishment. There was no menace to his gaze.

'Good evening,' he said.

'You – you can see me?'

'I can.' His voice had a faint Scottish lilt. 'Do you seek assistance, little stowaway?'

Kirsten tried to speak, but found it very difficult. She was *looking at* one of the ship's previous captains. Someone from another century, only alive in the ship's buried memories. And he, in turn, was looking at her.

Was *he* the truth? She glanced quickly at his hand, wondering if it was the same one she'd seen curled up in that glimpse of the ship's hidden memory. It poked out from his blue coat and she could admire his clean fingernails, but beyond that she was unsure. Kirsten rubbed her eyes. Her brain felt foggy.

'I'm looking for something,' she said. 'The truth? Do you know where it is?'

'Why do you need that, little stowaway?'

'Flatty said – I mean, I've been told to find it. It'll help me get home.'

His face softened. 'Home?' He glanced at an oval daguerreotype on the wall of a dark-haired woman, two young children on her lap and two standing behind her.

When he next looked at Kirsten, he seemed contemplative.

'You're awfully young to be alone on a ship like this, at a time like this.' He began to fill a pipe with strands of tobacco. When it was lit, he smoked it, then gazed at the ceiling. 'But strange things happen at sea.' A single plume of smoke curled round his head like a question mark.

'You seek the truth, you say? Whenever I want to think deep thoughts, I start with a moment of contemplation on deck. Maybe you could give that a try.'

He glanced at his pocket watch. 'And then you really must get back to bed. This evening is drawing to a close, and you know what happens to ship wanderers if they wander – or indeed, wonder – too long.'

The ship gave a sudden jerk, as if her sleep was coming to an end. It was a violent movement, and Kirsten felt something unwrap itself from round her stomach and fall to the ground.

'Thank you,' she whispered to the captain.

'Be careful,' he whispered back. 'Sometimes you can get lost in her.'

'That's okay,' said Kirsten. 'I've got a thing to keep me safe. Can't remember what it is, but I have it anyway.'

She felt a beautiful lightness.

She'd been in the ship's dreams for too long.

- 49 -
A FARAWAY CALL

KIRSTEN WANDERED OUT of the belly of the sleeping ship and on to the deck, and for a moment forgot everything. The sea in dream time was the most beautiful thing she'd ever seen, and an entirely different ocean to the grey-green waters of day.

This one whirled and swirled with rainbow hues, and each wave was made up of thick brushstrokes of colour and electricity, almost luminous with mystery and radiance. The ocean was lit up with it, while the sky itself, despite dawn coming, was dark.

Just beneath the surface of the water ran twisted, translucent ropes, thick and wide like cables, through which flew tiny sparks of light. Kirsten, to her delighted astonishment, knew instantly what these were: messages.

These were the thought telegrams the ship had been talking about. Some of them came from other ships across the seas and spoke of the ocean. Some of them came from shipwrecks. Some of them came from people and places. And they all danced and looped themselves round the ship in endless patterns, and the ship seemed to draw them in and send out her own thought telegrams in reply.

One skein of sparkling light in particular caught Kirsten's eye. It wasn't the brightest coil or the thickest. If anything, it was thin and seemed to flicker in and out of life quite weakly. But she couldn't stop looking at it, saw it wrapped round the ship, felt it tug at her heart and the heart of the ship too.

Kirsten regarded it, dazed and dreamy. She looked down and saw, delightedly, that her bare feet were turning to wood, as if they were becoming part of the decking. She was being pulled into the ship's dream for ever, and she didn't mind, as long as she could stand and stare at the ocean and its colours and words from the deep. That dark-haired captain she'd spoken to had been very wise. Here *was* the truth, and it was hypnotic.

All of a sudden, she thought she could hear the thought telegrams speak. As dreams always made sense at the time, so too did this ability to be able to understand the messages that flew across the ocean.

'*Once more*,' the flickering, frail message seemed to say. '*If I could see you just once more.*'

'Dad?' she said to the message, gasping. 'Is that you?'

Her thoughts grew sharper. She came back to herself, shook the wood off her feet. This was no time to be turning into the ship. She was a *girl*. She was *human*. If she didn't leave, she would literally become shipshape, and not in a good way. Kirsten gave her head a shake. She had to return to her room before the ship woke up.

She felt for her rope so she could wind her way back. But there was nothing round her stomach any more.

It was missing.

Fear drenched her. She must have dropped it. She would be swallowed up by this dream and lose her mind, just like Flatty had warned. She'd stayed too long. Tears poured down her face. This was failure. Only thing to call it.

Call it. Call it. Call it, the telegrams all said at once in agreement, and Kirsten sobbed.

Her eyes grew heavy. Her sight was dim. She heard something nearby breathing heavily. Death probably.

'What on earth are you playing at?' panted Olive. 'You didn't wake me up, and you dropped your rope! It took me *ages* to find you. I've gone round the whole ship twice! Do you not understand the fundamental rules of a quest? *You never drop your kit and you never go alone!*'

Olive shook her head, gave Kirsten a stern look and began to peer round the deck. 'Did you find it at least? The truth you were told to find?'

'I – so pretty – call it – look it – it's out there–' Kirsten raised one trembling finger and pointed at the water.

Her mouth worked. 'Thought telegrams. THOUGHT TELEGRAMS. Can you see them?' The sun was beginning to rise.

Olive widened her eyes as understanding dawned. '*Whoa*. Looks like you found maybe too much truth out here. I got to you just in time. You're going a tiny bit mad, aren't you?'

She laid a gentle hand on Kirsten's arm. 'Come with me. Hurry now. Bedtime. Before the ship wakes up.'

And she guided them back to their cabin, and put Kirsten back to bed.

- 50 -
A BABY
FRIDAY

WHEN KIRSTEN NEXT woke, she was ravenous. She checked her watch and her eyes widened. It was nearly 2 p.m., but the light that struggled in through the porthole was weak and thin. Where *had* that mist come from, and why wouldn't it lift? She pulled herself into a sitting position. On the blanket was a malt loaf, a handful of dried apricots and two stale digestive biscuits. She wolfed them all down.

She thumped her fist on the blanket. *Peer past the dreams and you will find the truth* indeed. She was empty-handed. So far, the only truth she'd found was that she was playing the hardest quest of her life, with no clear answers.

She had just three hours left to get to London and her chance to kick-start her flagging career and reputation. Impossible. It was never going to happen. What was Dad doing right now? Fielding off another call from their bank manager? Packing his bags as their house was repossessed? Was he stranded in the streets, trying desperately to find somewhere for him and Edwina to stay for the night?

Kirsten shoved the blanket aside and automatically reached for her school uniform. It was all still damp.

Her eyes drifted to the dark navy jacket and trousers Olive had brought her, and she dressed in those instead, but only because it was practical.

She attempted to comb her fingers through her hair, found it almost impossible, shoved her hat on out of habit, and left the cabin with bare feet, a sour mouth and a head full of writhing questions.

'You've been at it again, haven't you?' said the ship. 'Poking around. Trying to bring about an ending. I don't like endings, Captain. Haven't you understood that by now? And I *don't like people trying to take things from me.*'

Kirsten ignored her and roamed the ship, looking for Olive but also trying to clear her head. It was all very well the ship telling her not to go poking around in her memories or bring about an ending– *she* wasn't the one trying to get back to her dad. Kirsten didn't even *like* exploring the ship night after night. She was exhausted! And she wouldn't have to do it at all if the ship and the map would just play straight with her.

Why couldn't they simply tell her the truth, she thought crossly, beginning to stomp heavily round the ship, instead of making her go looking for it, in dreams and within riddles and old bits of parchment? Humans, she reflected, were so much more *honest*. If you wanted to know what someone was really about, all you had to do was *ask them* – they *never* kept secrets, or told half-lies, or concealed or disguised things, or . . . or . . .

She stopped suddenly and frowned into the darkness. '*Grrrrr*,' she said aloud, and she meant every bit of it.

'Easy there, Captain,' hushed a pallid woman. 'You'll wake the baby.' She gestured to a mannequin infant mewling on a blanket. 'Born last night, so she was.'

Oh great, thought Kirsten. *The mannequins are multiplying. Just like my problems.*

'Congratulations,' she said, taking in her surroundings properly. She'd stomped all the way below to the cramped quarters of steerage. It was very cold down there. Her breath came out in tendrils.

'Why that's all right,' said the woman in a kinder voice. 'Looks like you could fair do with a nap yourself, Captain.'

'You could say that.'

'Captain – are we going to be all right? Are we going to get back? I've heard rumours in steerage. They say we're in choppy waters. In the Mists of Longing or something. They say *you're not a* captain *at all*. That you're refusing the post. Are they telling the truth? Because—' And here the woman shivered, and pulled the dark, thin shawl round herself a little tighter. 'I'd feel ever so scared if we were at sea with no captain. No ship can come to any good without a captain, can it?'

She glanced down at the fitful baby – who seemed distressed, even in sleep – and her face clouded over with anxiety. The baby was turning quite blue.

Kirsten found herself taking off her jacket and handing it over to the pale woman. 'For the baby,' she said. 'Use it as a blanket if you want. It's quite thick. But try not to, um, sniff it.'

'Oh – thank you, bless you.' The woman tilted her head to the side, and her neck squeaked. 'Maybe you are the captain after all, Captain?'

But Kirsten walked away, unwilling to answer the question, leaving the woman to tuck in the baby.

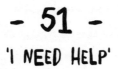

- 51 -
'I NEED HELP'

SHE PRACTICALLY FELL into the Captain's Cabin a few steps later. She hadn't been looking for it, but it must have been looking for her. For the first time, it was neither too big nor too small. But it *was* extremely cold.

She approached the map and stared down at it, her breath coming out in silver plumes, every hair on her body standing up. The vapour from Kirsten's mouth settled on the map's surface in a fine mist. Through the mist, she saw a very small indigo-ink ship bobbing aimlessly.

She idly reached down and stuck her fingers in the cold mist above the map, and slowly stirred them round. 'What's all this anyway?' she said, and the map began to write.

These are the Mists of Yearning, which can only mean one thing: you've reached the Lost Sea. Your second destination – congratulations.

Kirsten snorted. 'Never heard of it.'

The Lost Sea cannot be found on a normal map. It's very easy to lose. But, if you need it, it will find you.

'*Do* I need it?' Kirsten said uncertainly. 'It doesn't sound very nice.'

Oh yes, Captain. You certainly do. Anyway, loss isn't always bad, you know. Where do you think lost treasure ends up? Right here.

The map seemed to be putting a huge effort into making its words come out in jaunty little curls, as if it was trying to convince her.

'Unless it can get me back to Britain in under three hours' time, I don't want any lost treasure.'

Don't knock it till you've tried it, Captain. I've heard there's something quite life-affirming down there.

'Down where?'

Down at the bottom of the sea. Something you need more than you know.

'How are we supposed to get something from the bottom of the sea?' said Kirsten.

Not we. You.

'Why does it always have to be *me*?' said Kirsten.

This is your journey.

Kirsten had heard enough. She tried to move from the desk, but felt something small begin to prod into the back of her knees, like a small insistent goat.

'Hey—' She looked over her shoulder. The Captain's Chair had begun hammering itself into the back of her legs, as if to bend them. One particularly insistent shove later and her legs gave way. She found herself sinking into it, at which point it gave a squeak of satisfaction before swivelling her towards the desk.

She glanced down at the map. The Captain's Cabin had made its point.

'Oh, *all right*,' she said to the map. 'Tell me more.'

I've seen you can swim.

Kirsten had the grace to blush a little.

But how are you at diving?

Kirsten grimaced. 'Why have I got a terrible feeling about what you're about to say next?'

It's the only way you will ever return home. You know what to do. You know what you need. You've already seen it, in fact.

Kirsten sighed. It felt like she'd only just dried off. But she understood exactly what the map was talking about.

A while later, Kirsten eventually located Olive singing nursery rhymes with the mannequin children in the dining saloon, while Cook beat time on the table and the violinists plucked out a jolly jig. She lingered outside the little group, feeling awkward, until Olive lifted one of the smaller children off her lap and got to her feet.

'I guess I owe you a thank you,' Kirsten mumbled. 'You

saved me from going bonkers.'

Olive grinned slightly. 'Why did you leave without me though? I thought we'd agreed to explore together? I'd been –' she went a bit pink – 'looking forward to it.'

'I tried to wake you, but you were in too deep a sleep,' lied Kirsten.

Olive gave her a sceptical look.

Then Kirsten took a deep breath. 'Anyway, that was then and this is now. The thing is, Olive, I need help.' She was thinking of what they'd seen on their tour of the ship – a lifetime ago – though the memory of it made her shiver a little.

Olive seemed to suck in about five lungfuls of breath. 'Finally. I've been waiting to hear you say that for a while.'

'There's something heavy down in the engine room that we need to bring up. I can't do it by myself. Wait – what did you say?'

Olive's laugh was high-pitched and weird. 'Nothing. I mean – sure, fine. I'll help you.'

- 52 -
'ARE YOU SURE?'

'ABSOLUTELY NOT,' EXPLODED Olive five minutes later, in the ship's vast engine room. 'Nope. No way. Not in a million years.'

Together, they regarded the Victorian diving suit in front of them. 'It's at least a hundred and fifty years old,' she gasped. She shot the thing a wary look. 'I feel unsafe just *looking* at it. Imagine actually descending a million metres down to the seabed in it. You can't.'

It was, admittedly, a terrifying creature. As tall as a giant, with awful tubes snaking out of its body, completely still, and all the worse for that. It had three dark eyes in the middle of its forehead, and three dreadful black teeth in its chin. It had a large metallic chain snaking out of the top of its head.

The girls stared at it in horror. Mark Spencer, on the other hand, was delirious with joy. 'A *diving suit!*' he exclaimed, stepping forward and touching it. 'It's so beautiful!'

'Tell me again why you're even contemplating this?' said Olive.

'Basically, Flatty says that there's lost treasure to be found in this – um, Lost Sea, and I have to be the one to find it. It's right at the bottom of the sea apparently.'

Olive stared in concentration, then began to quote the map. '"*Some things must be lost. Some things must be found.*" And there are "*treasures to be treasured*".'

She looked back at Kirsten, realisation in her eyes. 'Oh. I see.'

'Exactly. And then I remembered this diving suit, from when we got shown around in the tour.'

Olive shot the old diving suit a look of deep distrust. 'What if it starts leaking or you run out of oxygen?'

'Run out of oxygen?' gasped Mark. 'In that? But it's the newest, most modern invention! It's the latest thing!'

Olive and Kirsten exchanged a look, and tried not to smile. Then Olive grew serious again. 'But, Kirsten – you can always say no to a level. Remember the Pond with Teeth on level five? We said it was too risky. Too many good wizards lost their lives in that pond and we decided not to.'

'But I have to do this,' said Kirsten softly. 'It's the only way to get us all going again. Otherwise, I think the ship will just stagnate here, and I don't know how long for. She's pretty good at evading capture and we're shrouded in this . . . mist. I don't think anyone will be able to see us.'

'And we don't have any means of calling for help,' said Olive thoughtfully, after a while. 'No phone. No radio. No reception. Nothing.'

Neither of them said it, but both of them thought it.

And the food stores wouldn't last for ever.

They had no choice. The quest was no longer merely a game. Their survival depended on it.

Olive looked at Kirsten levelly. 'Are you sure?'

'I am.'

And something came into Olive's sardine-coloured eyes as she looked at Kirsten, which made Kirsten feel, for all of a second, proud of herself.

'So how does it actually work?' Olive said, looking at the diving suit.

'This is an atmospheric diving suit,' said Mark reverentially, walking round it. 'It's connected to the ship with a winch, which will drop the suit into the ocean. Its weight will ensure that the diver keeps going down, but, because it's a pressure-proof, air-filled suit, it keeps the diver at atmospheric pressure, so there's less chance of getting the bends when they resurface.'

He barely allowed himself a small breath before adding: 'And it's got a small light outside its helmet for deep-sea diving. *And* that hook at the end of its right arm, which is perfect for any deep-diving salvaging needs.'

He looked up at Kirsten and his gaze was steady. 'If you don't want to go down, Captain, I will gladly go in your place. It would be an honour.'

Kirsten looked at the valiant boy made of old fibreglass, and for all of a minute, she was tempted to say yes. If he didn't need oxygen to breathe, how dangerous could it be?

'No,' she heard herself saying. 'This is not your responsibility. *I* must do this. But–' She surprised herself by putting a hand, for a moment, on his delicate shoulder. 'Thank you, Mark. It was very brave of you to offer.'

Kirsten eyed the Victorian diving suit, which seemed so much like a person in its own right she was still slightly frightened of looking at it head-on in case it went for her.

'Let's get it up to the deck,' she said finally. 'Gather the strongest mannequins.'

PART 5

'I almost fancied that the curtain was to fall'
Private diary entry, Isambard Kingdom Brunel, 1824

- 53 -
THE LOST SEA

IT TOOK NEARLY two hours of huffing and puffing from all the adult mannequins and Kirsten and Olive to lift and haul the diving suit up several flights of stairs and out on to the deck. The two girls were drenched in sweat and panting heavily by the time it was connected to the winch.

'Open it up,' commanded Kirsten quickly before she changed her mind. It took the cook and the soldier ten minutes to prise open the diving suit from the back with the aid of small kitchen knives. The smell hit her at once: mildew, damp, age. She wouldn't have been surprised if bats had flown out.

As the crowd watched in hushed silence, Kirsten stepped inside a small hatch at the back of the contraption. She slid her legs in first, and then her arms, into the heavy metal cylinders for her limbs.

And then, realising this might be the last time she saw anyone, she lifted her chin and contemplated the crowd before her. It was, without a doubt, the strangest bunch of companions she'd ever had in her life, and that meant something, because she'd once been part of the Brimmerton Brownie Unit.

'See you in a bit,' she said firmly.

'Godspeed,' said the soldier.

'Fool's errand,' murmured the cook.

'Bye, grumpy-guts!' shouted a small child in a sailor suit, before being immediately hushed by his father.

Olive just gave her a level smile. 'Go steady, Kirsten the Invincible.'

And then the winch lifted Kirsten until she dangled over the side of the ship like bait on a fishing line. The chain jerked. The diving suit dropped. And, at the exact same time that she would have been striding out on to the Jade Cooper studio floor, she was plunged into the Lost Sea instead.

It was like being injected under the skin of something huge, dark and alive. She was in the ocean's blood now. Despite the metal encasing her, she felt it almost attempt to nudge her like a dog, trying to get the measure of her by smell and by taste. She was entirely at the mercy of the chain and the winch.

Her head was encased in a metal globe so looking down within the diving suit was difficult, but, to her intense relief, her body remained dry. The diving suit held firm – no leaks.

The colours began to change,
grow darker.

The deeper she went into the waters of loss, the stronger the pressure became around her. **HER EARDRUMS THROBBED.**

She had to use all her concentration on not panicking, on not letting the cold and the dark and the isolation get to her. Her breath began to come in quick, panicked gasps, and she fought to get a handle on it.

Still she went deeper,
and deeper still.

When she could see absolutely nothing, when no light remained, when thousands of metres of liquid darkness pressed round her, Kirsten knew she had descended into the

deepest

heart

of the

sea.

The old headlight attached to her helmet flickered awake.

Just what was down here in the Lost Sea anyway? Things that needed to be found? Or things that ought to *stay lost?*

The weight of the ocean pressed against her, and in its fathomless depths she heard its questions.

Have you come to be lost? Are you lost? Have others lost you? What should I do with you?

Kirsten closed her eyes and thought carefully. *I'm searching for what is lost. I don't want to stay.*

DOWN,

down.

Clank,

S rattle.
L O
W E R
N O
W

Her breath misted up the glass pane in front of her. Time passed, but she didn't know how much. And then she felt her feet land on something. She hoped it was the seabed.

Tentatively, she tried to take a few steps, but was unable to move. The combination of the pressure of the water outside and the heaviness of the metal meant anything more than a twitch of her limbs was impossible.

What now?

Strange, otherworldly creatures swam round her, lit up by the light within them. Kirsten heard nothing but the sound of her own breathing; not even the chain in the water clanked. Everything was still.

She saw a small brown box lying nearby. The bronze clasp was faded and dented. It looked undeniably like every single treasure box she'd ever seen in a fish tank.

'I've found it,' she gasped. 'I've found the lost treasure!'

'I know,' said the ship inside her head.

'It's not as large as I thought it would be,' said Kirsten.

'Give it time.'

They were both quiet for a beat, while Kirsten contemplated the unusual peace of the ocean bed.

The ship began to speak in an oddly stilted way. 'Now all you have to do is bring it up, nice and quick. Oh, and, Kirsten? Don't take too long. The depths are an unusual place and full of eyes. And sometimes – sometimes things notice. You don't want to draw too much attention to yourself down there. Try only to bring the treasure up, won't you? Nothing else?'

Kirsten gazed at the miles of dark emptiness around her. '*Pardon?*' she said.

The ship hesitated. 'The depths get so few visitors, you see. So, if there's someone, or something, who wants to get out, they'll see you as a handy way of getting back to the surface. If such an entity senses you, it might try to piggyback off you.'

Kirsten let out a jagged breath of outrage that misted up the glass again. 'You can't *say things like that* while I'm down here,' she gasped. 'It's not good for morale.'

'Just trying to be helpful, darling,' said the ship, sniffily.

There was a ripple in the water. The small wooden box rose, then sank down gently on to the seabed again, sending up a tiny plume of sand.

Kirsten strained forward, tried to take a step towards it, but the Lost Sea pushed against her, as if to say: '*You didn't think I'd make it easy for you, did you?*'

Just as she was about to give up hope, there was another ripple, a sudden movement just outside the perimeter of her feeble headlight.

It must have been a very large, very dark nocturnal shoal

of fish moving just outside her field of vision. Or maybe something had fallen, like a stone, through the water?

Whatever it was, it made the box shift and move across the ocean bed. Kirsten held her breath, muttered a silent prayer and, to her immense relief, the box rose and floated nearer her, and its small bronze clasp miraculously hooked itself over the salvaging hook on her right arm. She had it. Now to get out of here *very quickly*.

'Pull me up!' she said.

Nothing happened.

Kirsten's breath caught in her throat. She looked around, trapped in the heavy suit, at the blackness that surrounded her, chest constricting. Was she now lost in the Lost Sea?

But then the chain above her, with a joyous start, clanged awake and began to lift her up.

She was so relieved she barely noticed how much slower the chain was moving, as she and the treasure rose through the darkness, back towards the **SS *Great Britain***.

- 54 -
MORE THAN TREASURE

THEY MUST HAVE made a funny sight, Kirsten thought with tired elation: a diving suit rising from the depths with a battered treasure box dangling off its hook. She felt like a strange firework shooting through a sky that few would ever see.

Up they went. There was an odd weight on the casing around her left leg, as if the ocean had grabbed hold of her and didn't want to let go.

Eventually, the darkness receded, the water became lighter, and then her head broke free from the Lost Sea. She rose through the air like a newborn baby, attached to the ship by a rusty chain.

And as she hung there above the deck, clammy and dizzy, desperate for release, she heard a chorus of shocked gasps and screams. When the winch brought her a bit closer to the ship, all the mannequins scattered in fright.

'What's going on?' Kirsten asked the ship. 'Why aren't they more pleased to see me? I found the treasure, didn't I?'

There was an eerie pause.

'You found more than treasure,' said the SS *Great Britain*. 'I did try to warn you.'

A second later, Kirsten felt herself being swung violently, like something stuck in the jaws of a dog. 'Is – is this really necessary?' Her body slammed from one side of the diving suit to the other. Olive and Mark were manipulating the winch to wobble her as much as they could.

Whatever they were trying to shake off her, she thought with a pang of fear, must have quite a tight grip.

'Has it worked?' gasped Kirsten, once her skull had stopped ringing.

'No,' said the ship.

Kirsten was pulled nearer the deck, but, for the first time since she'd actually climbed into the diving suit, she wished she could stay in it.

A few moments later, on the ship itself, the diving suit was opened up and she tumbled out, soaked in sweat, and then she finally realised why everyone had been shrieking and gasping when she'd emerged from the Lost Sea.

- 55 -
NO CAPTAIN

HE WAS SHORT and strong: a fist on legs. One hand held a harpoon. His other arm, latticed with scars, swung by his side like a pendulum. Although his skin was faintly translucent, everything about him pulsed with a dark vitality. He was clearly a ghost with a purpose.

He was slick with black oil, stank of it, and there were other smells to him too: animal suffering and flames and blood and the stench of a horrible hunt.

Kirsten stumbled to her feet, the treasure box forgotten. 'Who are *you*?' she asked uncertainly.

'I'm Obed Whitaker,' he said in a thick American accent. 'Who are *you*?'

'I'm – I'm Kirsten.'

'*Curse-ten*,' he said, making it sound like an insult. 'Well, Curseten, I'm commandeering this ship.'

'Wh-why?' she stammered.

He held up his harpoon. 'Whaling.'

'What?'

'You don't know what *whaling* is, Curseten? You ain't

lived if you ain't killed.' He reached for the smallest little mannequin nearby and roughly yanked him over. 'Say this kid is a sperm whale, right?'

The mannequin – a young boy from steerage – began to cry. Obed circled him, uncaring. 'Now, first thing is you loop the whale with your boat till he's confused and separated from his herd, got that?'

'Then –' here Obed lifted the harpoon and pretended to jab it into the small boy, making him cry even harder – 'you harpoon him till he bleeds. You'll know when it's gone in because the whale will start to thrash about in the water, and their death throes are always worth a watch. Then you kill him, lift him on to your boat, and render him into oil, meat and ambergris. You melt down that creature into money, hear me?'

He grinned and gave a mocking bow. 'Make killing your living and you'll be rich with it. That's how I made my fortune, and it was mighty fine. Until I fell, that is.'

'Fell? From what?' said Olive.

'My ship,' said Obed, looking bereft. 'The *Essex* – the finest whaling ship in all of America. We was torpedoed by a sperm whale with a grudge. And I don't know how long I been in that Lost Sea for, but now I mean business, and I need my own ship to do that. Luckily for me, I found you. A lost ship in the Lost Sea. I could practically *smell you* – a lost ship gives off a certain aroma of weakness. And a ship without a captain is the easiest of all to catch.'

'But – you're . . . you're *dead*,' gasped Kirsten. 'How are you even talking?'

'You'd be surprised by the preserving qualities of whale oil,' he said, shrugging.

He surveyed the mannequins and the two girls in front of him, and his gaze settled on Mark Spencer. 'You. Boy.'

'Mark,' muttered Olive.

'Boy, here's what I need. Coffee, thick and strong. A sizable collection of buckets, and some wood to build a fire for the rendering.'

Mark's eyes flickered from the whaler ghost to Kirsten and back again.

'What you waiting for?' demanded Obed.

The thin boy in the ragged clothes puffed his chest out. 'You're not my captain, sir. I can't take instruction from you.'

Obed pretended he'd been shot, and staggered a little on the deck. 'You wound me, boy. You wound me. Well, who is your captain? What fine figure of a man do I need to fight before you obey me?'

Kirsten shook her head emphatically, but Mark was a loyal mannequin and still believed in her. He lifted his finger.

'Over there. That's our captain, sir.'

Obed looked theatrically around. 'I don't see no captain at all, boy.' Then his taunting eyes met Kirsten's and widened with shock. 'Unless he's telling the truth? Unless a young maid with no place on this ship has some silly notion she's got captaining credentials?'

He sniffed. 'Well, Curseten? Are you the captain? Do you want me to disabuse you of that intelligence?'

Kirsten sensed everyone on the deck, as well as the ship herself, waiting for her answer. Even the ocean was still.

Was she the captain? Her mind ran quickly over the events of the last three days.

She'd abandoned the **SS *Great Britain*** in New York.

She barely knew how to talk to the mannequins.

She struggled to steer.

Not only that, but everything the map had asked her to do she'd failed at too. She hadn't managed to find *any* truth inside the dreaming ship. She'd gone down to recover some lost treasure, but had made a right mess of that as well.

Kirsten's head dropped. She was no captain. She'd known that all along, really, and now this ghoul knew it too.

She tried to ignore the dismay in Olive's face as she took off her captain's hat and handed it to Obed. 'Take it,' she said quietly. 'It was too big for me anyway.'

The inside of her head filled with a metallic roar. **'NO! NO! NO NO NO NO NO!'** but the minute Obed put the hat on his head, it stopped completely, and her head went quiet.

Kirsten thought she heard something small drop to the floor and, when she checked, saw two tiny splinters on the deck.

'I thought so,' said Obed, grinning triumphantly under the golden garlands of the hat. 'Look, I mean no real harm and, as long as you all do your jobs as I instruct, you'll find whaling as profitable and fulfilling an occupation as any other on God's earth. Now then, boy, hurry and make me that coffee, as thick and as black as the whale oil we'll all soon be drenched in . . .'

And he began to swagger round the deck, issuing instructions, pinching the cheeks of the bonneted women, and everywhere he went he left a filthy black oily footmark on the ship's polished deck.

Some of the littler mannequins were crying openly. Olive gave Kirsten an inscrutable look and went to comfort them. The cold grey mist they'd been surrounded by grew thicker and damper, like an impenetrable fog. Feeling helpless, Kirsten saw Obed strut into it, then disappear completely.

A few seconds later, the surprised laughter of the cook and the soldier rang out. She had a horrible sense the whaler was flattering them into obedience. Soon they'd pledge allegiance to this spectre, and then the ship and its people would be lost to a ghostly whaling expedition for ever, and she and Olive would be lost with them.

- 56 -
LOST TREASURE

THERE MAY HAVE been a golden, sunlit afternoon somewhere above the Lost Sea, but it was lost to Kirsten and all onboard the ship, which remained shrouded in the Mists of Yearning.

Through the muggy afternoon, the air rang with the sound of Obed's strident voice as he swaggered round the entire ship, ordering bunks to be chopped into firewood, constantly harassing Cook to bring him food and taunting the little children. The mist was freezing cold and everyone shivered, too chilled and stunned to do anything but obey.

Kirsten went to her cabin. Olive was in there, cross-legged on the top bunk, holding the damp treasure box.

'You dropped it on the deck.' Olive's voice was utterly expressionless. 'That *whale murderer* was about to kick it back into the sea. I thought you might as well open it.'

Kirsten shrugged. 'There's no point now,' she said. 'We've got a new captain. Which means the journey will have changed too, right?'

'Maybe,' said Olive. 'Why don't you open it anyway?'

Kirsten looked down at the box of lost treasure and shook it half-heartedly. And its bronze clasp clicked open.

Inside – buried underneath a few tendrils of seaweed and a crab, which scuttled away immediately – was a small, plain pocket mirror.

And that was all. Nothing else. No rubies. No diamonds. Just a mirror with a girl peering out from it back at her. Kirsten shook her head in disbelief and a grimy, sweat-stained girl with matted brown hair did the same.

She'd gone all the way down to the bottom of the sea, and brought up a whaling ghost, and risked life and limb, for – a pocket mirror? It wasn't even brand-new.

She peered into it again. 'What a mess,' she said quietly, taking in her tangled hair and grubby face. Olive got up and sat next to her.

Together, they silently contemplated the two girls in the glass.

'Lost treasure,' murmured Olive.

The girls in the mirror stared solemnly back at them.

'SOME THINGS MUST BE FOUND. THERE ARE TREASURES TO BE TREASURED,' said the mirror Olive solemnly.

Four girls looked at each other and seemed to wait for someone to speak first.

Then Olive broke the spell and turned to Kirsten.

'It's . . . us? We're the treasure? Us, together?'

'Um. I think so,' said Kirsten. She held her breath.

'Cheesy, right?' Olive's voice was quick and tight.

Kirsten flushed. *Fine.* 'Yeah. Bit obvious.'

'Exactly,' Olive said. 'Like – we've moved on. *We* don't care.' She turned her sardine eyes on Kirsten, and they stared at each other.

Kirsten put the mirror back in the treasure box. 'Yeah. Exactly.'

There was an awkward silence while her eardrums roared with pain and hurt.

'Why are you even here? On this ship?' It came out more rudely than she'd intended. If something wasn't scripted for her, she always messed it up. Just like now.

Olive's blush deepened and she glared at Kirsten. 'Why am I here? Good *question.* I'm here because I was the only one that cared enough about you to come back and get you! I was *worried* about you! Because when we all got off the ship after the tour, and Mrs Walia realised you were missing, she asked if anyone would go back and find you. Guess how many of your classmates volunteered, Kirsten?'

Kirsten found, all of a sudden, that she didn't feel like guessing. 'I . . . I didn't mean—'

'You'd been acting weird all year, *and* you fainted last week—'

Kirsten *had* fainted during assembly. She'd been skipping the odd meal here and there to lose a bit of weight before the chat-show interview. Edwina had suggested it, eyeing her tummy one day. Kirsten hadn't realised Olive had noticed her fainting; they always stood so far apart—

'—and I thought it might have happened again.' Olive's eyes were dangerously bright. Then she shook her head. 'I'm trapped on this ship with you because I wanted to be *nice*. Don't worry though – I won't make the same mistake twice.'

She grabbed the door handle and stormed out.

The room filled briefly with the sound of Obed shouting somewhere, before the door slammed and Kirsten was left alone.

- 57 -
HALF AN APOLOGY

FOR THE BEST part of the afternoon, Kirsten skulked round the darker, quieter corners of the ship, trying not to make eye contact with anyone. Not that it was hard. Olive was nowhere to be seen, and most of the mannequins walked past without really noticing her, as if she was becoming less visible now she was no longer their reluctant captain.

Kirsten's moping took her, eventually, to the rough wooden tables in steerage, where a lone mannequin sat in front of a plate of fake stale bread. He didn't look up when she sat down.

'Oh dear,' said an amused voice. It was one of the fighting women. She swayed down the narrow walkway towards Kirsten and rubbed a grimy finger against a scratched nose. 'I know a bad fight when I see one.'

'Bad?' said Kirsten uncertainly.

'Yes, dear. The one between you and your first mate that's been rumbling on since we left Bristol. Fights need to be short and sweet to be productive. Yours has been going on for far too long, and this –' she waggled a finger at

Kirsten, slumped at the table – 'is a frankly pathetic power move. How are you going to sort out anything properly like that? Who taught you to fight, a feather duster?'

Kirsten stared into her glass eyes. 'No one taught me to fight.'

'I can see that,' the woman scoffed, plopping down on the bench next to Kirsten and hiccuping slightly. 'Now, far be it from me to interfere, sweetpea, but you must *never* let an argument fester on a ship. It's the quickest way to make the entire voyage curdle. You need to go and find that clever girl and do some sail repairing, you hear?'

'Pardon?' said Kirsten.

'Stitch things up that have been ripped. Very important seafaring skill. Mend and repair, dear. You must restore what's been lost.'

Kirsten shifted in her chair suddenly, and the fighting woman gave her a wise but knowing wink and, for a tiny moment, Kirsten wondered if there wasn't a greater intelligence at work, one she couldn't quite figure out.

The woman got up and held out a filthy hand to pull Kirsten up.

'I don't suppose *you* know where Olive is, do you?' she asked.

'Yes, dumpling.' A cunning look swept over her face. 'Want me to take you to her? Only a shilling.'

Kirsten rifled through her trouser pocket. She pulled out one squished vitamin and fifty pence. 'Will this—'

They'd vanished before she'd even finished the sentence. 'Nicely,' said the woman, pocketing them in her skirts with the air of a magpie. She glanced down at Kirsten's school shoes. 'And those.'

'You want – my shoes?'

The mannequin gave a pointed look down at her own dirty bare feet and nodded. Kirsten sighed, unlaced them and handed them over. Once the fighting woman had slipped them on, and admired them for a while under her ragged hem, she looked back at Kirsten, eyes gleaming.

'I hope you got a head for heights,' she teased.

'Heights?' stammered Kirsten.

Kirsten followed the fighting woman up on deck. She peered round for Obed, but he was nowhere to be seen.

'He's in the kitchen,' said the woman, as if she could read her mind. 'Looking for sharp knives for skinning.'

The mannequin and Kirsten looked at each other and shuddered. A desperate sense of urgency filled Kirsten all of a sudden. Those oily footsteps Obed had left all over the beautiful deck filled her with anger.

'Oooh, that's better,' said her companion. 'I can see some fire come into your eyes.'

Then she pointed a finger up at the rigging, which stretched above like them like the ship's web. 'We've all been laying bets in steerage about when you were going to clock on. That's partly why I came to help you, to be fair, because I got half-a-crown riding on this and you're taking even longer than I thought.'

Kirsten looked in the direction of the filthiest fibreglass finger she had ever seen, and there was Olive, up in a small lookout basket at the top of the tallest mast. Olive gave her the tiniest of glances and then immediately looked away, as if she hadn't seen her.

'That's the crow's nest,' said the mannequin. 'You're going to have to climb the rigging to get there. It's easy . . .'

Kirsten gulped, feeling sick.

'. . . to start with.' Then her companion strolled away with a ribald laugh, holding up her coin to the sun with delight.

Kirsten gritted her teeth. *Mend and repair.* It was cold, and the Mists of Yearning around the ship were damp, and made the rigging hard to grip. Being barefoot didn't help either – her feet were freezing and numb and she kept slipping.

She glanced up. Olive crossed her arms and stared straight ahead at the horizon, making it clear that words of encouragement were not to be expected from her anytime soon.

Kirsten gritted her teeth and pulled herself up, inch by painful inch, repeat by a hundred. The rigging got narrower the higher she got; there was no room for mistakes. Her hands grew sore. She made the error of looking down. That wasn't something she was going to be doing twice. She gulped, felt dizzy. Everything in her body wanted to freeze.

'Come on, Kirsten,' she told herself.

When she was roughly a metre away, she looked back up at the crow's nest. Even tilting her neck back made her feel nauseous and unsafe, but she forced herself and this time, she noticed with relief, Olive was peering down.

'You *lost?*' she said, raising an eyebrow.

'Very funny,' said Kirsten. 'Look, um, Olive.'

'Yes?'

'I'm—'

'Mmmm?'

'Sorry. I'm sorry.'

Olive looked away into the clouds for a moment. 'What for?'

'For being rude. And ungrateful. It was nice of you to care about me, and come back to the ship. Honestly. I know we've not been the closest for the last few years—'

Olive stared at her, biting her lip.

'—and—'

The air around them filled with the sound of angry shouting. Kirsten discovered, all of a sudden, that she couldn't look down.

She pressed her face against the wires of the rigging and closed her eyes.

'Oh no,' said Olive quietly, peering at the deck below. 'It looks like Obed's got hold of Flatty.'

Kirsten swallowed. 'What do you mean, "got"?'

'I mean he's brought the map up from the Captain's Cabin,' said Olive. 'And, judging by the way he's holding it, it doesn't look like they're about to swap "bestie forever" necklaces anytime soon.'

- 58 -
WITCHCRAFT

KIRSTEN FOUGHT THROUGH her queasiness and clambered down the rigging as quickly as she could, landing on the deck moments after Olive. Without thinking, she ran towards the shouting, her heart thudding. *Flatty!*

The mist was thick around them now, but they followed the whaler's oily footprints easily enough until they found him by the large black funnel in the middle of the deck.

Even though the ghost had his back to her, it was clear what was going on. With one hand, Obed was thudding the rolled-up map into the palm of his other hand, as a group of mannequins looked on, making worried faces at each other. Kirsten remembered how old and fragile the map was, and she winced.

'Obed,' said Kirsten quietly. 'What are you doing?'

He whipped round, saw her and growled. 'I'm teaching this map a thing or two.'

'Why?' She knew why, of course, had often thought it herself, but there was a difference between thinking a thing and actually doing it. To her surprise, Obed lowered his ice and leaned in, bringing with him a foul smell.

'Because it's full of witchcraft,' he whispered. 'It told me
[a]l sorts of hocus-pocus . . .'

Kirsten suddenly felt a huge rush of affection for the
[m]ap.

'. . . and refused to answer any of my questions, and
[t]hen it said I was no captain!'

He gave the map another thump.

Kirsten winced. '*Stop* that,' she said.

He gave her a look of disbelief. '*Excuse* me?'

'I said stop that. This map doesn't belong to you. It
belongs to the Captain's Cabin downstairs. It lives on the
desk, not out here. Put it back.'

A short mirthless laugh split Obed's ghostly face. 'I'm
in charge here. I can discipline whatever I choose. That
includes maps –' *thump* – 'and disobedient members of my
crew!'

Kirsten saw a tiny rip appear in the corner of the map,
and that was it. She reached out and made a grab for Flatty.

To her horror, Obed held on tightly, and she pulled,
and suddenly the map ripped right down the middle.

Tears sprang to her eyes. She stared at the whaler. 'What
have you *done*? That map was alive! That was the ship's
brain!'

'Flatty!' cried Olive, coming up behind her. For a

moment, all they could do was stare at the ripped half in Kirsten's hand.

One small ball of ink formed on the thin paper, peeled itself open at them, like an eye, and then closed slowly. No words appeared.

'Give me the other half,' Kirsten pleaded. '*Please.* I can try to fix it.'

But sneering, Obed balled the other half of the map up and threw it on the deck. Kirsten gasped and tried to grab it, but Obed was too fast for her. He put his oily arms round her and wrestled her away. She began to flail at him, with hands and feet, and suddenly she felt the harpoon jab her in the back.

'You're going in the hold for gross insubordination,' growled Obed. 'And your accomplice. And you can rot in there for all I care.'

Kirsten tried to argue, but the sharp harpoon tip sticking through her shirt was very persuasive.

As they were prodded and poked all the way down the stairs, all she could do was hold her half of Flatty as carefully as she could to protect it from any further harm.

But, she thought with a sinking heart, as she glanced down at the damaged scrap in her hands, it was possibly already too late.

- 59 -
THE QUEST IS CHANGING

OBED HAD MARCHED Olive and Kirsten all over the ship, dripping his stinking whale oil wherever he went. Eventually, they stopped outside the

mop room where they'd first discovered Mark Spencer.

'That looks suitably dark and uncomfortable,' he barked. 'Get in there and stay in there, you snivelling ingrates!' He jabbed them in with his harpoon, and they'd barely had the chance to turn round before the door slammed shut and they heard the sound of the key turning in the lock.

'And this key is going straight in the waves, along with that map!' he shouted through the door.

'No!' shouted Kirsten, but the only reply she got in return was a mocking laugh and the sound of his footsteps fading as he swaggered back to the deck.

The silence and the darkness pressed in around them. Kirsten sniffed. 'Do you think he really will throw Flatty in the ocean?' she asked Olive quietly.

'I do unfortunately,' said Olive. 'I think he likes to cause suffering.'

They went quiet as each remembered the awful sound of the map ripping.

'Is it – very bad?' said Olive delicately.

Kirsten's lips trembled a little. 'Very.' She held out the half in her hands. 'And it's not saying anything.'

Just like the ship.

She unfolded Flatty and stared at the torn fragment, urging it to help her, to tell her what she should do, but the old map just stared back at her blankly.

Time passed. There was the sound of heavy footsteps down the corridor.

Kirsten and Olive jumped up and began to hammer on the door with their fists. 'Help!' they shouted. The footsteps stopped. 'Who is that?' It was Cook.

'It's us!' said Kirsten. 'Your old captain? And Olive, the first mate!'

'Don't know them,' said Cook, and he moved along.

Olive hit her head with her palm. 'Of *course*,' she said. 'They're morphing to fit the new world of the quest. If you're not the captain any more, they aren't technically your passengers, so their memories are changing. They won't have any loyalty to us, and won't do what you command. Elemental quest rule.'

Kirsten tried to understand. 'So . . . what does that mean?'

'It means we're basically stuffed. The ship and the quest are changing to suit that awful whaler. I can feel it happening already, can't you?'

Kirsten knew what she meant. Just in the short while they'd been locked in the broom cupboard, the air had grown thick with a malevolence that hadn't been there before. Even her brain felt toxic with it. She could feel the whaler's influence seeping into everything and everywhere . . . Her thoughts grew horribly sticky, dark with the shadows and destruction Obed had brought onboard.

Maybe I'll wait to see what Obed wants us to do, maybe spearing whales is fun, you never know until you try it . . .

No. Kirsten gathered her thoughts and mentally shoved the whaler out. 'If we want to get out of here, we've got to do it alone.'

'Yes,' said Olive, and despite the lack of light in the broom cupboard Kirsten could see her eyes shine, could see the way Olive had tilted her head and was looking at her curiously.

'Right then,' said Kirsten. She turned and grabbed the old mop in the corner and, with one end, began to hammer at the keyhole. She banged and she bashed and she hammered at the door, but all she succeeded in doing was breaking the mop.

She threw it in the corner and stared into the shadows. She felt ashamed of herself – of how easily she'd handed over her captain's hat to Obed without a fight. She thought about how Mark Spencer had insisted she *was* his captain, right in front of the whaler. And she'd let him down. Kirsten hung her head.

She'd never expected to find so much devotion in an old mannequin. Which just went to show – her brain began to race – *you could find loyalty in the most unexpected places.*

Her heart thumped. She gasped.

'Kirsten?' said Olive. 'What's going on?'

'I've got an idea,' she said. 'There's one place on the ship that might take longer to switch allegiance to the whaler. Somewhere that always found me when I least expected it. I just hope it might still be there.' *And that I deserve its loyalty.*

'Do you mind holding Flatty?' She handed the torn fragment gently to Olive, then picked up the broken wooden mop handle and began, wincing, to rub her hands up and down it.

'*What* are you doing?'

'The first time I boarded the ship, I fell on the deck and got two splinters, which somehow kick-started all this,' Kirsten said. '*Ow!*' She looked down at her hands and grinned. 'I need to prove to the ship that I'm sorry so I thought I'd better get some new ones.'

Then she hurried to the door and put her palms on it.

'Now, I'm just going to send out some – um – thought telegrams,' she muttered. She leaned her head on the door and tried to think.

I know I haven't always appreciated you, she thought fiercely. *But I need you. We need you. Please, come to me now, as you have before. Please.*

For an awful moment, nothing happened.

And then she heard a whooshing sound, and the sound of furniture flying through the air. A door opened. Something small and insistent scraped towards them.

Then hesitated.

'I promise I'll repay your loyalty this time,' whispered Kirsten. 'I will make it good.'

And very slowly, then faster, something began to batter at the door like a determined goat.

'What's *that*?' gasped Olive from behind her.

'It's the Captain's Chair,' explained Kirsten, grinning with relief. 'Get back!'

They pressed themselves up against the back of the broom cupboard, and the small plucky Captain's Chair hammered and bashed away until the door broke apart in a hundred splinters.

Kirsten brushed tears from her eyes. She felt incredibly humbled all of a sudden. That room had still believed *she* was captain, not Obed, and came to her when she needed it.

She picked her way out of the broken door and patted the chair gently. 'You did a good job, you clever thing. Thank you.'

The chair did a proud little jig on the carpet, and then made several jerking movements in the direction of the stairs.

'I will,' said Kirsten. 'I promise.' She turned to Olive. 'Come on! Back on deck!'

She went first. She didn't see Olive's proud smile as she followed her.

- 60 -
BEATEN

OUT ON THE DECK, the Mists of Yearning swirled thickly among the mannequins, who were drifting through the fog, looking lost and confused. They stared at Kirsten as if she was a stranger.

Kirsten spotted Mark Spencer by the funnel, standing in a strangely hunched way. 'Mark!' she said. 'Mark!'

But he didn't reply. 'Boy?' she whispered, and he looked up dejectedly.

Kirsten gasped. His entire torso had been speared several times. Despite the holes being bloodless, there was something awful about his injuries all the same. And she could guess why they'd been inflicted. Because, out of all the mannequins, he would have refused to obey the whaler.

'Where is he?' she said in a low, furious voice.

Mark lifted a finger and silently pointed into the mist. Kirsten peered into it and, as the ship lurched violently from side to side, she suddenly knew where she'd find Obed. She was about to break into a run when she saw that Mark was holding something small and flat in his other hand.

'You saved half of Flatty?' she said, moved beyond measure. 'Is *that* why he speared you?'

Mark nodded. 'I wouldn't hand it over,' he said through chattering teeth. 'It wasn't right.'

Kirsten turned on her heel and, closely followed by Olive, flew down the deck, narrowly avoiding the other mannequins, determined to confront the whaler.

At the prow of the ship, she was relieved to see that the steering wheel was proving just as difficult for Obed to manoeuvre as it was for her.

'Get your hands,' she snarled, '*off my ship.*'

'How did you get out, Curseten?' said Obed, frowning through the mist. 'I'll have to make you walk the plank next if you won't even stay in the hold.' He let go of the steering wheel and put his hands to his mouth. 'Boy!' he shouted. 'Boy! Find me a—'

'He'll do no such thing,' hissed Kirsten.

Obed seemed unimpressed by her rage. In fact, he rolled his eyes. 'I've made whales angry,' he drawled lazily. 'Ninety-six of them to be precise. And, when my adversaries get angry, it normally means I'm winning. So get angry if you want to. Let me command my ship.'

'No,' said Kirsten. 'I won't. She's not yours. She's *mine.*'

The mist grew thick around them, moving in and out of the deck in dense curls. Suddenly she could see no one else; it was her versus the whaler.

And then he was gone too, swallowed by the mist. But she sensed that he was there, waiting to attack.

She whirled round, blindly flailing. A flicker of movement in the corner of her eye. She spun but saw nothing.

Where was he?

Then she felt a shove and, staggering backwards, slipped on whale oil and landed, with a heavy thud, on the deck.

The mists cleared just enough for her to see Obed's face lit up with dark triumph. 'Where's your bravery now, hmmm? If it's your ship, why won't the crew help you? I'll tell you why. It's cos they know – and I know and you know – that you're useless. You're a charlatan. You're just pretending at all of this, aren't you? That's what you *do*. You go through life pretending. The ocean always reveals the truth, Curseten, and we've just found yours.'

He was like a demon, staring at her with glittering dead eyes.

Kirsten looked up at him and felt the fight leave her.

He was right. She *had* spent the last four years of her life pretending to be someone she didn't really want to be.

Obed turned his back on her with an air of grim triumph and disappeared into the mist.

- 61 -
I'M THE CAPTAIN

BUT, TO HER surprise, Kirsten found herself getting back to her feet and following him - ragged, dirty, but not yet quite beaten.

As she staggered about in the mist, barefoot, grubby, with a face she hadn't washed for three days and tangled hair, spoiling for another fight, even though she'd probably lose it, she began to laugh. Something Obed had said cracked Kirsten's heart wide open and revealed a truth. She *had* been pretending. The Bramble brand was, she could see now, a *total lie*: a sweet story blown up into a bloated soap opera, and she'd been stumbling about in it just like she was stumbling about in this mist . . .

She thought suddenly of the girl that the old pocket mirror had shown her. A feral, wild girl reborn from the ocean, sitting side by side with Olive . . . a version of herself she much preferred.

What had the map told her? *Some things must be found.*

She felt the ship's huge metallic heart suddenly roar into life.

WHOOSH, WHOOSH, WHOOSH,

Her stride became more confident. Tendrils of mist parted and there was Obed on the deck, right in front of her. His eyes widened at the sight of her.

'Why don't you learn to stay beaten, girl?'

But, all of a sudden, he seemed smaller. Either he'd shrunk or Kirsten had suddenly grown.

She reached out, grabbed the captain's hat off his head, put it firmly on top of hers and said: 'I'm not beaten. You are. I'm the captain of this ship. And I command you to leave it.'

The SS *Great Britain* gave a joyful lurch. Kirsten's head rang with the sound of the ship's delight.

'Finally, darling. I always knew you'd realise. I didn't anticipate it would *take quite so long*, but there you are. Late bloomers have their own strengths—'

The mist began to clear and Kirsten heard the mannequins give surprised gasps as they returned to their former selves. They began to gather behind her, trusting in her again, and she felt them there, and their presence gave her added strength.

'*You* need to go back to the Lost Sea, Obed,' said Kirsten in her new firm voice. '*You* need to stay lost. That was what Flatty meant.'

All of a sudden, she forgot who she was looking at, and she began to speak to someone else, to other people who weren't on the ship at all but back on land. 'Leave us alone now,' she said, and her mouth twisted in strange, strong shapes she hadn't been expecting. 'I brought you here by accident, but you've got no place here.'

For the first time since boarding the ship, Obed looked uncertain.

Kirsten focused again and looked him in the eyes. 'I'm sorry – I *am* – that you lost your ship, but that doesn't give you any kind of excuse for stealing this one. Your time has gone.'

Obed's hands dropped from the steering wheel, and he gave Kirsten a grudging look of respect. 'You might just be a small calf,' he said faintly, 'but you're awful strong when you blow.'

And then his harpoon crumbled and, a few minutes later, he had disappeared.

Kirsten felt a hand on her shoulder. 'Well done, Captain,' said Mark.

A tiny, cold hand slipped into hers, and she didn't pull away.

'You were very brave, Captain,' said a small child. 'Do you want to play with my train? You can have it for the whole afternoon.'

- 62 -
NO TiME TO WASTE

EVERYONE WAS EXHAUSTED after all the excitement. Some of the smaller mannequins fell asleep in a huddle on the deck, like a bunch of kittens. Cook and the soldier began a game of cards down in the promenade saloon, others began to mop up the oily tracks Obed had left throughout the ship and the fighting women had a new bone of contention: Kirsten's school shoes and who should own them.

Kirsten and Olive tried to mend the holes in Mark's torso, but they were too wide and too large. In the end, Kirsten gave him her school shirt instead, which, although grubby, was in better condition than his, and at least covered up his injuries.

The three of them gently took Flatty back below deck. The Captain's Cabin appeared immediately, and the chair and the desk hopped up and down on the spot, overjoyed to be reunited with Flatty once more.

Sadly, they couldn't fix the map either. They put both halves as carefully on the desk as they could and waited, biting their lips, hoping that would be enough.

For a moment, Flatty remained utterly blank.

And then one tiny line of watery ink appeared. Kirsten was surprised by how much she felt like crying.

I owe you my thanks, said Flatty, and the words struggled slowly from one half to the other, like someone struggling over a stile.

'Oh,' said Kirsten. 'You're okay! Oh, thank *goodness*.'

Enough sentimentality, Captain. We must persevere with our voyage. Time has never been more scarce.

Your next destination is . . .

For the next few seconds, the map appeared to be struggling.

Th Flknd slnds, it finally produced in very wavery, spluttery ink, as if it was running out of reserves.

Olive and Kirsten looked at each other. 'Are there any vowels to go with that?' said Olive gently.

e aa la, the map added tiredly.

The letters sat on top of the parchment flatly, like broken shards of china. The girls stared at them for a while, and then Olive gave a start.

'I know what that means.' She glanced at Kirsten. 'And you do too, right? Remember those pictures? Remember the story Flatty told us that night – about where the ship ended up after being damaged in a storm?'

Kirsten did. Port Stanley – where the ship was mutilated

and broken. Sparrow Cove – where she was abandoned. Both of them had been at– She glanced at the map again and understood finally what the letters meant.

'*The Falkland Islands*,' and the words felt heavy and sad in her mouth. 'Where bits were stolen from her.'

Flatty seemed to groan, as if with a gargantuan effort, and then wrote: **And parts that are missing must be restored. All these things must be done on this journey, and only then can it end.**

Kirsten remembered the dreams inside the ship, how the passengers had flown over the floor of a rotting wreck.

'They took from her, they used her and then no one wanted her,' muttered Kirsten, tears pricking her eyes. 'What an awful thing to happen to . . . the ship.'

Olive gave her a piercing look. 'Are you okay?'

'I'm *fine*. I know why we're going there,' said Kirsten. 'To get those bits that were stolen back from the islanders, and bring them back to the ship. They need to make amends.' She turned to the map. 'I'm right, aren't I?'

What you do when you get there is up to you. Are you prepared? the map wrote slowly. **This is the hardest part of the voyage. You may find it . . . Painful.** 'Yes,' said Kirsten. 'Take us there immediately.'

**Put your hands on the steering wheel. She
will need your help for this bit. She is tiring.
Can** you tell?

Kirsten glanced round the Captain's Cabin. The
wallpaper was fading by the second. The carpet seemed to
be fraying. As they watched, the old compass swung slightly
on the wall, and then fell to the ground with a clatter.

Kirsten turned to Olive and lifted her chin. 'Get ready,
First Mate. Tell the crew. We're off again.'

Olive grinned and saluted. 'Aye aye, Captain. Oh, I've
been waiting to say that *for ages.*'

They gave each other shy smiles.

Then Kirsten ran up to the ship's wheel.

- 63 -
FURTHER, FURTHER

THIS TIME THE ship didn't fly like a falling star across the waves. Instead, she zigzagged and stumbled down the North Atlantic Ocean towards the Brazilian coast, her path increasingly erratic and occasionally dangerous. Now and again, her entire hull made pinging noises, as if screws and other vital bits of her were weakening and falling apart.

What had the map warned? ***This is the hardest part of the voyage***.

Time passed in a blur. They crossed the equator and moved into another ocean. Kirsten would look up from the wheel, see an island speed past, catch sight of a curious albatross flying parallel to the ship, and feel strangely calmed, then slip into a steering trance again.

She fell asleep on the deck and would wake and begin steering again, pausing only to eat whatever Cook or Olive pressed into her hand. Urging the ship on through the night sky, she could feel the pistons of the engine somehow moving in unison with the beating of her own heart: but the ship remained jittery and hard to control, as difficult to steer as a rusty supermarket trolley. Kirsten's arms screamed with pain, but she wouldn't stop. *She was the captain.* And she was so close to ending the journey and returning to Dad.

'I won't rest,' she muttered through cracked lips. 'I know what I'm doing.'

Every now and again, she would remember that awful picture: the stripped, wrecked ship, her beautiful deck mildewed and rotten, the stumps of her masts lying askew on the deck, and she'd shiver, and shake, and then the unexpected sadness would harden into determination again.

The ship lurched and flew through the South Atlantic Ocean, driven on by Kirsten in a fever. She had no control over what wreckage of a life would be waiting for her back in Bristol, but she could do something about this – she could fix what had been broken. Fury rose up in her, and she thought it was on the ship's behalf.

Kirsten didn't know what day it was by the time they pulled into Port Stanley. It was a pretty harbour dotted with small white houses, the flat green fields of the Falklands behind them. The ship had practically limped into the port and remained at a wary distance from the town.

Kirsten unpeeled her tired, blistered hands from the wheel, straightened her captain's shirt and planted her bare feet on the deck in what she hoped was a true stance of authority.

A few moments later, they saw a convoy of small rowing boats coming out to greet them. 'This will be the islanders now,' said Kirsten, narrowing her eyes in a way she hoped looked intimidating.

'I can't wait to give them a piece of my mind.'

INTERLUDE

BACK IN BRISTOL, quite a lot had happened over the last few days. Kirsten's disappearance had made Mick Bramble take a long look at what their life had become. He believed his beloved daughter had run away on the SS *Great Britain* because she was unhappy. Then he wondered if *he* was unhappy.

Then he thought some very deep thoughts, aided by a fortifying bowl of salted peanuts.

His phone wouldn't stop ringing. It was always someone connected to the show, or his agent, or the press. He started to ignore it.

Reassured by the reports that the SS *Great Britain* had been spotted in New York, and people had seen Kirsten having what looked like a little swim, and that she was therefore still alive, he had decided to go on *The Jade Cooper Show* all by himself. Where, realising he had nothing to lose, he'd gone *very* off-script.

'I don't like being in a reality TV programme actually,' he said, staring straight into the camera. 'I miss my daughter very much. Edwina Clippity and I have separated. And, when all this is over, *I'm* going to go back to my true love, which is teaching maths to secondary-school children in Brimmerton in Bristol. And that – um – is what I think you call a wrap. Cheerio.'

He'd pulled off his mike, given his best melancholy smile to the audience, thanked them for their time, and walked out of the studio a lighter, happier man.

Then he went back to the harbourside and stood at the empty dock again, watching and praying for his daughter's safe return.

- 64 -
RETURN WHAT YOU HAVE TAKEN

HALF AN HOUR after the SS *Great Britain* arrived at Port Stanley, the mayor of the Falkland Islands had sped out on a small boat. It was now bobbing by the side of the ship. Kirsten lifted her chin defiantly and made her glare more ferocious, not fooled by the mayor's gentle smile.

'I think you know this ship,' she said curtly, looking down at her.

'I do,' said the mayor, a friendly-looking woman with a nose stud and tanned skin, smiling up at Kirsten. 'I'm stunned to see her. We heard reports that the ship was on the move again, but I'd never have believed it if you hadn't come here.'

'No more small talk,' said Kirsten dramatically. 'I'm here for one reason and one reason only.'

'Oh,' said the mayor. 'You're here for one reason, are you? Righto. What's that then?'

'For you to make amends. I'm the captain of the SS *Great Britain*, and I've come back to claim what is rightfully hers so that I can bring my journey to an end, lay some ghosts to rest, ease the pain of her ill-treatment and return home.'

The mayor tilted her head to one side. 'Claim what is rightfully hers?'

'Yes. The things your people stole.'

'You mean her masts and stuff? We'd love to–'

'I won't take no for an answer,' warned Kirsten. 'Oh. What?'

'I said we'd love to. Completely. Give me an hour or two to make some calls, and we'll get what we can ferried over here straightaway. I've often wanted to do this. We've got an entire *mast* of hers – you can have that too.'

Kirsten gave Olive a look. Olive raised her eyebrows back.

'Um, can I ask for two more things while we're at it?' said Kirsten ferociously.

'Of course,' said the mayor. 'Anything.'

'Well – firstly – could we get some hot food while we wait? Er, please?'

The mayor punched some buttons on her mobile. 'Consider it done,' she said. 'And secondly?'

'Can I borrow that?'

The mayor threw her mobile up and over the deck. Kirsten's hands shook a little as she keyed in Dad's number. She was half prepared to leave a message, but to her surprise—

Dad answered.

'*Kirsten?*' he gasped. 'Is that really you, sweetheart? I've been so worried. Everyone's been combing the ocean for you both, but your ship – she seems very hard to spot apparently. Like she's slipping in and out of different places or something? Every time they think their radar's spotted it, the ship gives them the run-around again. It's like she's occupying a completely different map they can't see or something–'

'You don't know the half of it, Dad,' said Kirsten through a tight throat.

'Where are you, lovely?'

'I'm in the Falklands.'

'I'll tell the navy,' he said. 'I'll tell everyone. Stay right where you are. I'll fly out.'

And Kirsten – who a few days ago would have begged him to do exactly that – said: 'No! Not right now! Dad – just stay on the line a bit. I want to talk – there's so much to say–' but now Dad was speaking again.

'I wish I'd been able to help more.' His voice went crackly then.

Kirsten hunched up as much as she could round the small device, desperate not to lose him.

'I've been flying over the Atlantic in a helicopter whenever I can, but I can't ever see you. But listen. I went on *The–*'

The line went crackly too.

'–*Cooper Show* by myself. I told them–'

The line went crackly again. Kirsten fought back tears. 'Dad,' she said, trying not to cry, 'I'm so sorry for letting you down—'

And then, miraculously, the line cleared. She heard him speaking as if he was right next to her.

'Darling, I've been proud of you since the day I met you. You haven't let me down; you'll *never* let me down. You carry on doing what you're doing. I've got a feeling about this. It's important for you, isn't it? It's – it's bedrock. It's that important. So you carry on, my girl. Oh, and by the way – been meaning to tell you – sad news I'm afraid, but me and Edwina are no longer—'

The line went dead.

Kirsten stared at the mobile.

No longer what? No longer in the house? No longer under contract? No longer *what*?

'Everything okay?' said Olive, reaching eagerly for the mayor's phone. 'Can I borrow that?'

While Olive called her mum, Kirsten puzzled over what she'd just heard. Dad had gone on *The Jade Cooper Show* by himself? Then what? He hadn't told her off though. He hadn't begged her to come home.

He'd told her to *keep going.*

- 65 -
TRUTH HURTS

KIRSTEN HAD TO hand it to the people of the Falkland Islands: despite the treatment shown to the ship in the past, now they were kindness itself. While Kirsten and Olive were passed flasks of hot soup, cake and fruit, bottles of water, and toothbrushes and toothpaste, a call went out among the islanders to bring any **SS *Great Britain*** heirlooms to the port.

Within a few hours, another sailing boat was dispatched to the ship loaded with bookshelves, cigar boxes, trunks and bits of mast: all parts of her original wooden deck that had been stripped and turned into souvenirs. These fragments of the ship were brought up by rope and placed delicately on deck.

Kirsten half expected the ship to miraculously drink in those relics, for the wood to liquefy and then be reabsorbed back into the planks somehow. Instead, the retrieved artefacts just – lay there, looking old.

But the mayor seemed expectant, so Kirsten said: 'Thank you.'

'And thank you for the food and things as well,' added Olive quickly.

'There's one more thing,' said the mayor. 'Something I personally would like to do.'

She got down on one knee. Then she said loudly, so everyone could hear: 'I beg your forgiveness, **SS *Great Britain***, for taking things from you when you were in our care. We should have treated you with more courtesy.'

The air went very still then. Kirsten felt, rather than heard, the ship soften around them.

THERE ARE PEOPLE THAT MUST BE FORGIVEN.

'Thank you,' said Kirsten.

'Now then,' said the mayor, 'because you're underage, and technically shouldn't be in charge of a ship, I should, by rights, contact the authorities to get you stopped—'

Kirsten held her breath.

'—but I'm not going to do that. If you've got this far on your own, you can get back on your own. Besides –' she gave a wry smile, and looked up at the ship with glistening eyes – 'I can't tell you how wonderful it is to see her on the move. And something tells me she won't be stopped anyway.'

Kirsten gave the mayor a grateful smile. 'You could say that.'

Once they'd said their goodbyes, and the mayor had

sailed back to the port, the mannequins drifted away, Olive following them. Kirsten, however, remained where she was.

'Well?' she asked the ship.

'What do you mean, *well*?'

Kirsten rolled her eyes. 'How about a thank-you for restoring *things that have been lost*? Don't you feel a bit more complete or something? Repaired? Fixed?'

The ship's rigging jangled heavily, as if she was letting out a big sigh. 'Captain, haven't you guessed yet?'

'Guessed what?'

'I had made my peace with what happened here. It was a long time ago, and although it hurt at the time, honestly it did, the Falkland Islands, for me, are a site of both pain and hope. This is my worst place and my best.'

'Why?' stammered Kirsten.

'People stole from me, and abandoned me here, but people also came for me, and brought me back to life, thanks to that wonderful man—'

'But you were *betrayed* here.' Kirsten couldn't understand why her heart was thudding so much.

There was a very long pause, and Kirsten felt the SS **Great Britain** taking great care over the words she spoke next.

'I think what's actually making you angry is *your* past, not mine. That's why we're here. This destination was as important for you as it was for me. I knew as soon as you came onboard. I could tell you felt broken. And it's now clear to me *you* needed to come here – to realise that.'

For a moment, Kirsten wanted to cry hot, angry tears. Her hands curled into fists instead. '*What?*'

'*You* feel as if you've been stolen from. Things have been taken from you too, haven't they? Your life was completely stripped, and altered, then rebuilt by other people, right? And it's been going on for years.'

The ship paused.

'Oh yes, Captain. This journey has never just been about *me*.'

- 66 -
RUNNING AWAY

KIRSTEN BEGAN TO shout. 'Where do you come up with all this stuff? Do you dredge it up from the sea?'

A corner of one of the flags on the ship rose up, as if the ship was raising a tiny little eyebrow. 'You think I don't understand you, Captain? I've *carried you*. I've held you in my arms while you slept. I can read your depths like the seabed. While you've been peering into my dreams, guess who's also been looking into yours?'

Kirsten felt a white-hot stab of rage and grief build inside her, like a geyser getting ready to explode. 'How *dare you*—'

'Captain?' prompted Mark. 'Are things going as you expected?'

'No,' snapped Kirsten.

'Well look, you've done it now,' added Olive, gesturing at the returned bits of the ship on the deck. 'The quest? Everything the map asked of you has been done, right? This must be the truth hidden deep inside the ship, right?'

Kirsten looked at her, unable to speak suddenly.

'You must be chuffed,' said Olive. 'I am too. It's

definitely been interesting, a proper quest, but I'm ready to get back now . . . and, between you and me, I think all the mannequins could do with a rest. They're exhausted. They weren't built to move about so much, and even the ship is looking a bit ragged. I'm sure I saw some rivets ping out of her on that last bend—'

But, as Kirsten watched Olive's lips move, she was struck by a strong realisation. And a terrible plan began to form in her head.

I don't want to go back home. Not now.

She'd missed the Jade Cooper interview. She was on a runaway ship. The papers must be having a field day. She'd be a laughing stock when she got back. They were bound to lose their new contract. Keith O'Keefe would probably dump them. And, even though Dad had tried to sound encouraging, how could he genuinely be proud of her when they were having such terrible money worries?

And – she gulped and finally faced the truth – Edwina *wasn't* her dad's true love, was she? Edwina had only applied to the show so she could become famous. Her dad had gone along with it because everyone around them was very persuasive. It was such a complicated mess.

She thought about what the ship had said. *Had* things been stolen from her? She turned on her heel suddenly and began to pace the deck.

The last four years . . . Kirsten sighed. How many quiet, uninterrupted evenings or weekends or holidays had she had with her dad? What friendships could she have forged at school if she hadn't been – well – famous? What *fun* could she have had if she hadn't always been worrying about being camera-ready? She thought, angrily, of how she'd actually skipped *meals* to lose weight she didn't need to lose, how Edwina had suggested it and she'd just *gone along with it*. How much had *she* wanted to become a reality-TV star? Had it ever been what she wanted? She got told it was often enough, but . . . actually, all she'd hoped for had been a girlfriend for her dad.

Who, it turned out, didn't even want one. That was what he'd always told her, hadn't he? But she'd just gone ahead, determined she knew best. And now being famous was all Kirsten had. And she didn't even like it. *No, I don't. I hate it.*

Her deeper thoughts, ones she didn't know she had, were swirling to the surface of her mind out here in the ocean.

She grew cunning, and afraid. That was it. Her mind was made up. She would keep going for ever and ever. If she kept travelling, she'd never have to deal with life back on land. Now the wander-thirst was on Kirsten, not the ship, and it was the strongest thing she'd ever known, like a sea fever. The tables had turned. Now *she* wanted to go on.

She turned to Olive. 'The journey isn't over.'

'Hold on a minute,' said Olive, eyes flashing. 'What about me? I can't live on this ship for the rest of my life. My teeth hurt. I miss my bed. I miss my–' Her lower lip wobbled. 'I miss my brothers, and Mum–'

Kirsten could barely keep her irritation in check. 'Olive, we're going to have more adventures. More quests. Doesn't that make you happy?'

'No,' sniffed Olive. 'I've had enough. I want a hot bath. I want to go home. And so does everyone else but *you*.'

She wandered away, followed, a few seconds later, by Mark, who gave Kirsten an unsettling gaze before he left.

Kirsten watched them go, then squinted into the horizon, feeling her jaw clench as a twisted, lonely pride stole over her. They'd spent so many days telling her she was the captain, hadn't they? She'd fought off a whaler, hadn't she? And she'd activated the ship in the first place. This was *her* ship. No one else's. She was in charge so she'd make some decisions for a change.

Right?

She strode to the ship's stern and put her hands on the wheel.

'I command you to move.'

'Very well,' said the ship flatly.

'I thought you'd be more pleased to hear me say that.'

'I'm beginning to wonder if endless beginnings are all they're cracked up to be, darling,' she replied softly. 'I'm feeling my age. But go ahead. Proceed. Just don't be surprised if I'm harder to steer.'

'Why *can't* you make the steering a bit easier for me, ship?'

'You're running away. That's not the same as exploring. This doesn't feel like a proper voyage so don't expect me to pretend it is.'

Slowly and reluctantly, the ship moved away from Port Stanley.

- 67 -
SUNDAY OR MONDAY

FOR AN ENTIRE day, Kirsten stood at the steering wheel, forcing the ship and the crew onwards, fuelled by nothing but the urge to put miles and miles between her and the Falkland Islands. Olive came nowhere near her.

Kirsten became increasingly glittery-eyed with pride and a manic sort of sleeplessness as the hours ticked by, bossing Mark about, barking at the mannequins to leave her alone, mindlessly eating her way through food whenever she was hungry at the wheel.

The only mannequin she would allow near her, occasionally, was the surgeon, but even he got on her nerves, as he kept talking about brain fever, sea lust and the heebie-jeebies, and telling her to rest. In the end, she waved him away. The ship's erratic movements and difficult steering wheel took all her concentration to manage. Kirsten had no idea where she was.

She felt cheated. She felt humiliated. She'd gone to all that effort to restore to the ship what had been taken from her . . . and it had all been flung in her face. The ship seemed to shake and shudder with every passing mile.

As the sun set and she began to tire, Kirsten reflected on the entire trip. All of their destinations, she suddenly realised, were eerily tangled up with various points in her own life, right up to now.

In New York, she'd seen how fickle fame could be.

The Lost Sea had been about confronting her lost friendship.

And the Falklands were about realising your entire life was a wreck.

She sighed with despair. She felt completely lost, and freezing cold inside and out. The ship was right. She *was* broken.

'Captain Kirsten?'

'Yes?'

Mark Spencer saluted.

'Ah,' she said. 'Have you come to bring me something to eat?'

'Not at all,' he said.

'Oh. Weather reports?'

'No,' he retorted, looking cross. 'Look – you're putting the ship in danger and I don't think you should. You're being selfish.'

Kirsten scowled at him. 'Oh, *really*? Well, who are you anyway? *I'm* the captain of this ship. If I say this journey isn't over, then it isn't over.'

The sun was just about to set behind the water, and the light seemed to infuse his waxy face with a pink glow. He looked, for a moment, just like a human.

'Captain—' He hesitated. 'Do you really want to be this sort of skipper? Don't you think the ship deserves better? Shouldn't you be looking after her? Have you learned *nothing*?'

He put a hand out then and laid it gently on the steering wheel, and he looked up into the ship's rigging, and there was something about his face that made Kirsten suddenly slump where she was standing and come back to herself in a way.

He was right. The ship was right. This wasn't a journey. What was she going to do – sail the ship till they both fell apart?

'Yeah,' she said softly. 'Point taken.' She took her hands off the steering wheel and the ship's movement slowed.

They looked at each other. 'I just . . .' Kirsten said. 'I don't want to go back. It'll be awful. Everything I thought was right wasn't right, and everything that's left will be wrong. And there'll be an awful woman bossing Dad about . . .'

Mark Spencer reached out and grabbed her hand. She stared at him in shock. With the other, he pointed at the ocean around them. 'Aren't waves amazing, Captain? Look at them. They just keep going. Even if they break, they rise up again.' And he looked straight at her.

Kirsten felt suddenly exhausted. 'Will you look after the ship for a bit, Mark, while I just grab forty winks?'

His glass eyes went very wide and very shiny. 'Really?'

Kirsten nodded, fighting back a yawn.

'I—' His voice faded, as if speech was impossible, as he placed his hands gently on the spokes of the wheel with devotion. And, even though he could barely see over it, Kirsten sensed that it didn't matter.

Wearily, she staggered to the room she shared with Olive. She could see her huddled under the blue blanket on the top bunk.

Kirsten didn't even bother taking off her captain's clothes. She fell into bed and was asleep within minutes.

- 68 -
OLIVE THE MIGHTY AND KIRSTEN THE INVINCIBLE

LATER THAT NIGHT, the ship's snoring shook the entire vessel. She rattled and wheezed like an old lung. From the corridor outside came the sound of things falling to the floor, rivets and plates pinging and crashing, as her reverberations tested her structure, pushed it right to its limits. Even Kirsten's bunk felt as if it was hanging on by a thread.

Olive was right. Mark was right. The ship was weakening. This journey had cost her more than she'd ever admit. No matter how young or how strong and timeless the ship believed herself to be, or *wanted* to be, she was also vulnerable. Her journey *had* to come to an end. And only Kirsten could bring that about by finding the ship's ultimate truth: the final one in a journey of several. This was the last remaining riddle.

Kirsten groaned in her bunk, contemplating her next steps. First of all, it meant getting up: an epic challenge in itself. What came after that seemed even more impossible: hunting something invisible inside the ship. Something the ship didn't want her to find.

PEER PAST THE DREAMS AND YOU WILL FIND
THE TRUTH.

Better see this scene through, she thought, grinning a little.
Come on, Kirsten Bramble, give them a bit of the old razzle-dazzle.

She pushed back her blanket, groggily grabbed her rope
and tied it round her stomach. She'd got as far as turning
the door handle when she stopped. Tiptoed back to the
bunk. And gently shook Olive Chudley awake.

'Third time lucky,' she whispered shyly. 'Just wondered
if you fancied coming with me this time? To find the truth
in the dreaming ship? I thought we could complete the
quest properly. Together.'

It was dark in the cabin, but she saw the gleam in the
other girl's eyes clearly enough.

'Yes,' said Olive. 'I really do. Immediately.'

They grinned at each other.

Olive leaped out of the bunk and stood, wincing a little
at the feel of ship's soft floor.

'You'll get used to it,' murmured Kirsten.

Olive wrapped her school cardigan round herself and
slipped into her grey trousers quickly, but, after glancing at
Kirsten's bare feet, left her socks and shoes off too. 'Let's
do this,' she said, firmly tying her own rope round her
stomach.

'Quest o'clock,' they whispered, smiling.

'Okay,' said Kirsten, more serious, in a low voice. 'Just remember: don't wake her up. No noisy footsteps or shouting.'

'And we can't outstay our welcome,' murmured Olive. 'Or hang about in the dreams too long, or we'll lose our minds.'

'That too.'

'It's an almost impossible challenge, with outrageously high stakes and multiplayer characters,' whispered Olive, shivering all over with a mixture of cold and delight. 'It's *awesome*.'

Together, they left their cabin and stepped out into the dreaming ship.

'I'll never forget this for as long as I live,' muttered Olive some time later.

They'd seen the waves crashing through the corridors, admired the miniature ports floating in the washbasins, watched the dancing Victorians and stood on the ship's remembered galaxies. Dream whales had swum overhead and allowed themselves to be tickled on their smooth stomachs. The walls had pulsed with 200 years' worth of conversation, and they'd heard nursery rhymes, heated arguments, jokes and earnest vows that the ship must have stored from her favourite journeys.

Walking through rooms of sleeping mannequins and remembered Victorian passengers alike, Kirsten suddenly felt how she was simultaneously very lucky and yet also in danger. Wandering through memories so rich brought with them a temptation to stay there for ever. It would be so easy to stare until you no longer knew yourself.

But she was the captain. That meant remembering her duty to the ship. Her heart thudded. That was what being a captain meant. It wasn't just about a hat. (Although that was obviously hugely important too.) It was about *caring.*

An hour or so passed. They were cold and tired from dragging their ropes behind them. The Captain's Cabin materialised instantly, between the galley and the pantry. Here they were able to sit with the kind dream captain from the past and warm up with a few sips of his whisky, which burned their throats and made them gasp.

'And did you find the truth in the end, little stowaway?' he said to Kirsten, sitting back in his chair with a smile.

'Not yet,' said Kirsten, getting up and tying on her rope again, mindful of the consequences of spending too long in the cabin. 'But I hope to.'

'It's not land you're searching for, is it? And it's not a coordinate on a map either, I suspect. It's something inside you.'

'No,' corrected Kirsten. 'Not inside me. I'm looking for something inside *her*.'

He laced his fingers under his chin and stared at her. 'Maybe it's both.'

'We never got your name,' said Olive softly.

'I'm Captain Gray. Longest-serving captain of the ship. We were together for eighteen years, and I loved every plank of her.' He looked right at Kirsten. 'Just like you, I'll wager.'

Kirsten had that same strange sensation she'd had when Flatty had read her. 'Yes,' she said, nodding softly. 'Just like me.'

He was right. How had he guessed it?

She wasn't sure when exactly her love for the ship had been formed, between which waves on the ocean. Maybe it had started earlier: the moment she saw the ship from the car park. Perhaps it had started even earlier than *that*, and the ship had drawn Kirsten towards her with all the might of her metal, like a strong magnet that had sensed that Kirsten Bramble was also exploding and needed to land somewhere safe.

Whenever it had come and crept into her heart, it was a love she could never have prepared for. There *was* no knowing what, or who, you might love in your lifetime. She'd certainly never imagined it would be a 3,400-tonne nineteenth-century ship, but there it was. And it hadn't come with boxes of chocolates and bouquets of flowers either. It had been born out of something entirely different.

Kirsten stared round the room, trembling a little as things fell into place. Real love had been in her life – and her dad's – all along. True love wasn't just something that you could orchestrate, as she'd tried to. And it didn't just have to be the romantic sort of love. You could find real, true, life-changing love between *anything*. A daughter and her father. A man and his maths. A girl and a ship. Two friends.

She *loved* the ship. Perhaps that was the secret to being a captain after all. And, while she was in no doubt that on an ordinary ship, knowing about winds, or currents, and what bits were called what would be essential, on *this* ship it wasn't. Maybe the most important thing was to love the ship you were in charge of. And the people inside her, whatever they were made of: memory, fibreglass, parchment, wood or flesh. It was love for others that made someone a proper leader.

And with that love came a responsibility: to understand the ship's story once and for all.

'We must go,' she whispered. 'Time is ticking.' She brought her hand up to her temple in a smart salute. 'Goodbye, Captain Gray,' she told the dream.

'Godspeed, Captain Bramble,' he said softly, lips curling

in an unexpectedly dashing smile at her look of surprise. He nodded at Olive. 'First Mate.'

'Is this goodbye for ever?' muttered Olive to Kirsten, as they stood in the doorway, looking back. 'It's sad to leave him alone.'

But as they watched him settling into his chair with another dram of whisky, glancing into the golden glow of the oil lantern on his desk, they realised he wasn't alone at all. He had his ship.

He barely looked up as they tiptoed away from the warm cabin.

69

A FAIR SWAP

'I THINK,' MURMURED Olive earnestly, after another fruitless hour of quietly searching the ship, peering into nooks and crannies, but finding nothing, 'Captain Gray had a point when he talked about finding something inside you.' She rubbed her nose. 'What I mean is . . . maybe, if you want to find the ship's truth, you have to give yours.'

'Huh?' whispered Kirsten, distractedly peering under a bunk in steerage.

Olive stared at her solemnly. 'So – in all quests, you give something, then you get something. A trade.'

'A fair swap?'

'Exactly. Can you give her some of your truths? Maybe something secret, something important?'

The sound of the mannequins snoring filled the air around them. Kirsten found herself staring at the smallest child curled up in a bottom bunk with a threadbare teddy. 'Something important?'

'Don't worry about scripting it,' said Olive. 'This isn't an episode of your show. You're allowed to make mistakes in real life, you do realise that? It doesn't have to come out perfect.'

Kirsten stared at her, lost for words, unexpectedly touched by her wisdom.

Olive gestured into the shadows around them. 'Just – erm – open your mouth and start to speak. You know. From the heart. Be honest. Then you might find what she's been hiding too. She might give it to you. I dunno. Worth a shot.'

Kirsten looked at her ex-best friend and finally found the words that had been buried deep inside her. She told the truth, in hushed tones, because that was the best way to tell it.

'I miss you, Olive,' she whispered. 'I *really* miss you. I wish we were still best friends. I let you down. That audition was a nightmare. I can understand why you didn't want to get involved. I walked away when you needed me. I let that programme ruin our friendship. You're really clever, and brave, and kind—'

'—and brilliant at quests—' added Olive helpfully. 'Don't forget that.'

'—*definitely*, that too – and I wish we hadn't fallen out.'

Everything about Olive's face went still. Her eyes grew large and brimmed with emotion like buckets of water.

THERE ARE PEOPLE THAT MUST BE FORGIVEN. It had been Kirsten all along.

Kirsten took a deep breath. 'I'm sorry. For putting you through that dreadful audition and thinking that you could be replaced. India-Rose is *paid* to be my best friend. She's not a real one, not like you . . . were. I'm really, really sorry. About everything.'

She'd had to go halfway round the world, and down to the bottom of the sea and back up again, and fight off a whaler ghost, and explore dream times, and fall into cahoots with a talking ship, and eat a *lot* of food past its sell-by date, but . . . she'd got there in the end.

'Will you forgive me?' she asked quietly, surrounded by a chorus of snores.

'Yeah,' Olive grinned. 'I will.'

They smiled at each other. Then Olive took a deep breath. 'But you know what? I don't think it was totally your fault. I mean – yeah, you turned into a right show-off at the start, but I've thought loads about this and actually, if anyone's to blame, it's the grown-ups who let you down really. Not your dad – he was manipulated too – but the telly people. They *used* you. So be kind to yourself. You were trapped in that show. You were the child. They should have looked after you, but they didn't, not really.'

Kirsten rubbed her eyes. *THERE ARE PEOPLE THAT*

MUST BE FORGIVEN. She needed to forgive herself?

'I'd never thought of that before.' Her mind whirled. 'You mean . . . I never did anything wrong?'

Olive nodded firmly. 'That's right,' she said. 'And, if I'd been you, I'd have driven a car into the sea too. So stop blaming yourself.'

Kirsten felt unbelievably light all of a sudden. She'd been carrying something heavy and dark inside her for many, many years, and it had just vanished.

'Wow,' she whispered. 'That's made me feel so much better.'

'Stick around,' Olive said. 'There's loads more where that came from.'

Kirsten giggled. *And parts that are missing must be restored.*

'Will you be my best friend again from now on, please?'

Olive hesitated. 'Would - would I be filmed?'

'Definitely not. Don't worry about that stupid TV programme. I'm going to quit it all as soon as we get back home.'

Olive let out a huge sigh and smiled. 'Good. In that case, yes.'

They grinned happily at each other.

'It was bad, right?' asked Kirsten.

'Shocking by the end,' agreed Olive. 'Although I did quite like *Rambles with the Brambles*, but only because you kept getting chased by cows—'

Kirsten gently punched her on the arm, but happily. 'I think the only person who actually enjoys filming is Edwina,' she whispered.

Olive began to laugh quietly. 'Well, it's just as well the camera loves her, because your dad *definitely* doesn't—'

Kirsten's eyes widened in shock, and then she started to laugh too. At first, their giggles were quiet, but the more they tried to stop, the worse it got, and they couldn't stop themselves from staggering around, bent double.

The ship twitched. She stopped snoring.

'We've woken her up,' moaned Kirsten. 'We were too loud!'

And then suddenly there was a pull in the air around them, and something invisible seemed to tug on their ropes, and they both began to stagger forward.

It felt like they were being sucked into the ship's rage and distress. The pull in the air grew stronger, and drew them on like a magnet, ripping them from their tethers. Their ropes fell to the ground and they were whooshed down corridors and through the galley, bashed along the floor and walls, wincing and crying out with pain.

Kirsten, drenched in icy fear, remembered how the map had warned her about exploring the dreams: *IF SHE SENSES YOU TRESPASSING, YOU MIGHT GET INJURED.*

She heard the ship mutter thickly, as if half asleep: 'Stop meddling! Stop your thieving! Get *out*! Don't dredge up the past . . . makes me feel sad . . . makes me feel old . . .'

Kirsten and Olive couldn't stop – everything inside the ship was whirring round them like a cyclone: whales and stars and petticoats and top hats spun round them, the surprised faces of dream passengers, old trunks, palm trees, tins of tripe . . .

After a few more agonising twists and turns, they were flung into the darkest part of the ship, and spat out like discarded sweet wrappers on to a cold, hard grid floor.

The whirring, beating noise was all around them now. They had landed in the engine room.

As they staggered to their feet, wincing and brushing themselves off, Kirsten suddenly realised this was where the ship kept her ultimate truth.

And knew what it was.

It was grief. It was metallic, and huge, and too big for Kirsten to see properly, but that's what it was. She could *feel it* herself: it was like standing in the middle of an earthquake and sensing everything shatter. That's why the ship grew so cold at night. Her iron heart was breaking.

The **SS *Great Britain*** was very, very sad about something, and she hadn't wanted anyone to know.

That was the truth Kirsten had needed to find.

But why? Why had she needed to keep her sadness a secret?

She looked deep into the engine and saw that vision of a human hand again, curled right up in the middle of the grief, and all of a sudden she had a hunch she knew who it belonged to. The ship had even mentioned him, and so had the map, but Kirsten hadn't picked up on the clues, not then.

'Get . . . *out* . . .' moaned the ship softly.

It was dawn. The ship was awake, they were out of their beds, and both were within moments of danger.

'Hurry,' hissed Olive, grabbing Kirsten's hand. They ran as quickly as they could out of the engine room and skidded into their cabin just as Kirsten's temples felt as if they were about to explode.

'Talk in the morning?' said Olive, hollow-eyed with triumphant exhaustion and shock, as she climbed into her bunk.

'Talk in the morning,' promised Kirsten.

Olive was asleep within moments, but Kirsten stayed awake a while longer, puzzling things out, until she finally understood.

70

STORYTIME AGAIN

WHEN KIRSTEN OPENED her eyes the next morning, her cabin was full of golden light. Yawning, she stretched, then winced. She was covered in bruises from being whirled through the ship. But she grinned despite the aches. She'd managed a few hours' sleep and, better than that, she had solved the puzzle. She'd found the truth. It was time for the next destination.

She got up and glanced over. Olive was still asleep. Rubbing her eyes, Kirsten left the room, grabbed her hat and wandered down the corridor, stopping to smile and chat with the mannequins.

She couldn't remember the last time she'd brushed her hair or had a bath. She actually kind of loved how grubby she'd become. She smelled like she'd *lived a little*. Adventure and risk and truth-seeking, she realised, were never going to make you smell like washing powder.

From now on, she would treat people who smelled with respect; she would see them as the true explorers of the cosmos. If they smelled of the wind, and salt, and sweat, and fear, if they walked barefoot and slightly wonky, as if they'd spent a long time on a ship, she would tip her hat to them and make way for them on the street. She would listen to their stories and ask about their journeys—

'How's the fever, Captain? Has it broken?' said the surgeon, coming round a corner.

'I'm not entirely sure actually, Doctor. I sense it might still be lingering? Or maybe I went a tiny bit mad in the end, from staying too long in the ship's dreams? I feel good though.'

'That's the main thing,' said the mannequin lightly. He stared at her intently, in that way he had. 'Yes, I think your diagnosis is correct. Still—' He drew back and nodded. 'You appear to be thriving on it. Those heebie-jeebies have totally vanished. Total recovery. Well done.'

They smiled at each other, and the surgeon walked smartly away, and Kirsten turned and there was the Captain's Cabin, right in front of her.

The walls stayed right where they were. The room looked utterly delightful to her: the wallpaper seemed as fresh as the day it had been pasted; the lights were at a pleasing height; it was the right temperature and the right size. It fitted Kirsten perfectly.

That was always the way, she thought, walking up

to the desk. Things were always the most comfortable towards the end, like a pair of favourite shoes. Like a Captain's Cabin that had grown to fit you.

She bit her lip, let the sadness wash over her and, when it had passed, approached the torn map.

One tiny blue line seemed to blink open, like an eye. Blearily, the eye regarded her for a while. And then:

Ah, it wrote. **Hello. You seem different.**

'Do I?'

Oh yes. Your outlines are . . . **changed.**

'I found the truth last night. What the ship couldn't bear to admit to herself. I know why we're here. I know what this voyage is really about, and how it needs to end. I know what I have to do.'

Tell me.

Kirsten hesitated. 'You told us, that first night, that there was a man who saved the **SS Great Britain** from falling to bits in the Falklands – when everyone else had given up on her. He was the one who brought her back to Bristol, wasn't he? Can you tell me his name?'

The map did better than that. It produced a name and a picture.

His name is Ewan Corlett.

Kirsten looked at his kind face and felt an echo of the grief she'd uncovered in the ship the night before.

'He's – well – he's at the heart of all this, isn't he?'

Cor . . .

rect.

Kirsten pulled out a pen from her pocket that she'd brought just in case this happened. She stamped on it and gave the map a good long drink of ink. Then she made herself comfortable in the Captain's Chair, giving the arms a little pat as they held her.

'Tell me,' said Kirsten. 'Tell me everything.'

The SS *Great Britain* **was on the verge of breaking in two, out in Sparrow Cove.**

Ewan Corlett was just an ordinary man who had been given a picture of the SS *Great Britain* **as a present. That was all it took.**

Wh— Pardon?

Yes. It's impossible to take a bad picture of you. That's right. Yes, you are extremely rewarding to paint. Many, many artists have said so.

May I continue?

When he found out that she was falling to pieces in Sparrow Cove, he was shocked and decided she must be rescued, before it was too late.

Everyone said it was impossible to lift her out of the sand. That it couldn't be done. He decided it must be done.

He wrote a letter to The Times. He helped raise money. He fought to save her. He brought her back to Bristol and helped restore her. From a wreck to a star once more.

'And she never forgot him,' whispered Kirsten.

Never.

'She loved him.'

Completely. And, when an iron ship loves someone completely, it's . . . Well, it's something.

'It is,' said Kirsten. 'It really is.'

But she had been stolen from before. In Port Stanley and Sparrow Cove. She'd felt everything ripped out and taken away. And so she'd learned to keep her most precious things hidden from people, so they couldn't be stolen again.

That's what she did with her love for Ewan Corlett, with her memory of him. She squirrelled it away, in her deepest, darkest recesses.

'Her engine room.'

Where she could keep it safe, and private, and far from prying eyes and thieving hands.

But, if you hide your love too long, it can be difficult to face it. It can break your heart if you don't bring it out now and again.

Kirsten thought of the voice she'd heard, coming across the ocean the second time she'd explored the ship's dreams. The flickering, frail skein of thought telegram that had wrapped itself round the ship.

One last time. Just one last time. Let me see her one last time. That hadn't been Dad. It had been Ewan Corlett, calling to the ship.

'He's . . .' she whispered, the final piece of the puzzle falling into place. 'He's dying, isn't he?'

He is. His journey is coming to an end.

'And he sent out loads and loads of thought telegrams, right? Hoping they might get through?'

Yes.

'But she resisted, because to see him would be an . . . ending.'

And she doesn't like those.

- 363 -

Kirsten blinked. 'But . . . she has to see him before he dies. It would break her properly if he went before she got a chance to say goodbye. And I've never met this Ewan Corlett, but I'm guessing if his thought telegrams were powerful enough for even me to hear them, then his love for her must be pretty strong too. Seeing her would mean everything to him.'

It would, I agree, be a very . . .

sp . . .

. . . ecial reunion

'You're fading, aren't you?' Kirsten whispered. 'This is your last voyage.'

Yes.

'And now – now you need me to get you both to him.'

Yes.

Kirsten put one hand, very gently, on to the soft parchment and dark blue ink began to appear, weakly, round her hand, as if to touch her gently.

'It would be my honour,' she said, 'to take her to him. I'll help in any way I can.'

Captain? wrote the map slowly.

'Yes?'

You're not the witless dullard I mistook you for.

'Thank you, Flatty,' Kirsten whispered through her tears. 'That's very, very sweet of you.'

PART 6

'**O**ur hopes gratified, on we fly'
Private diary entry, Isambard Kingdom Brunel, 1824

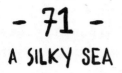
- 71 -
A SILKY SEA

AND NOW, SOMEWHERE in an undisclosed spot in international waters that *no* navy would never be able to find, because the ship liked to do things her way in her own time, and she and the oceans went way back, and they were happy to bend the rules a little, just for her . . .

. . . a grubby, barefoot girl, with a thatch of unbrushed hair and some *very* dirty fingernails, reached, once more, for the ship's wheel. Her heart was bursting.

'Come on then,' she whispered to the **SS *Great Britain***. 'Do you think you can shoot – like a star – one last time? To . . . him?'

The ship's bowsprit shook vehemently from side to side.

'No,' she said, her voice cracking. 'Absolutely not.'

Kirsten had expected a bit of resistance, but not an outright refusal.

'Don't you *want* to see him?'

The ship sighed. 'Not if it'll be the last time,' she said sternly. 'I'd rather never see him at all than see him like that. If I don't say goodbye to him, things will never end.'

Kirsten bit her lip and stared at the weathered deck. 'But . . . he so desperately wants to see you. And I *know* you want to see him. I saw that in your dreams—'

The flags of the rigging flapped vigorously, and all the metal snapped and flapped in a sharp rebuke. When the ship next spoke, it was with iron and fire.

'You know *nothing*, Captain. If I see him, it's to accept that nothing lasts for ever. I'd rather remember him as he was than face the fact that he's dying. That something else precious is being taken away from me. I hate goodbyes. They're just like being robbed, all over again. Hate them more than anything.'

Kirsten thought hard about everything she'd seen in the ship's dreams. She remembered that man with ink-stained fingers she'd met on the docks, who loved the ship he'd designed so much he'd travelled through time and space to see her; who'd designed her with so much care that he'd created something extraordinary.

'You've got it wrong,' she said suddenly. 'If you love someone, or something, you help them last for ever. Love isn't a weakness. It's a strength.'

'If I see him, he'll die. He's holding out for me, isn't he? If I never see him, perhaps he'll live. Staying away from him is the kindest thing I can do. It will make him last for ever.'

Kirsten smiled. 'Humans don't work like that though.

When it's time for him to go, he will.'

The ship sniffed. 'Another example of your terrible engineering.' But she seemed to be listening – everything about her was very still.

Kirsten thought about Captain Gray and the passengers that the ship carried safely in her dreams night after night.

'If you love someone, it makes them immortal in some way. That's what Brunel did for you. And that's what you've done to Captain Gray, isn't it? And all your past travellers? They all live on in your dreams.'

'Y-yes,' admitted the ship shakily.

'So then – ' said Kirsten, growing in confidence – 'that's what you'll do for Ewan Corlett. Showing him you love him—' She swallowed. 'It's your way of returning the favour, isn't it? Staying away won't make him last for ever. Seeing him will. You'll make him always last like that. You'll always carry him inside *you*.'

'What if they take my love away?' said the ship quietly. 'What if they steal my memories? They stole so much before.'

'They won't,' said Kirsten. Kirsten, who had struggled to speak emotionally for such a long time, now found it was as easy as anything. 'No one will. I promise. I won't let them. They won't *dare*.'

For a moment, they were both silent.

The **SS *Great Britain's*** entire hull swelled, then shuddered. 'It won't be as fast as before, but I can get us there by nightfall.'

Kirsten felt a huge rush of pride in her. 'Do you know where you're going?' She peered at the grey ocean around them. 'I can steer you, but have you got any directions? Because, between you and me, I have *literally no idea* where we are.'

'I'll follow his thought telegrams,' said the ship quietly. 'They're all around me now.'

And the steering wheel moved – finally – like a dream. It was so responsive: she only had to touch it lightly for the ship to move through the water. Kirsten steered their way through huge waves as easily as gliding.

'Why are you so easy to move *now*?' she said, confused.

'You know why,' said the ship.

Kirsten did. This was a proper journey: not running away, but going *towards*.

She grinned and held on to the steering wheel a little bit tighter. Standing at the back, with the entire majesty of the ship laid out before her, and knowing she and the ship were in perfect accord, was an experience she didn't want to waste a second of. It felt like she and the ship were one.

All the mannequins, as if they sensed something magical was happening, came up on deck, followed by Olive.

As they flew over a silky sea, all of them together, quiet, joyful, lit up from inside, their faces glowing in the setting sun, Kirsten knew she'd carry this moment inside her too for the rest of her life.

Many hours later, they skidded to a halt just outside the harbour of a sleepy seaside town. It was dusk. Rain was falling. The air, Kirsten realised, smelled faintly of mustard and madness.

'Where are we?' said Olive, walking slowly down the deck. 'Brazil? Thailand? Venice?'

'Somerset,' said the ship quietly. 'Little Greenport. He's here. Somewhere. I don't know where. But I'll find him.'

Kirsten grinned at the irony of it. They'd travelled a thousand miles, yet Somerset was just next door to Bristol. What had the map said? *We're going the long way round.*

The ship stuck her pointy bowsprit into the air, like a loyal dog sniffing the air for a beloved friend.

'Ah,' she said. 'Found him.'

'Do you want me to try to get him down here somehow?' asked Kirsten. 'Alert him?'

'That won't be necessary, Captain, but thank you all the same,' said the ship. 'You see, *we're* going to *him*.'

- 72 -
X MARKS THE SPOT

AND THE SHIP began to move, at a determined clip, right towards the shops and cafés and people of the harbourfront, her bowsprit pointing straight ahead doggedly the entire while.

Kirsten, Olive and Mark grabbed the rails.

When the ship had overtaken four small fishing boats and was almost within spitting distance of the harbour wall, Kirsten began to panic.

'Um – ship? You might want to slow down? If you don't stop, we're going to crash *right through that wall.*'

'Love knows no barriers, darling, and you can't make an omelette without breaking a few eggs,' said the ship firmly.

They'd reached the small sandy cove in front of the harbour, scattering seagulls and a few dog walkers as the ship ploughed up the beach. And still she moved, hauling her hull over the sand with utter single-mindedness.

Kirsten peered through the drizzle. The harbourfront was lit up by the cosy cafés and a few streetlamps. She suddenly saw what the ship was aiming straight towards.

It was a small white building on the high street, with five windows, a smoking chimney, a pink rose that climbed up one side and a sign in the front garden that said:

10 PLEASANT STREET
A COMFORTABLE RETIREMENT HOME
WITH SEA VIEWS
FOR RETIRED GENTLEMEN

On the front of the building was a Roman numeral chiselled into its façade.

X

Kirsten remembered. X *marks the spot.*

She laughed. It was too good. *That map*, she thought, wiping her eyes. *That tricky, delightful, maddening map.*

Then she stopped laughing because the ship's bowsprit had smashed right through the bottom window of the nursing home.

And the ship finally stopped.

AT LAST

THE THREE BAREFOOT children ran and skidded down the damp deck of the ship and stood, silently, at the front, in the fo'c'sle, the narrowest part of the ship where the bowsprit began.

They were just a few metres away from the smashed window of the nursing home. Within a few seconds, there was the high-pitched sound of a woman screaming, then a furious monologue:

'What on *earth* is going on? Mr Barker, have you been throwing cricket balls indoors again? Mr Date-Bah, why are you sitting there, grinning like that? Have you been at the sherry again? And why is the entire tea set on the carpet? I leave you three alone for *one minute* and the amount of mischief – *what is that thing sticking through our window?* And Mr Corlett, why are you getting out of your wheelchair?'

There was the faint sound of very, very gentle scuffling.

'Mr Corlett. Mr *Corlett!* Stop it! Don't fight me! I'm only trying to help! Get back in your wheelchair at once! You'll have a turn! Stay away from that window! *Don't touch that white pointy stick – we've no idea where it's been!* Don't stand in the breeze – you'll catch a chill! For a man approaching ninety-seven, you're behaving just like a *child*, Mr Corlett!'

And then the three children saw an old man at the window of the nursing home.

He was stooped, and slight, and the hand that hovered above the ship's bowsprit was trembling a little. He peered out into the gloom and, when he saw his beloved ship just a metre away from him, his mouth turned into a perfect O.

He stared at the **SS *Great Britain*** for at least an entire minute without doing anything, just drinking in the sight of her. And the ship, in turn, said and did absolutely nothing. There *was* nothing to do for the time being. All they needed was to be near one another again: one man and the ship he'd believed in so passionately.

Everything seemed to hold its breath around them. The dusk grew extremely soft. The lights of the harbour twinkled extra brightly.

Ewan Corlett rested his hand on the bowsprit, and then, a moment later, bent his head and rested it gently there too.

The ship started a little, like a horse, and her engine began to rotate, loud and true and fast. After a while, Ewan Corlett looked up, and peered past the broken glass into the dusk once more. This time he saw the three children gathered at the front, and rewarded them with a tremulous smile.

'Thank you so much,' he said softly, and the sound carried in the still evening air. 'I'd almost given up hope of seeing her again. I have no idea how you managed to bring her here, but I'm much obliged to you all.'

Kirsten wondered if she should tell the old man how hard the ship's heart was beating, and how much the ship loved him, then realised he probably knew already.

His crooked back straightened and, with some effort, Ewan Corlett gave them all a smart salute and, for a minute, he looked like the blazing, wonderful human who wouldn't, all those years ago, take no for an answer, who had brought the broken ship back home when everyone had said it couldn't be done.

And – as if they'd been born to do it – Olive, Kirsten and Mark saluted him right back.

Just as they were all enjoying the peace of the moment, the evening air and indigo hue of the sleepy harbour village were riven by the sound of a very large, very determined warship pulling up outside the harbour.

'Uh-oh,' said Mark.

'Oh no,' said Olive.

'Let's go,' said Kirsten.

But they couldn't. HMS *Destroyer* was blocking them in again.

- 74 -
BUBBLES

BUT THIS TIME, Kirsten realised, the officers onboard the *Destroyer* didn't look quite as disappointed or telling-offy as before. (Even though the warship itself was still hands down the most terrifying thing Kirsten had ever seen.)

'Kirsten Bramble,' shouted an officer with a megaphone. 'You have somehow sailed the **SS *Great Britain*** halfway round the world while evading capture, without any basic seafaring knowledge, no provisions, no fuel, and yet are mysteriously back in British waters safe and sound.'

'Oh?' said Kirsten lightly, playing for time. 'Have I?'

'Well, we're absolutely stunned. And rather impressed. And we'd like to know how you did it. These are, frankly, extremely important seafaring skills that our crews must be trained in.'

Kirsten laughed. 'Have you got an old, slightly grumpy map onboard? You need to start with that.'

'And lots of Fruittellas,' added Olive, grinning. 'And some very brave mannequins. And a decent knowledge of computer-quest games.'

While the two officers threw puzzled glances at each other, Olive took a deep breath.

'So – officers – are you saying that we're not in any trouble? Are you going to arrest us or anything? Because you do *look* quite scary – you know that, right?' shouted Olive, hands on her hips.

'No, we're not going to arrest you. We just wanted to check you were all right actually. Do you need anything?'

Kirsten was longing to see Dad. But there was something else, something important, she wanted to do.

'Well, seeing as you asked,' she said, 'have you got any champagne?'

That night there was a big joyful party on board the SS **Great Britain**, and Ewan Corlett was the guest of honour, along with his friends from the retirement home. The Royal Navy ordered the finest food in the village, and brought it in, laid it all out and then left them to it, smiling. The huge dining saloon was filled to bursting with delicious food for Ewan and his friends, and Olive and Kirsten.

Cook was finally able to serve his finest tripe to all the mannequins, who proclaimed it delicious and asked for thirds, and he wiped his eye with his apron and was happy.

There was champagne for the guests, and dancing, and the violinists took requests. The fighting women fought, but they did it very respectfully, and they demonstrated their infamous ear-ripping move and everyone clapped. The children were allowed to stay up as late as they wanted. The men threw their hats in the air and danced, the women in bonnets undid their corsets and were the wildest dancers of all, and the doctor and the surgeon and the soldier and the man with the not-really-bleeding hand played with the train set and threw marbles for the children.

The party went on for hours, and they danced all through the ship, and once in a while Kirsten caught a glimpse of a short man in a top hat smoking a cigar and looking very happy with the way things were going.

Underneath it all, the ship's metal heart whooshed and whooshed and whooshed, and sometimes you could almost hear her purring.

At around midnight, Kirsten saw Ewan Corlett slip away to bid farewell to the ship one last time, and then he came back and thanked her. He put his hands over hers and squeezed them.

'You have made an old man very happy,' he said, before disembarking, pushed in his wheelchair by his friends. Kirsten waved them off, knowing it was only a matter of time before Ewan Corlett would be carried by the ship in her dreams. *Perhaps he might even share a whisky with Captain Gray.* The thought pleased her.

The mannequins began to take themselves off to bed. Olive was sitting with Mark, chatting quietly.

Kirsten grabbed a nearly full bottle of champagne and took it up to the top deck by herself.

Under the full moon, she took one sip, held it in her mouth and drank it ceremoniously. (Then she took one more sip, because the first one was so delicious.)

Then she held the bottle aloft, over the railing, and threw it at the side of the ship as hard as she could. There was a smash. A pause. A very quiet slurping noise.

'Bollinger,' sighed the SS *Great Britain*. 'The best. Thank you.'

It was a beautiful night. Kirsten glanced at the silver clouds, and the harbour around them, and was at peace. She and the ship had healed each other. She had helped the ship become a bit more human. The ship had given her iron and strength.

And she thought of what the map had told her.

You will learn something from each destination and, when the time is right, you will choose the final destination, and that will be the most important one of all.

She pressed her lips together very tightly. 'We've got one more place to go, haven't we?'

'Have we?' said the ship brightly, as if she was trying to pretend everything was absolutely fine. 'And where's that?'

Kirsten had to choose this one.

'Home.'

'Yes,' said the ship, after a moment. 'It's time.'

Kirsten bit her lip. 'Will you be okay? What with it being – I dunno – an ending, in a way. Of us? Of *this*?'

There was a very long pause. Kirsten's heart jumped around a bit.

Then the ship said lightly: 'Actually, Captain, I'm beginning to think endings aren't all that bad after all. They just need a new name.'

'Like what?'

'Well, I'm still working that out. I'll report back once I know.'

The ship went quiet then.

Kirsten looked, one last time, at the harbour, and the stars peering through the clouds as if to see what had happened to their old friend. She sighed a very happy, sleepy sigh, and finally went downstairs, where she crept through the ship's cabins, as everyone lay sleeping, and tucked them in properly.

Only then did she go to bed herself. And she slept like a baby, held firmly in the world's strongest embrace.

- 75 -
A HERO IS BORN

THE NEXT MORNING, the SS *Great Britain* – aided by the Royal Navy – began her homecoming procession down the River Avon, back towards the city of Bristol. She was slightly sleepy, a bit bedraggled in places, but still utterly radiant obviously.

Most of the passengers and crew were on the deck, some rubbing their heads, some their bellies. But inside, Kirsten was tidying up: pulling blankets tight, straightening tablecloths, coiling ropes and storing them safely. The last thing she did was change out of her captain's clothes, roll them up carefully, put them into her rucksack, then dress in her crumpled, stained school uniform. Minus the shoes.

She gave one final fond look round her berth and left.

Then she paid the Captain's Cabin one more visit, where the light was as dark and rich and full of new beginnings as soil.

'I've come to say goodbye,' she whispered. The torn, thin parchment under its green lamp gave a tiny ripple in response.

Goodbye, Captain. Well done. Capital journey.

Then Flatty's ink gave a startled splutter as Kirsten bent over the parchment. **What are you doing?**

'Where I come from,' said Kirsten, '*people* read *maps*. Don't worry, I'll be gentle.'

She peered right into the grain and ink of the parchment and stared and stared until she gave a satisfied nod and pulled back.

The map was silent for a moment. **Well? What did you see?**

Kirsten patted the map with the gentlest fingertip. 'I saw goodness. And wisdom. And a nice green, soft valley of peace and retirement too, with your name all over it. Right ahead.'

It sounds n . . .

. . . ice

'Hold tight, map,' whispered Kirsten. 'We're nearly there.'

She wiped her eyes, grabbed her rucksack, saluted the walls and slowly walked towards the staircase that led out on deck. On the top step, with a rectangle of blue sky beckoning her, she stopped and took one final sniff of the ship's labyrinthine insides: that curious, wonderful aroma of the past, secrets and voyages made.

Glancing over her shoulder, back into the shadows and

colours that played and ran through the corridors beneath her, she began to tremble all over. Everything inside her head felt technicolour. She had an eerie feeling of having been swallowed up whole by something and that she'd never be the same again.

'Thank you,' she said under her breath.

Then she took two steps into the blue rectangle.

One.

Two.

Just like that.

She was on the deck, out in the world; a barefoot girl with a white-and-gold garlanded hat on her head.

She walked down the deck and joined everyone.

Once they'd gone under the Clifton Suspension Bridge, the mannequins and children heard a funny noise coming from the city.

It sounded like a party. A welcome party.

Once they'd turned into the harbourside, they finally saw it. The celebration that the SS *Great Britain* had wanted all along was being held at home.

'Oh my goodness!' she said. 'Here it is.'

'Better late than never,' said Kirsten, smiling, yet hugely nervous at what she'd find beyond the celebrations. Would Dad know she was back? Would – would Edwina be there? Her heart sank at the prospect.

A massive brass band erupted into a joyous tune, and flags and cheering filled every single corner of the harbour. The entire city of Bristol had turned out to welcome their ship back – *again*.

But Kirsten had one more thing left to do before she could start scanning the crowds for Dad.

She turned to Mark and took off her captain's hat – feeling a slight twinge of sorrow as she placed it on his head. His eyes grew wide and he reached up then, and tried to take it off to give back to her. Concern rippled over his features.

'I can't take it off. It's actually stuck to my head, Captain.'

'That's because I'm not the captain any more, Mark. You are.'

He pressed his lips together, very tightly, and looked up into her face.

'You'd better assume a new position at the steering wheel,' said Kirsten quietly. '*Captain* Spencer.'

She knew it was right. *He* was right. Mark had always been right for the job. He was always up before everyone. He'd volunteered to go down to the sea depths. He'd told her off when she needed it.

Kirsten unzipped her rucksack and began to pull out clothes. 'You were *made* to be captain,' she said, handing over the dark blue captain's jacket and trousers next.

They fitted him perfectly. Olive and Kirsten looked at him, stunned at the transformation. 'Now *no one* will throw you in the broom cupboard.'

They were getting nearer to the ship's dock. The broken caisson had been cleared away. A huge crowd of well-wishers were gathered. Everything looked spick and span, waiting to welcome them back.

'You'd better go to the steering wheel, Mark Spencer,' murmured Kirsten, sensing he was too modest to take the captaincy.

'And then you'll always be above,' added Olive shrewdly.

'I'd like that,' he confessed quietly, glancing at the blue sky, the fluttering flags he loved so much. 'It's my favourite place.'

They looked at each other, knowing what was going to happen when they pulled into the dock.

'Mark,' said Kirsten, looking firmly into his shining eyes, 'it's been an honour to have sailed this ship with you.'

'It really was,' said Olive. 'We'd have been lost without you, to be honest.'

'The honour was mine,' said Mark, glancing shyly at them both. 'I'm so glad it was you. Please come back to say hello. I might not – you know – be very talkative, but I'll know you're here all the same.'

'We will,' they said. 'Promise.'

All three saluted each other then. As Mark lifted his arm to his face, Kirsten noticed how his movements were slowing, how his face seemed to be hardening.

It was happening, she thought, her heart clouding with pain. But she gave him her biggest, most dazzling Bramble smile, dazzling because she meant it, and it was enough to make him finally turn round and assume his rightful place at the steering wheel. He took up position, the captain's hat on his head at a jaunty angle. He gave them one final look of devotion, and then looked out where the bowsprit pointed to the sea and went completely still.

Then Kirsten and Olive turned and looked at all the mannequins: the brave, frightened, fighting, wonderfully complicated Victorians who had embarked on a new life with them.

'Goodbye,' murmured Kirsten, trying not to cry, watching as they all went back inside the ship. 'Goodbye. Thank you. Goodbye.'

One of the fighting women sidled up to her. 'Can we keep your shoes, Captain? We've decided to split the pair. Right down the middle. It will solve a lot of rows, we think.'

'It won't,' said the other.

'Will.'

'Won't—'

'Yes,' said Kirsten, laughing and blinking hard. 'Good idea.'

For a moment, she simply stood, struggling to get her heart rate back to normal. *So many goodbyes.* Now she knew how the ship felt.

The ship executed a triumphant circle until her stern was facing the back of the gift shop again, and then she slowly backed up into the dock once more.

'Do you know,' said the SS **Great Britain**, as she manoeuvred herself back into place, her golden-unicorned behind facing the gift shop, her white bowsprit pointing out to adventure for ever, 'I have finally come up with a way of looking at endings that I find more satisfactory.'

Kirsten blinked back her tears, exhaled hard. 'What's that then?' she asked finally.

'Endings,' said the ship grandly, 'are just beginnings in different hats. They're honestly the same thing, except endings are cleverer because they know the whole story.'

Kirsten's heart and the ship's engine beat in perfect accord. 'You're right,' said Kirsten. 'They still hurt though.'

'Well, of course they do, darling,' said the ship. 'They wouldn't be half as special if they didn't.'

'Will we ever talk again?'

'Anything is possible with the right calculations,' purred the ship sleepily. 'Although I'm *definitely* never leaving this dock again. Anyway, right now you've got another journey to undertake. Haven't you?'

Kirsten looked over the railings. And then she saw him. *Dad.* He was right at the front of the crowds. He was smiling his happiest most melancholy smile and waving proudly. She looked either side of him. There was no sign of Edwina.

No cameras either.

Then he lifted up one finger and traced a simple shape in the air. A square.

'Two triangles,' whispered Kirsten. 'Just us. Perfect.'

She gave him a thumbs up, and he grinned and gave one back.

The ship eased herself back into the dock with a satisfied groan and finally, finally stopped.

For a minute, everything went still. A few seagulls made surprised squawks at each other, then began to circle the deck, shrieking out elated noises of welcome.

Kirsten looked at Olive and then down the length of the ship. She longed to leave, but she longed to stay on the ship just as much. Her legs were shaking.

There was the sound of a determined little clatter. Something persistent and loyal ran up the stairs and flew down the deck, head-butting her on the leg. Then it stopped, quivering with emotion.

The Captain's Chair looked up at her. She looked down at it.

'Goodbye,' said Kirsten through wobbly lips.

The chair butted against her leg again.

'Take it,' said the ship. 'You'd make us both very happy if you did. I've never seen that chair take to anyone like it has to you.'

'Really?' gasped Kirsten. 'I will. Thank you.' The chair gave a happy jig. 'I'll put you by my desk,' Kirsten told it.

Wherever that might be. Probably not True Love Heights, but that's fine. My home is with Dad and near Olive. She made herself a firm promise. *I'm going to lead a life that I like. My way. The moment my feet feel land again, it will be a fresh start.*

'Wait here a sec,' she told the chair, 'and I'll come back and get you. I've got to say hello to someone first.'

She looked ahead. Olive was waiting for her by the tiny bridge. Beyond her was Dad.

At first, Kirsten walked, but, by the time she got to the bridge, she was running. Two tiny splinters fell out of her hands as she ran, and she felt them go, but the ship remained a part of her, all the same.

SOME HISTORICAL NOTES
(AND SOME NON-HISTORICAL ONES)

ONCE IN A while in our lifetimes, if we're lucky, we stumble across something that calls to us. It might be a box of paints, a tree in a wood, a ship in a dock . . . it can be *anything*. There's no preparing for it and, best of all, it will find you when you're least expecting it. Whatever this glorious object is, it will give you what you need, even when you don't realise you need it.

I saw a ship, and a hundred other things as well. Beauty, imagination, hope, despair, adventure . . . I saw a story, which is all of those things, of course, and more.

I have taken poetic licence with some of the elements of the SS *Great Britain*, but not many. I hope, in the main, that I have done justice to her *incredible* story, and her astonishing engineering. Any mistakes are either entirely accidental or very deliberate, in order to make it even clearer how wonderful she is, which is, of course, only what she deserves.

Isambard Kingdom Brunel, Captain Gray and Ewan Corlett really did exist. Almost everything I wrote about them I believe to be completely true – especially the depth of feeling the ship inspired in each of them. The ship really did go to New York, and the Falkland Islands, and many more places besides.

William Patterson, who doesn't feature, was the shipbuilder who worked with Brunel on his designs for the **SS *Great Britain*** – not forgetting the men who built the ship themselves. Unfortunately, Patterson's company archives, which would have included the names of those who worked down in the dockyards, have not survived. This means the names of the people who constructed the ship so well have sadly been lost, but I'd like to acknowledge them all the same.

I honestly think something incredibly special happened when the ship was created by all those people. Some mysterious power, something supernatural, collided with the efforts of people trying to make something the best it could possibly be, working things out as they went along, and somehow in this way actual *magic* was created. That is something I have not had to invent. All you have to do is look at her to see it for yourself.

The **SS *Great Britain*** might be a ship, but she's also a mirror. To look at her is to see the best and the worst of us. She shows how we can create something wonderful that will change the world for good. How readily we can abandon things when we've grown tired of them. But most importantly she's a symbol of hope. She is a ten-metre high monument to it: to the fact that we can repair what feels beyond repair. To what is possible, if we believe it's possible. The ship reminds us that anything can be done, that almost nothing is hopeless, and that we can survive almost anything.

I hope if you ever see her, you will feel the same.

Ewan Corlett is not, sadly, in a cosy retirement home down by the sea, much as I'd love him to be. He died in 2005. But I became so impressed by what he achieved that I yearned to give him one final reunion with the ship he brought back to life.

Lots of wonderful people work in the television industry! But *some* reality programmes can be a tiny bit exploitative, and fame isn't always what it looks like. Just saying.

Obed Whitaker, the whaler ghost, ends up banished back to the depths of the sea in the book, but, tragically, commercial whaling – the business of killing whales – still continues, even though it was officially banned in 1986.

The people who altered and then abandoned the ship in the Falkland Islands are easily judged by modern standards, but at the time they were probably just being practical. There is still one of the ship's masts at Port Stanley.

It's still in excellent condition.

Isambard Kingdom Brunel kept many work diaries. But, to date, only one personal diary of his has been discovered: his 'locked diary', which he wrote in 1824, aged eighteen. This was a much more different diary – an incomplete and never revisited journal, and relatively short at only thirty-five pages. It's full of doubt, ambition, dreams, hope and despair. It's a complex record of a person struggling to become the man he wants to be and, as a Victorian under a huge amount of pressure to keep his emotions reined in, it's all the more powerful and poignant for that. (His handwriting is as beautiful as the ship.)

These diaries can be seen at the Brunel Institute in Bristol, which is right next to the **SS *Great Britain***. It was there I learned that Brunel spoke of everything he designed with a great deal of love (he called one of his bridges 'his darling' and was always distraught whenever any of his ships ran into trouble) and I realised that engineering was full of emotion, risk and passion. And that a man who felt that way about a ship would probably create a ship full of feeling too.

The **SS *Great Britain*** herself is now docked at Great Western Dockyard, Gas Ferry Road, Bristol. You can find out more about her, and plan your visit to see her, here: www.ssgreatbritain.org.

ACKNOWLEDGEMENTS

IT REALLY IS true that every time Brunel sat down to draw and measure his ship, she grew bigger. Understanding her shape took him a while, and so it was with me. Writing her and Kirsten's story wasn't the most straightforward journey and the following people helped keep me on course, when at times I was desperate to abandon ship. (And those are the first, but by no means last, hilarious shipping metaphors I will use.)

Ben and Polly, thank you for your love and support. Thank you for naming Pricky Bill. Thank you for everything really. This story took me far, far away at times, and made me smell, and made me mad. But I'm home now, and I promise I'll have a bath.

My endlessly patient editor, Nick Lake, who helped with the fundamental engineering of this story, put up with it when it was basically just one huge tentacled mess, made some genius suggestions and believed in this story even when I didn't. Thank you for your craftsman . . . *ship*.

Everyone at HarperCollins Children's Books who worked

on this book and its launch. Thank you for working through an exceptionally strange time.

Kirsty Applebaum for reading an early draft of this story, for your wise, calm, insightful feedback, for always being at the end of the line whenever I needed to chat.

Megan Barker, who is as strong as the ship. I will never get bored of your stories or your many voices.

The Swaggers. I am staggered by how kind and supportive and encouraging you are to each other and to me. Also, thank you for making me laugh so hard I once pulled a muscle in my neck.

Anna James, thank you for reading this story and seeing stuff I didn't. Thank you for your encouragement and hugely epic conversations. Thank you for your friend . . . *ship.*

Any teacher, child, blogger, bookseller, librarian or reader who has ever taken the time to let me know if they enjoyed *Bloom* or *Storm*. You helped add a tiny bit of coal to my flagging engine, and gave me the fuel to keep writing. (Honestly, these ship metaphors just keep coming. I hope you're enjoying reading them as much as I'm enjoying writing them.)

Speaking to anyone who knows anything about ships is like unlocking a door into another world. Thank you, Paul Miller, Master Mariner, and Paul Dean, partner at shipping law firm HFW, Jim Scott, Sam Jefferson, Carol Bishop at the Falkland Islands Company and those who helped with my queries at the Brunel Institute: Joanna, Mollie and Nick especially.

Thank you to Michael Oates of the Geologists' Association for his help in explaining to me where the iron from the SS *Great Britain* could feasibly come from. Any email that starts, '*First, I'll take you back at least five hundred million years,*' is always going to be a total winner.

Finally, thank you to all the staff and volunteers at the SS *Great Britain* Trust and the Brunel Institute, who care for and love and protect the ship to this day. Your dedication to keeping her story – and *stories* – alive is an inspiration. If you ever see a short woman with unbrushed hair crying outside the ship, that will be me. They're happy tears, don't worry.

BIBLIOGRAPHY

Corlett, E., *The Iron Ship: The Story of Brunel's SS Great Britain*, 3rd ed., Bradford-on-Avon, Moonraker Press, 1980

Vaughan, A., *The Intemperate Engineer: Isambard Brunel in His Own Words*, Shepperton, Ian Allan Publishing, 2010

Lavery, B., *SS Great Britain, Enthusiasts' Manual*, Yeovil, J. H. Haynes & Co Ltd, 2017

Goodman, R., *How to be a Victorian*, London, Penguin Books, 2014

Philbrick, N., *In the Heart of the Sea: The True Story of the Whaleship* Essex, London, Penguin Books, 2017